WATFORD UNDER WOOD

Lynn Phillips

Pen Press Publishers Ltd

First published in Great Britain by
Pen Press Publishers Ltd
39-41, North Road
Islington
London N7 9DP

ISBN 1-905203-34-9

Printed and bound in the UK

A catalogue record of this book is available from
the British Library

Cover design by Jacqueline Abromeit

Acknowledgments

I would like to acknowledge the help and support I have received from the following in the writing and production of this book:

Readers' Comments

'I just finished 'Watford' and was more than suitably impressed. Normally I don't care for 'detective novels' but this one was a jolly good read! (I couldn't resist this bit of English.) I am so impressed that you could put it all together and tie all the loose ends up in such a tidy manner at the end without getting obvious, silly or outlandish. We are looking forward to great things for you in your literary future.'

Bebe Zigman

'The Watford portrayed in her novel Watford under Wood is in many respects a familiar one, but with the sort of intrigue that would have local newspaper journalists salivating. There is murder, sex, corruption, cover-ups and more…'

Martin Booth, Watford Observer

'Greta Pusey is the plausible and determined young detective assigned to investigate this truly complex case. In Watford under Wood, Lynn Phillips has accurately captured many of the frailties that Police officers experience.

This an interesting "warts and all" tale.

Inspector Neil Collin,
Officer Commanding Ruislip Police Station,
London Borough of Hillingdon

'Readers who relish the combination of a gripping detective story with a wealth of recognisable geographic details have a new location to savour. To Morse's Oxford and Rebus's Edinburgh is now added - Greta Pusey's Watford.'

Northwood Residents Association Newsletter

'I just finished "Watford" and was more than suitably impressed. Normally I don't care for "detective novels" but this one was a "jolly good read". I am so impressed that you could put it all together and tie all the loose ends up in such a tidy manner at the end without getting obvious, silly or outlandish. We are looking forward to great things for you in your literary future. Let us know as soon as you receive your first invitation to Buckingham (Palace) or anything else that would excite envy in the hearts of lesser mortals.'

San Diego Book Club, California, USA

'I've just finished reading your book and was highly entertained. Many congratulations. When's the next one coming out?'
PS Is the Watford police station really in Shady Lane?'

London reader

'This is a great book, compelling and intriguing. Lynn Phillips has the ability to keep the reader hooked until the very end. An excellent read.'

Reader's review on Waterstone's/Amazon's website

Watford is a pleasant town, unjustly derided by some. But Lynn Phillips knows better. After a work history zigzagging through different countries and occupations, her final job before becoming a full-time writer was in an office a few hundred yards from Shady Lane Police Station - in Watford. With a background as diverse as a cowgirl in a farm in Suffolk, running a laundry on a kibbutz, and for many years as the International Advertising Manager for Outspan, she now keeps her hand in by working part-time for the Hillingdon Police. She has had a number of prize-winning short stories published, and Watford Under Wood is the first of her Watford series of novels to appear in print.

Chapter 1

Great things happened to me that month. First I got my Black Belt in karate, just when I was beginning to wonder if I could do it. Much more important than that, though, was that at last my transfer to CID came through, and I was no longer WPC Plod, but Detective Constable Greta Pusey! In plain clothes! Yippee! Then, thirdly, just to put the cap on everything, there was my first murder case.

Oh yes, I nearly forgot. There was a fourth thing that happened, but it wasn't nearly in the same class as the others. It was just that I slept with Jim Robinson, the Long-Distance Lorry Driver, for the first time. Not what you'd call a thrilling event, but it certainly was another first.

But anyway, because I've always been so career-minded, the most exciting things at that time were becoming a DC and going on my first murder case. Well, it wasn't really my case, and I didn't really get it. But I was sent with my minder, Detective Sergeant Alfie Partridge, to attend.

It turned out that this woman had dialled 999 and said she'd done a murder, so they sent a couple of plods to check up, and sure enough, she had. So then the doc and the usual team and DS Partridge and I were sent to the scene. The old girl was in a bad way, all shaking and crying, wearing just a blood-stained nightie, with her hair hanging over her blubbery old face and blood all over her hands. Alfie Partridge told me afterwards that he thought I was going to faint when I first saw the body.

'Me, faint!' I scoffed at him. 'That'll be the day. Just don't hold your breath waiting for Greta Pusey to go all girlie!'

But I have to admit I did go a bit swimmy and sick-feeling. I'd never seen a murdered body before, although I had seen a dead one, when my old Gran died. And of course in uniform you see all kinds of messy things, accidents and so on. But a body with a great carving knife sticking out of it is a lot different from one that's just peacefully passed on, or even a traffic smash, right?

I quickly pulled myself together and asked the old lady, 'What's your name, dear?'

'Gladys Trulove,' she sobbed. 'Oh Jules,' she went on, addressing the corpse, 'why did you make me do it? You know I never meant it.'

Well, no mystery murder there. No great detecting qualities called for. What could be called a cut and dried case, I'd say.

That was when I encountered Sergeant Alfie's First Rule of Policing.

'Never take things for granted, my girl,' he solemnly instructed me. 'Just because things look straightforward, that's when you should expect complications in this job.'

I was so busy at the time trying not to give him a sharp answer for calling me his girl that I didn't altogether take in the sense of what he said. But since then, I've learned over and over again that he was right. And I've also found out that 'girl' is what he calls every female he talks to, so I don't take it personally any more.

Anyway, from the point of view of the guilty party, this murder case certainly was open and shut. Gladys Trulove was obviously telling the truth when she said she stuck a knife in the deceased. It was the rest of the story that was a bit perplexing.

'Good practice for you, girl,' Alfie said. 'Sorting out this little lot will give your brain a bit of exercise.'

From my notes, this is how it went. In the notes, I'm ME and Gladys is SHE.

ME: The name of the deceased?

SHE: Jules Verne.

ME: Really?

SHE: I should know.

ME: Why did you do it, Gladys?

SHE: He was untrue to me, the rotter. I found out he was having it away with Bertha Collins from number forty-four and Maggie Burke from number sixty-eight as well. (*Crying*) And when I asked him if it was true, he just laughed and said why not.

ME: So you just picked up the knife and—

SHE: No, *he* picked up the knife and taunted me. 'Go on,' he said, 'if you're so upset, stick it in me.'

ME: So you did?

SHE: No, I said to him, 'What about Vera?' I said.

ME: Vera? Who is she?

SHE: Vera Verne, my best friend.

ME: Vera Verne? What is her relationship to the deceased?

SHE: She's his wife, isn't she.

ME: Is she? Is that really their name? Jules and Vera Verne?

SHE: I already told you. (*Crying*) She'll be upset when she hears. Who will she have to go to the bingo with, if they're going to put me away. She's got nobody else, only me.

ME: I think we should postpone the rest of this interview until you feel a little better, Gladys.

What I really meant was that I needed a break from this farce, and also to find out a few facts for myself. On the one hand, it was daft to think that Gladys Trulove actually didn't know the real names of her best friend and her own lover, who happened also to be her best friend's husband. On the other hand, impossible to believe that there were living – and dying – people in Watford called Vera and Jules Verne.

Alfie came to the rescue before I lost my sanity so early in my career as a DC. He'd sent one of the plods door to door, while he went up the road to interview the so-called Vera Verne himself. The answer came back loud and clear.

Bertha Collingrove (not Collins) and Maggie Brooks (not Burke) both confirmed that the Great Lover of Watford was indeed married to a lady called Vera, who did regularly go to bingo with her best friend, Gladys Trulove. On those occasions, Julius *Varney*, husband of Vera and long-time lover of Gladys, did have trysts alternately with Bertha and Maggie. Portly, middle-aged and balding, Julius Varney had some personal magnetism which rendered him irresistible to the local female population of a certain age. It certainly wasn't apparent when he had a knife sticking out of his middle, nor even when the police surgeon had pulled it out.

Poor Gladys was notorious in her street for getting names wrong. Bertha and Maggie were resigned to sometimes being called Brenda and Martha. Julius Varney obviously didn't mind being confused with a famous French writer. But to Gladys, Vera was always Vera. Maybe she just couldn't think of another name beginning with V.

Still, as Alfie said, it was a good introduction for me into the mysterious ways of life and death of the Great British Public. Especially the part of it that lived in Watford.

What puzzled me about that remark was, what was wrong with Watford? Why were people always joking and sneering about it? I love it, I've always loved it. I was born here, I've lived here all my life. What if it's got a pedestrian precinct that allows buses, cars and bikes to use it? Suppose it *has* got a shopping mall that's usually empty. So it's a place that people whiz past on the motorway – so what? I still can't see anything wrong with it.

Turning all that over in my mind brought me back to how it all started with Jim. It was funny really. When I was still in uniform, I'd had to wave him down and point out that some of his load was coming adrift. I told him it looked as if something was hanging out of his back door, and he tried to make some dopey joke about it. After that, he tried a sad go at chatting me up, and although he looked quite a likely sort of fellow, for a long-distance lorry driver, I wasn't having any. After all, it's true to say plenty of others have been after me. They tell me I'm wasted in the police – too beautiful, they say – I ought to be a model. Oh yes, right. Anyway, then I clean forgot about Jim.

But about a fortnight later, I came out of the station house in Shady Lane, and there he was, hanging about. Turned out he'd been there for hours, on the off-chance that he'd bump into me. Well, we went for a drink or two at our favourite local, and I came in for a bit of a ribbing from a few of the others from the nick who were there, and off he went.

But then he started to make it a regular thing, every two weeks I'd come out and there he'd be, waiting for me. And the rest was just a natural chain of events, as you might say.

After that first night, which was no fireworks, I might add, we kind of fell into a pattern that every time his work took him through Watford he'd stay at my place. So eventually I gave him a key and let him come and go as he pleased. He was OK, once I taught him a few things about the facts of life, such as the difference between women and lorries – you don't just get in and put your foot down, for example. And it was useful to have a man sort of on tap, without strings and without him expecting me to be available every night of the week.

Soon after 'my' first murder case, Alfie invited me to supper at his home. I was very flattered. True, he'd been kind to me on the job. But for a sergeant to actually befriend a rookie DC was rare.

Alfie's was an unusual family. At first, I was confused by all the names, and I thought Alfie had four children. After all, if you're told in one go about four different names, as I was on the way to Alfie's home, it's understandable. Touch of the Gladys Truloves there, maybe. But I got his wife's name right away, and there was no mistaking her. If I'd met her in a supermarket, I could have made a good guess whose wife she must be. They fitted together like hand in glove. She's a lovely lady, Betty. About my height – that's a bit shorter than Alfie's six four – but with a physique like a wrestler. More solid than me, I'm sort of more curvy. She's a good match for Alfie, who's built like a brick shit-house, if you can imagine such a thing with a fine ginger beard and moustache and a big booming voice to match.

That's why the others were such a surprise. They had two kids, twins, in their late teens, and a weedier couple you couldn't expect to meet lounging on a street corner. Not only were they nothing at all like their fine sturdy parents, but they were both so skinnily identical and colourless, that it was hard to make out which was which. They hardly spoke, and when they did, they had the same warbling contralto voices, so that was no help. Their mother was very sharp with them, but Alfie looked at them both beamingly all the time, and said now and again to Betty, 'No, leave them, girl, they're all right' or some such unhelpful rubbish. Was this the scourge of the layabout youth of Watford?

So by this time it was hardly a shock to be introduced to the other two, who turned out to be the twins' pets. Neil's dog was a fat slobbery creature who occasionally put a large paw on my leg and, gazing soulfully into my eyes, tried to hypnotise me into giving her titbits from my plate.

'She likes you,' one of the twins – probably Neil – said fondly. 'She hardly ever takes to strangers like that.'

Maybe, I thought. But she's not getting any of Betty's excellent grub off my dinner.

Carole's cat, on the other hand, took an immediate dislike to me, and tried to bite my leg under the table when she thought nobody was looking. When I was sure none of them knew what was going on, I gave her a good kick, and that was the last of our association.

But that Betty Partridge – what a marvellous cook! So although it was a bit odd, I had a really enjoyable evening. And after we'd cleared up, Betty showed me the photograph album of when Alfie was in the Army. I could see why she was proud of him. He was what used to be called a fine figure of a man.

'We've always been together,' she told me. 'Born next door, went to school together, got married at eighteen. Everybody said we was too young, but we've never regretted it, have we, Alfie?'

'That's right, girl,' he boomed, and turning to me, he asked in his usual tactful way, 'and what about you, girl? About time you found someone, isn't it?'

'Yes,' Betty added, 'lovely girl like you, you must have plenty of chances. Hope it's not because you're too choosy, being so good-looking an' all.'

I took no notice of the compliment, but decided not to tell them about Jim. I gave what I hoped was a girlish laugh.

'No, career comes first for me,' I said. 'I'll think about men and marriage when I'm Assistant Commissioner at Scotland Yard.'

I could see from their reaction that they thought I was joking.

I wasn't, though. I was dead serious. All I cared about was The Job.

Chapter 2

When Alfie and I clocked in at Shady Lane next morning, it turned out we'd missed some heavy drama through being off duty the night before.

'Don't go telling young Greta any of the details,' one of the sergeants told Detective Constable Dusty Miller – whose real first name was never mentioned, by the way. 'We don't want her fainting all over the place.'

I squared up to him, Detective Sergeant or not.

'I've told you before, *sir*, I never faint, and I don't want any special treatment.'

I was about to go into overdrive, when he backed down.

'No, no, I didn't mean because of you being female. We've already got Dusty to show us that women are OK. What I meant was, because you're new on the job—'

'We see plenty of nasty stuff on the uniform side,' I wasn't letting him get away with that. 'It's nothing new to me—'

'OK, OK,' the Inspector interrupted, 'let's not make a macho contest out of this. We're here to do a job, right, not prove a point.'

We all subsided, muttering.

Even on my first day I'd had to put up with a few cracks. I suppose every newcomer gets a certain amount of stick from the regulars, but even in these supposedly enlightened days, women get more of the sharp end of it. I'd had to put a couple of the blokes straight about not putting an extra 'S' in my surname – big joke, right? They'd just love to call me Pussey, wouldn't they.

And I'd heard them making stupid schoolboy jokes about not calling Dusty Miller Busty Miller, because she was decidedly lacking in that department. Strangely enough, she showed no signs of solidarity with me against them, so I supposed it was every woman for herself.

Anyway, about the overnight case. It turned out that they'd been called out to a nasty accident at the fairground. One of the cars of one of the rides – Devil's Loop it was called, suitably enough – had come uncoupled from the main drive, and had gone sailing off into the next field, with all its occupants still in it, shrieking their heads off. Naturally, the uniforms had got there first, then the ambulances, so by the time our lot arrived on the scene, there wasn't much visible. The amazing thing was, nobody was actually killed.

Of course, the Health and Safety bods had to be involved, but where we were concerned, the question was, had someone tampered with the mechanism? Was there something faulty in the works? Had the Health and Safety checked it out as OK and issued a certificate before the fair started? If so, then it was really fishy. That would certainly be something for us to investigate.

Then again, police nosing about amongst the Health and Safety officials would be a lovely juicy scandal for the press to get hold of. We just had to hope it wouldn't come to that.

But there was enough for big headlines to start with. Although there were no fatalities, some of the injuries were pretty nasty, and no doubt in the end somebody would be suing somebody. Probably the ambulance-chasing photographers had got into the hospital already.

It was the details of the damage to the 'passengers' that had been under discussion when Alfie and I arrived. Dusty Miller didn't seem a bit upset.

'One broken pelvis, one leg, three arms, one concussion, one collarbone, four adults, two children,' she droned out from her notes.

'Still OK, Greta?' she asked in a pretend considerate voice. 'Don't want you flaking out, do we.'

Bit of a bitch we've got here, I mused as I flashed her my best warm friendly smile.

'Right, Pusey, got a little job for you. You won't need your minder with you on this,' the DI interrupted. 'Over to the hospital, sharpish, and get statements from all the injured. Probably won't help, I expect we could sit here and write them ourselves, but we've got to stick to the form. Freddy,' he said to DS Forbes, 'you and Dusty come with me to interview the fairground people. Alfie, Charlie wants you to go with him to talk to the Health and Safety people. Come on, you lot, chop chop, we've got a job to do here!'

And he bustled us all out in his usual pompous manner, leaving only Alfie hanging around waiting to leave with Chief Detective Inspector 'Cheerful Charlie' Chester.

I'd learned on my first day that CDI Chester's first name was actually David, but for some reason he was always known as Cheerful Charlie. Turned out this wasn't to do with the fact that he was always cracking fifth-rate jokes and falling about laughing at them, though that was bad enough. No, it was something about some old-time comedian of that name. That was another difference between this branch and the uniforms: their liking for nicknames. Well, I'd have to try to make sure that I didn't get one. Just Greta or Pusey would do for me.

Anyway, as instructed, I hot-footed it round to Watford General to see the injured. Like the DI had said, it was probably useless, but somebody had to do it, and as the latest newcomer, naturally it fell to me to do the most pointless duty. And of course I didn't need Alfie with me on this one.

My old Gran used to be a Matron in a hospital in the old days. She was one of the last of that breed. My job would have been easier that day if things were done in her old-fashioned way. As it was, I got a right old run-around trying to locate these six accident victims. Arrows and signs pointed all over the place, and there never seemed to be anyone around to ask where everything was.

Finally I found the kids, the Paediatric Department being the most straightforward to locate. They both had broken arms, but they'd recovered quickly from the shock, as children do. They would have been sent straight home if their parents had been available to take them, and not been patients themselves, in another part of the hospital. As it was, the kids had to hang around until their grandparents came to collect them.

But the grandparents themselves were visiting the other injured, who had all been enjoying a fun night out when they got tossed out into empty space. This was the first I knew that all the victims were from one family.

The children were cousins, both ginger-haired, freckle-faced and about twelve. There the likeness ended. Rosie was tearfully worried and asking to see her parents. Alan was proud of the cast on his arm, already well autographed by the nurses, and anxious to get to school to boast about his adventure. Neither of them could tell me anything except that they had thought at first that sailing off into the next field was just another exciting part of the ride on the 'Devil's Loop'. The next thing they knew was the screaming and shouting. Then came the sirens and the ambulance men, who were 'very nice' according to Rosie, and 'good fun' from Alan's account.

I dutifully wrote it all down, and went in search of the rest of the family. I didn't know that Watford General had mixed wards, but it was good luck for me that day. All four of the injured parents were in the same ward.

'Can I speak to the Bennett family who were brought in after the fairground accident last night?' I asked a nurse. 'I'm afraid I haven't got all their names, but I've seen the two children.'

'Well, not all of them. Anthony Bennett was severely concussed and hasn't recovered consciousness yet. And his wife, Joan, has suffered a fractured pelvis and clavicle, and is still heavily sedated. You'll have to come back this afternoon to see them.'

'Excuse me, but is there anything about these names that strikes you?' I interrupted.

She looked blank. 'What do you mean?'

I didn't take it any further. I expect I was just being silly. But how could anyone not notice that in one family they seemed to have Alan Bennett, the famous writer, Tony Bennett, the singer, and an old-time film star called Joan Bennett. Probably nurses had to concentrate on more serious matters. And maybe I still had the late 'Jules Verne' on my mind. I was beginning to get a hang-up about names.

After a pause, the nurse went on, looking at me with pity, 'But you can speak to Jonathan Bennett. He's only a fractured tibia, and a few scratches and bruises, and he'll probably be discharged later on today. I don't know about his wife—'

'Never mind,' I interrupted again. 'I'll start with Jonathan.'

It looked as if this was going to be even more of a waste of time than I'd expected. I showed Jonathan Bennett my warrant card. He turned out to be the ginger and freckled father of little Rosie, who was so worried. Clear family likeness with both of the kids, but only in appearance. Different sorts of personalities altogether.

'I gather your brother is still unconscious, Mr Bennett, and his wife is still under sedation, so it's up to you to make the first statement.'

And then, I don't know what came over me, but I couldn't seem to help myself. I added, 'Is your brother a good singer, can you tell me?'

But before he could answer, I pulled myself together and hastily asked him in more formal tones, 'What can you tell me about the accident, Mr Bennett?'

'Accident? Accident!' he suddenly roared at me. 'That was no bloody accident! I inspected that ride myself, inch by inch, only two days ago, and I can tell you there wasn't a bleeding thing wrong!'

This was more like it. Something interesting at last.

'May I ask how you came to inspect it, Mr Bennett?'

'What do you mean, how I came to – It's my job, isn't it! I'm the blasted inspector!'

'Oh, I see,' I said, scribbling furiously. 'Have you anything with you that will establish your identity—?'

'Of course I bloody haven't, you idiot!' he yelled, clearly beside himself with rage. 'They cut all my clothes off and took them away, didn't they!'

Then, calming down a little, he pointed a shaking finger at two people hanging about at the door of the ward, and shouted, 'Ask them! They're my mother and father! Ask them who I am and what I do! Go on, ask them if you don't believe me!'

'I'm sure that won't be necessary, sir. So are you willing to make a formal statement to the effect that it's your belief that the mechanism was tampered with?'

He nodded, still breathing hard, and I went on, 'And this must have been done, according to your knowledge, during the two days between your inspection and the incident last night?'

'Yes, that's right. And look what it's done to my family. My brother and his wife still unconscious, the two kids with broken arms, and look at me! And I haven't even seen poor 'arry yet—'

'Harry?' I was puzzled. There had been no mention of another man.

I could see that Jonathan Bennett was beginning to fizz up again, but I couldn't understand any reason for it this time. Now that I was getting a bit more of the story, it was obvious it was his involvement as the HSE inspector that was making him so agitated, as well as concern for his relatives. But what was this about Harry? Harry who?

'What's the matter with you people?' he bellowed. The nurse came hurrying up, followed by the two parents who'd been hanging around, waiting for me to go before talking to their son again.

'Please, Mr Bennett,' the nurse said. 'You're disturbing the other patients. Officer, could you please leave him alone for a while. You can see you're upsetting him.'

I turned to Mr Bennett senior, and introduced myself.

'Can you tell me, sir, who is this Harry your son is referring to?'

He gave me a wintry smile.

'He's talking about his wife, Ariadne. She's from Cyprus. He calls her Ari.'

He pointed down the ward. 'She's in that bed.'

I thanked him and left him and his wife to pacify Jonathan Bennett, while I went to interview Ariadne Bennett. At least she didn't have a famous name, too.

She was lying back with her eyes closed, her black hair spread over the pillow in what could only have been a careful arrangement. I cleared my throat. No response.

'Mrs Bennett? I am Detective Constable Greta Pusey, from Shady Lane Police Station,' I started.

But her eyelids didn't even flicker. I touched her face very gently. She moaned and opened one eye a little.

'I am injure,' she stated in a husky murmur. 'No more perfect. No more beautiful. End of all.'

I took a good look at her. She had nothing to worry about in the looks department. It wouldn't be an exaggeration to say she was as stunning as any film star I've ever seen. And after all, she seemed to have suffered nothing more serious than a broken forearm. Apart from that, there was not a bruise or a scratch to be seen.

'I'm really sorry to bother you, Mrs Bennett,' I put as much sympathy into my voice as I could manage, 'but I have to ask you for a statement.'

She came to life so fast I took a step back away from the bed.

'My 'usban' is a fool,' she announced at full volume. ''E say is safe on the stupid machine we go on, now look. All go flying off, landing with pain, children screaming, all injure.'

'Er, would you care to add anything to that statement, Mrs Bennett?'

'Is all I 'ave to say,' she pouted. 'Is no more to say. If I 'ave no more career, is because my 'usban' is a booby. I am actress, you know. Maybe you seen me on TV? The Beel. You watch? Maybe you learn somethin'.'

I thanked her and left. I didn't want any lectures about watching *The Bill* to learn my job. Anyway, I had enough material for the team at Shady Lane to puzzle over.

Jonathan Bennett must have done his job properly, otherwise surely he wouldn't have taken his own family on to the ride. It followed that somebody had tampered with the mechanism in the two days between his inspection and the accident. The malice couldn't have been directed at him, since nobody could have known that he'd go to that particular carriage. So it was probably a rival funfair family, trying to run this lot out of business. Seemed like a cut and dried case to me.

But what would I know? I was only a rookie detective. And as Alfie had so wisely pointed out in the Trulove case, just when things look straightforward, that's when you should expect complications.

On the way back to the nick from the hospital, I was pondering various things. Of course, the most important was the mystery of Jonathan Bennett inspecting the Devil's Loop and then being injured – along with his family – on the very same funfair ride. You'd think, wouldn't you, that he'd have enough of those things in his everyday working life, and wouldn't want to go near them for enjoyment. But then again, maybe the kids were keen... But he certainly wouldn't risk all their lives on something he wasn't a hundred per cent sure was safe. So how come?

Then, at the same time, I was wondering if I was getting a bit silly about names. After the Gladys Trulove/Jules Verne case, somehow I'd noticed that I'd interviewed a little boy whose name was the same as a famous writer, and failed to interview his parents, who seemed to have been named after an even more famous singer and a film star of the thirties. The strangest thing was that nobody else seemed to have noticed these coincidences. It must be me, I shrugged. Getting a bit fanciful. Seeing myself as the great lady detective, finding clues where there weren't any.

Another thing I'd noticed, early on in this new part of my career, was that everybody else in our department whizzed about their business in cars, whereas I was trudging to and fro on foot. True, I'd got used to pounding the beat. But I'd expected to put all that behind me, once I was a Detective Constable in plain clothes and not a common or garden uniformed PC any more. Maybe it was because I was the youngest and latest to arrive in CID in Shady Lane.

When I finally got back from the long walk from Watford General to Shady Lane, the plod on the desk told me there were two people waiting to see me. They turned out to be Bertha Collingrove and Maggie Brooks. Well, right away I could see why the late Julius Varney had had a bit on the side with them whenever his wife and mistress were off to the bingo together. Bertha was a big bosomy blowsy blonde, almost my height (and I'm nearly six foot) in her four-inch heels with her platinum hair teased up to another three inches. Maggie was a tiny sylph-like redhead who barely came up to Bertha's armpit. The mystery was why the deceased had ever bothered with Gladys Trulove when he had these two at his fingertips.

Perhaps it was their voices. It was very off-putting that they each had the voice that went with what the other one looked like.

'We want to talk to you about poor Gladys,' big Bertha husked in a breathy Marilyn Monroe-type sexy little voice.

'Yes,' foghorned little Maggie in a voice which sounded more like a man's, that would have been more suitable coming from big Bertha, 'we want to give her a character reference.'

'See, it wasn't just she got so muddled about names,' Bertha explained, shyly twisting her fingers round each other. 'She was always a bit confused about everything. We know that's no excuse for what she did—'

'I'm sorry, ladies,' I interrupted, 'but the matter is no longer in my hands. It's all with the CPS – the Crown Prosecution Service – now, and you'll have to speak to Mrs Trulove's solicitor. I'm really sorry I can't help.'

'If we go and tell her solicitor that he should talk to her doctor,' Maggie boomed, 'will that help her case?'

'Yes, yes, that's an excellent idea,' I agreed eagerly, showing them out of the room, the entrance, the front door of the station.

'Something else,' Bertha breathed at me as I was shovelling them out. 'Have you talked to Vera? I think you should.'

I nodded my thanks for this helpful suggestion, but I was more keen to get rid of them than to ask why this would be a good idea. I just wanted them to go so that I could get on with the current case. As far as I was concerned, the Trulove case was over except for court appearances.

'Good luck!' I cried after them as they toddled down the road, looking like some wacky variety turn from the music halls of long ago. No wonder I was getting a thing about names, I mused. My whole life seems full of them.

I trudged back upstairs, and no sooner I'd got back into the office than DI Gerry Graves positively pounced on me with, 'Well, Pusey, what have you got?'

'Not a lot, Guv—' I started, but he interrupted, 'What haven't you got, then? What's missing?'

I thought this was a bit unfair, but I tried to explain, 'I've got an interview with the Health and Safety Inspector who gave a safety certificate to the ride—'

'Sergeant Partridge and Chief Inspector Chester went to speak to the HSE people,' he positively yelled. 'Who told you to muscle in on their investigation? I sent you to the hospital to interview the victims, didn't I?'

'Yes, Guv, and one of the victims—'

He shouted me down again.

'Just sit down and type your report, Pusey, and shut up.'

Feeling deflated and baffled, I sat down at the nearest keyboard, as Gerry Graves marched out of the room, looking like thunder.

Dusty Miller came and sat on my desk, pushing my notebook aside. I expected her to tell me what was eating the DI, or at least to offer me a bit of sympathy. Instead, she just smirked at me and said, 'Not off to a good start, then, Greta? You'll have to do better than that if you want to be a successful detective.'

I didn't answer. Just pulled the notebook back and started typing. But I made up my mind I'd get those other two interviews at the hospital, even if I had to sit there all night waiting for them. It probably wasn't important to get their versions of the accident, but at least nobody could say I didn't do the task I'd been assigned. In the meantime, I needed to tell somebody that the HSE inspector who'd passed the ride as safe was also one of the injured. Surely that was important.

On the other hand, Dusty was the only one around, apart from the storm-cloud Gerry Graves. I wondered if it was wise to tell her anything, apart from the fact that she didn't really look her best in a skin-tight tee-shirt.

'Dusty,' I started cautiously, 'what should I do with some information that I came upon by accident? If it seems important?'

'Tell it to me,' she answered, too promptly for my liking. 'I'll steer you right.'

I wasn't at all sure of that, but thought I'd have to give it a go.

'Well, it's one of the victims of the fairground accident,' I told her. 'It turns out that he was the one who inspected the ride and gave it a safety certificate.'

She burst out laughing.

'Not very good at his job, then, is he?' she guffawed. 'Was he badly hurt, the silly bugger?'

'What should I do?' I persisted. 'Should I tell someone? Surely it'll affect all the rest of the investigation?'

'Just put it in the report of your interview with him,' she said, getting off my desk at last and strolling over to the coffee machine. 'Silly cow!' she shot back over her shoulder.

Thank you and good night, I thought, as I went on typing. But I took her advice, just the same.

It was only when I'd finished my report and handed it in to a still scowling Gerry Graves, that I realised what I'd left out. I hadn't got any home addresses of the victims, and I hadn't got Jonathan Bennett's office address, either. And come to think of it, I should have got the name of his boss at the HSE. Oh well, I'd already decided to go back to the hospital to see if the others were fit to be interviewed yet, so I could probably get all that at the same time.

On my way back there, walking again, I thought about why I seemed so unpopular with my new workmates. I could guess why Dusty Miller didn't like me. If I looked like her, I wouldn't like anyone who looked like me. Bit of sexual rivalry there, maybe, though there was no need. But none of the guv'nors seemed keen on me, either. Looked as if Alfie was going to be my only friend, as well as my mentor.

The situation at the hospital had changed in the few hours since I'd been there. Jonathan and Ariadne Bennett had gone home with Mr and Mrs Bennett senior, taking the two children with them, and Anthony Bennett had been moved to the Intensive Care Unit. But his wife Joan was conscious and able to be interviewed.

'Does this mean that Anthony Bennett's life is in danger?' I asked the nurse.

'No, he should have been taken there right away – it's usual with head injuries. And don't you go saying anything to alarm his wife,' she added.

My talk with Joan Bennett was helpful. She was well-spoken and made more sense than any of the others. And by the way, she referred to her husband as Anthony, so I could forget any silly jokes about singers called Tony Bennett. As I'd guessed, it was the children who'd wanted to go to the fair and then on to the unlucky ride. The grown-ups in the family had only gone along because the kids teased them about being scared. Pity they hadn't just admitted that they were, and left it at that. There were only six seats in the car, so there were no strangers with them.

'But there was never any question about safety,' she assured me. 'We knew Jay had been responsible for checking all the rides at the fair, and we'd all trust him with our lives.'

'Seems as if you did,' I murmured. 'So does everybody call him Jay?'

There I go again, I rebuked myself, going on about names. It must be that Gladys Trulove – she's really got me going. Anyway, it turned out that yes, everybody did call Jonathan Bennett Jay, even his boss at the HSE office.

'What will happen now?' Joan Bennett asked me, and I was tempted to give her the standard answer, 'Buggered if I know'. Instead I gave her all the routine guff about forensic investigation, and interviewing rival fairground operators, and so on.

This time I remembered to get her home address, and addresses of the other branch of the family, as well as Jay Bennett's office. I even checked again with the nursing staff to find out if they could give me an idea about how Anthony Bennett was doing, and when I could interview him. So I was quite pleased with my efficiency and thoroughness, and ready to leave, when my curiosity won again. I went back to Joan Bennett's bedside.

'Is your sister-in-law Ariadne really an actress?' I asked her.

What a change in a woman's face! Until then, she'd been a sensible matter-of-fact witness, quite likeable and fairly good-looking. Now she looked at me like thunderclouds over Vesuvius, face all twisted.

'Yes, she is,' she spat, 'she never stops acting. But if you mean does she get paid for it, is she a professional, the answer is: in her dreams.'

And she shut her eyes. The interview was at an end. I can take a hint with the next person. I crept away.

Chapter 3

I woke up the next morning wondering what had happened to me. Somebody had Velcro'd my tongue to the roof of my mouth and then done various unlikely things to the rest of my body. Although I could tell that nothing was broken, there seemed to be bruises where there was no accounting for them.

Then I remembered. I glanced across the bed, trying not to move my head. Yes, there was Jim, snoozing peacefully away, giving out little beer puffs with every outward breath. What a pong. I had to get out of range. I creaked my way quietly to the bathroom and glared at myself in the mirror with hatred. Some model!

It had all started as a favour to Alfie Partridge, which of course I couldn't refuse. He'd asked me to take his two weedy twins to a karate class, to build them up a bit, he said. Well, I'd soon been able to sort out which of them was which, and no mistake. Neil was as puny and feeble as he looked, and I couldn't get him to make a single move. But that Carole! What a goer! She gave me a run for my money, all right. And me a Black Belt, too. She said she was going to take it up seriously. But Neil said it was too tiring.

None of that was so bad. But when I got home, ready for a nice soothing sudsy bath, there was Jim, waiting to have a celebration because he'd got some great contract or other. So we had a few drinks and one thing led to another. And it ended up with me showing him a few karate holds, too.

And here was the result, pink eyeballing me back in the bathroom mirror. With a heavy day coming up at Shady Lane, too, I wouldn't be surprised.

I was right about that. The first bit of bad news was from the hospital. They'd phoned to say that Anthony Bennett's condition was more serious than at first suspected, and he was on the danger list.

'So it might turn out to be a murder enquiry?' Dusty Miller asked in her eager way. She didn't quite lick her lips, but it was that kind of attitude. Like she didn't care about the man himself, still less his wife and child, but if it was going to be murder, it was more exciting.

'Hardly murder, even if he does give up the ghost,' CDI Chester corrected her. 'Manslaughter, maybe. But let's hope it doesn't come to that. The situation is serious enough. Give us a run-down, Gravesy.'

DI Gerald Graves said, 'As you've discovered for yourself, Charlie, Jonathan Bennett is considered a serious and conscientious officer of the Health and Safety Executive, and his chief expressed the opinion that if he said the mechanism was perfectly safe, it was. But they still have to suspend him, pending investigations, and even though he's still not fit for work yet, apparently he's very upset at the slur on his work. He insists somebody must have mucked about with the ride after his examination. Forensics are pretty sure it's been tampered with, too, so that would seem to clear his name. But, and this is a big but, the fairground people insist that all their equipment is absolutely secure from any kind of interference. Also, they say they've got no rivals for that particular site, so there's no reason for anyone to try to sabotage them.'

'So, a big mystery then,' Cheerful Charlie Chester said, not looking at all worried.

I looked at Alfie for enlightenment, but he avoided my eye and stayed expressionless. Why did none of them seem bothered about it, I wondered. I'd have to get hold of Alfie later and ask him to explain. If Jonathan Bennett hadn't been careless in his work, and nobody could have got at the Devil's Loop after he'd examined it, but Forensics found it had been tampered with, how could that be? It seemed to me that *how* it was done was far more baffling than who dunnit.

After all, there were only three possible sorts of culprits: vandals of the sort who threw paving stones off bridges, or somebody wanting to do down the fairground operators, or thirdly, somebody trying to discredit Jonathan Bennett. By this time, I was longing to blurt all this out and ask for a round-table discussion. But I had a feeling, looking at Alfie's wooden expression and the way he was refusing to look at me, that I'd better keep my furry tongue still. Anyway, if I'd said anything, the way I was feeling, it would have come out like a raven's croak.

'Pusey,' DI Graves barked, causing me to jump up and clutch my head, 'what's the matter with you? Pull yourself together and go back to the hospital and talk to Mrs Bennett – the one whose husband is critical. Get some family background, and keep a check on how he's doing in Intensive Care at the same time.'

I gave him a smart enough 'Yes, Guv,' but I couldn't help wondering what was the point of this errand, apart from giving me another long hike back to Watford General. Didn't dare query it, though.

As I went past Alfie, he muttered in his quietest rumble, 'Come round tonight for some pie, Betty says.'

Something was wrong, I knew it. But I couldn't begin to figure it out.

Mrs Joan Bennett was wide awake, although still in pain when I got to her bedside. As soon as she saw me, she told me she'd been refusing painkillers so as to stay alert.

'I want to talk to you, er... what am I supposed to call you, anyway? I can't keep saying Detective, and DC Pusey sounds so formal. Am I allowed to address you by your first name, or is that not proper?'

'Yes, call me Greta, and tell me what you wanted to say. And anyway, what's the news of your husband?'

'Well, they let me see him earlier this morning, and he seemed to know me, although he was a bit hazy and groggy, but they say the scan shows no brain damage. Whatever that might mean.'

'It sounds promising,' I offered. 'Is he still in Intensive Care?'

'No, he's in another ward now, and they've said I can go home later today. My in-laws are coming to fetch me and I'll be staying with them and Jay and Ari and the two children. Good thing they've got such a big house in Radlett, so they've got room for us all.'

This time I was bright enough to get the address from her, and she even gave me directions how to get there. Of course, she was assuming I went everywhere by car, having seen on the TV that's what all the police do. That was another thing I'd have to ask Alfie about. Why was I walking everywhere when everyone else had a squad car? Anyway, never mind that, there was something more important to think about just now.

'See, Greta, I have to talk to you about Jay. You know he was the one who inspected every one of the rides at that fairground, and checked all the mechanisms? Well, what I've got to tell you is about that. Jay told my husband this, in strictest confidence, because he was so worried about it, and Anthony told me, although I suppose he shouldn't have done, because it was a secret between brothers. But now I feel I ought to tell you.'

'You mean there *was* something wrong, after all?'

'No, of course not! You'd never find a more honest, ethical man than Jay Bennett. We'd all stake our lives on him being absolutely incorruptible – well…' she broke off with a bitter laugh, '…I suppose we all did, in a way. No, it was quite the opposite. He told Anthony that he'd got an anonymous phone call, telling him that it would be worth his while to pass all those rides and issue certificates on their safety, *without inspecting them*! He couldn't understand it.

Nor could Anthony, when he told him about it. I suppose that was why Anthony told me, because he thought I might have an idea what it could mean.'

She was silent for a moment, easing herself round in the bed into a more comfortable position.

'Then when he did check them all, and they were OK anyway,' she went on, 'it was even more puzzling. Of course he'd checked everything even more thoroughly than he normally did, just because of that call, but there was absolutely nothing wrong. Otherwise he wouldn't have passed them, and it goes without saying he wouldn't have let us and the children go on that blasted Devil's Ride if he thought there was the slightest risk. What do you make of that, Greta?'

Just as I was starting to get my brain into gear, there was a big noise at the door to the ward. A small mob surged in, turning out to consist of most of the Bennett tribe – Jonathan and his parents and the two children – although not, I noticed, the beauteous Ariadne. Shoving me aside, they descended on Joan Bennett with anxious noises, bunches of grapes, flowers and boxes of chocolates.

She objected, 'No need for all this, I'm coming home today,' but I could see she loved it, so I crept away and left them all to it.

I managed to get a brief interview with Anthony Bennett before the family got to him, too, but his recollection of everything to do with the accident was so hazy, I need not have bothered.

What now? I asked myself. Back to Shady Lane? Not keen, I answered myself. But I must do something. I can't just skive off.

A light went on in my head.

I went to see Vera Varney. I had no reason, specially since I'd decided I had no more to do with that case. I just thought I would. Anyway, dumb as I seemed to be lately, at least I had a note of her address. It was just down the street from Gladys Trulove's.

Vera Varney could have been Gladys Trulove's sister, they were so alike. The difference was that Vera had clearly put a lot of effort into improving on nature. Although, to be fair, I'd never seen Gladys at her best, so maybe she'd tried, too, on her better days. Vera was a sort of poor approximation of the late Dame Barbara Cartland – about the same proportions and type of make-up, but the shade of pink was a little different. Or maybe it was the reflection from the walls and carpet of her hall.

Blinking, I told her who I was.

'Oh, do come in, Detective,' she shrilled hospitably, and led the way into her sitting room. It was done out in that one colour too, a sort of orangey pink.

'I see you're admiring my décor, Detective,' she said, seating herself in a swirl of netting on a couch of the same colour, and not quite disappearing. I noticed that her hair was roughly the same shade as everything else in the room. 'Everybody who comes here compliments me on my taste. It's my favourite colour, you see. Apricot.'

'Pardon?'

'Apricot,' she said, her gracious hostess manner slipping for a moment. 'My favourite colour,' she explained.

There was only one reply possible to this, and I made it.

'Oh,' I said.

Then I pulled myself together.

'I'm sorry for your loss, Mrs Varney,' I said formally, 'and I'm sorry I haven't called on you sooner.'

'Yes,' she said, 'poor Gladys.'

Not quite the reply you might expect from the widow of a murdered man about his murderer. Poor Gladys, indeed.

After a short silence which I couldn't think how to break, she offered me a cup of tea, which I accepted gratefully– I was even more grateful to see it was in a white cup. I didn't think I could stand any more apricot.

'That was a terrible business with the Bennetts at the funfair,' Mrs Varney suddenly said, startling me out of my apricot daydream. 'My Julius worked there, you know.'

'At the funfair?'

'No, of course not. At the Health and Safety Executive. Didn't you know? I'd have thought you'd have found out all about him by now.'

'You mean, you mean, he knew Jonathan Bennett,' I stammered. 'What, what did your husband do?'

'Oh, nothing posh like an Inspector, like Jonathan Bennett, no, not my Julius. Well, I'm not sure exactly, but he was just some kind of clerical person. And sometimes he did a bit of driving, as well. He used to talk to me about Jonathan, Jay, he called him. Said he was a very nice feller, but didn't know the ways of the world.'

I got out my notebook. 'And what did you understand him to mean by that, Mrs Varney?'

'Well, you know, there's always a bit to be made on the side, specially if you're friendly with the boss. But my Julius said to me, only a few nights before Gladys stuck that knife in him, "That Jay Bennett is a proper thorn in the side of some of the people at the HSE," he said. Another cup, Detective? Have one of these little cakies – they're filled with apricot jam.'

*

By the time I got to the Partridges that evening, my head was in an even worse state than it had been when I woke up that morning. What with the confusion of all the names, and the sudden connection between my first two cases, and all the bits of hidden agenda that seemed to be bobbing about – I was badly in need of some guidance from Alfie.

It should have been a good evening, with just the three of us. The twins were out with the damned dog, the aggressive cat was off somewhere on her own pursuits, and Betty had produced another of her superb meals. But neither she nor I could get more than two words at a time out of Alfie. This was so unusual that Betty got worried.

'Come on then, Alfie Partridge,' she barked at him, 'spit it out. We can both see there's something you don't want to talk about, can't we, Greta?'

I wasn't sure how to react to this. If there was something he didn't want to talk about, surely two women going on at him wasn't going to make him open up? On the other hand, Betty must know how to deal with him. I kept shtum, to be on the safe side.

Alfie then went through a most peculiar performance, sighing, shaking his head, groaning a bit, and finally walking up and down and muttering to himself. Betty sent me a signal with her eyebrows which I just couldn't begin to understand. This was turning out not to be the evening I'd hoped for.

Finally, Alfie flung himself back into his armchair, and said to me, 'You really got Carole going on that karate business. She's gone to enrol in the local beginners' class tonight, and Neil and Freda have gone to watch. Me and my Betty want to thank you for that – they needed a hobby.'

'Stop that, Alfie Partridge!' Betty cut in sharply.

'Stop what, girl?' he gave her his most smarmy smile.

'Trying to change the subject. You know as well as I do, there's something you've got to get off your chest, and you're just trying to get away from it. Come on now, Alfie, out with it.'

She certainly knew her man. He coughed it up right away.

'Alright then. It's nothing I actually know, see. Just when you've been on the Job for long, you get a feeling. There's something wrong with this case. There's something the guv'nors know, and it's not good.'

'Is that why you were avoiding my eye earlier today?' I asked him, and when he gave a glum nod, I went on, 'But what sort of thing do you mean? We can all see how puzzling it is that Jay Bennett inspected the ride two days before the accident, and nobody could have got to it to interfere with the mechanism, and yet it happened. Well, surely it's our job as detectives to work out how that could happen? What's wrong with that?'

'No, girl, you don't understand,' Alfie groaned. 'What I can smell is graft.'

There was a shocked silence.

'Alfie, what are you saying?' Betty whispered. 'Are you accusing your own superior officers?'

Alfie shook his head miserably.

'I don't know what I'm saying, girl. I honestly don't. All I can tell you is, there's something wrong, and I shouldn't be talking about it, neither to you nor to this here rookie what I'm supposed to take under my wing. Not give her potty ideas about corruption, when I've got nothing to go on.'

My headache had gone. I was shocked, thrilled, excited. I was in the middle of something that made major national scandals!

Just a minute. No I wasn't. I was just listening to a copper who was letting his imagination run away with him. No, it couldn't be that, either. Nobody could accuse Alfie Partridge of fantasising. I wasn't shocked, thrilled or excited. I was confused.

'Er, Alfie, is it anything to do with what I told you about Vera Varney?' I offered nervously. 'You know, that her husband said Jay Bennett was a thorn in the side of some of the people at the HSE? And Jay telling his brother about that phone call saying it would be worth his while to issue certificates for the rides at that funfair without actually checking them?'

'No,' said Alfie, firmly putting an end to all my theorising. 'No, it's more that they don't seem to *want* to get to the bottom of things. Then when CDI Chester and I got to the HSE office, it turned out that he and Jay Bennett's boss were old friends. Golf,' he explained. 'The Super goes to the same club, as well.'

'Superintendent Wood and Cheerful Charlie play golf together?' Betty asked. 'How do they get the time?'

'Good question,' said Alfie moodily.

Just then there was a bang from the kitchen as Muriel the cat came in through her cat-flap, trotted into the sitting room where we all were, and made straight for my foot with her claws out. Time for me to go.

I was gloomy when I said my goodbyes and thanks to Betty, and she didn't need to ask me why. I felt a bit cheered by her invitation to come again in a couple of days, though. And I could tell she liked me, which helped a lot, too.

But I hadn't really had a chance to ask Alfie all the questions that were churning round in my poor buzzing head, specially the one about why all the detectives in our department got to ride about in cars – all except me.

Still, by the time I'd rollerbladed my way home, I felt terrific. Blading beats running any time. And made me feel a bit better about the conversation I'd had earlier that day with Dusty Miller about transport.

'There's a limited number of cars at our disposal, you know,' she'd said in her sneery way, 'and if there isn't one available for you, you can always use your own and put in for your mileage. There's a set rate according to the size of your engine. What's yours?'

So I'd had to put up with her disbelieving laughter when I admitted I didn't have a car – at present, *at present* – I emphasised. But it was no good, the damage was done, and I knew I was going to be in for a lot of heavy ribbing, thanks to friend and colleague Dusty Miller spreading the amazing news that poor Greta Pusey didn't even have a car! Blowed if I was going to explain to her that I'd had to choose between affording a car or a flat of my own, and the home had won. And as for telling her that my preferred personal transport at the moment was either a bike or the trusty rollerblades – well, wild horses would have to pull my teeth out first. I hadn't even told Alfie and Betty that much.

As a matter of fact, I'd told Betty more about myself than I'd told anyone for years now. It wasn't so much that she was nosy (well, she was, actually, but in a nice way) but when she asked me questions about my life, she did it so kindly and in such a sympathetic and interested way, that I didn't feel I had to put her off with cagey answers. Like I did with Jim, for instance.

So I told her about how my mother had had me at fourteen and my Gran had looked after us both until my mother topped herself at sixteen, out of her head with amphetamines by that time. And how my Gran had been more like a friend, being only in her thirties when I was born, so I'd never actually had any girlfriends of my own age, especially being a bit touchy about my past. None of us had any idea who my father was, and as my grandfather had died before I was born, it was just us two girls together. I suppose it was Gran being a Matron in a hospital and Granpa having been a cop that made me so determined to join the police and make a big success of it. Sort of picking up on the idea of public service. Good thing I didn't seem to have inherited anything from my birth mother.

Very gently, Betty said, 'And now you're on your own? What happened?'

I couldn't go so far as to tell even her, understanding as she was, about Gran dying. I just changed the subject and started talking about karate, and Betty understood and left it.

Anyway, what with one thing and another, I felt quite OK by the time I got back to my little flat, and relieved to see that Jim wasn't there, so I could be quiet on my own for a bit. Time to think things over.

I didn't, actually, do any thinking. I went straight to bed and was fast asleep before my head reached the pillow.

So when the phone woke me in the middle of the night, I couldn't make out what was going on. I'm a very bad waker at the best of times, even after a full night's sleep and the alarm going off at a reasonable hour. I've never been one of those who leap out of bed with a smile and a song, jump into a track suit and go for a five mile run before a quick work-out at the gym and then a healthy breakfast before getting to work at 7 a.m. No, I'm one of your bleary-eyed mumbling staggerers, unable to work out my own name until I've had a life-giving cup of tea and a slow ponder about what to do next.

I managed to focus on the face of my giant spotlit alarm clock. Ten-past three! It must be that lunatic Jim. I'd have to give him a piece of my mind.

It wasn't. It was Alfie!

'Listen, girl,' he rumbled, 'I'm really sorry to wake you up at this hour, but I couldn't sleep, and there's something I've got to say to you. It's been on my mind since you went home, and I had to phone you now to tell you.'

'Go on, Alfie, it must be urgent and important for you to phone me at three in the morning,' I muttered bitterly, almost awake by now.

'It's just this, Greta. I want you to forget every word I said this evening. It was all rubbish, and it was stupid of me to say such daft things. I don't know what came over me.'

'But—'

'NO,' he was almost shouting now, 'just wipe it out of your head, you hear!'

And he hung up.

That was really out of character. And worrying.

*

The next week passed in a blur of inactivity for me. Everyone else seemed busy, rushing around, barking terse words at each other, answering phones and reading and writing reports – but it was all incomprehensible. I tried to look part of everything, but I've never been any good at faking, and I probably looked as baffled as I felt. It was obvious that the fairground case was ongoing, and other cases rolled in with normal regularity, but somehow I was not actually given anything to do. Worst of all, when I tried to talk to Alfie, in the office or canteen, or even at his home on the phone, he remained monosyllabic. A long word to explain a series of grunts.

The worst of it was, I had nobody to talk to. I couldn't just go and chat to my old mates in the uniform branch. It would have been like admitting I'd made a mistake in trying so hard for this transfer. I had a few sort-of friends outside the police, but they wouldn't have understood. Even Jim might have at least given me his ear, but he was off on one of his long trips. So, failing Alfie, that left Betty. I phoned her one day from a box at Watford Junction Station.

'I'm sorry, dear, but I don't understand,' she said, after I'd poured out my tale of confusion. 'What was it you wanted Alfie to explain? I'm sure he'd be only too pleased to give you any help you need. He's properly taken you under his wing, you know. Tell you what, Greta, come round to supper tonight and we'll have a long chat together. It'll be alright, you'll see.'

That evening I really hit rock bottom. Even Betty had to admit something must be wrong. When Alfie saw that I'd come to supper, he muttered something about forgetting something, and rushed off out. And he still wasn't back when I left at eleven.

'He wouldn't miss a meal,' Betty said worriedly. 'He's too fond of his tummy. Course, I'll keep his hot for him, whatever time he comes back. But it's not like him. You must be right, dear, he's avoiding you. I wonder what you could have done to upset him so?'

My misery and confusion were gradually being replaced by anger. I was beginning to think, not so much what I could have done to cause Alfie to behave like this, but more what I would like to do to upset him still further. But all I could do was wait it out.

Finally, of course, things changed. In a most unexpected way. I had a phone call from Jay Bennett.

'I don't want to talk to anyone else in your department,' he said. 'Can you come and see me, unofficially and outside your working hours? We could call it a social call, if you like. Come to tea on Saturday. We're all still at my parents' house at Radlett. You've got the address, haven't you?'

Well, it wasn't work and it wasn't any help about my weird situation in the department. But it was something to do. I cycled over to Radlett.

The whole Bennett tribe was there, and en masse they were a bit overwhelming. Eight Bennetts in one room was rather a lot. But it looked as if they were the sort of family that believed in togetherness. Made me a bit envious, really, not having any.

The two senior Bennetts, not having gone to the funfair with the rest of the family, were naturally quite OK. They and the two kids, clearly not at all bothered by the plaster casts on their arms, were the only properly mobile ones, and they all trotted about, serving tea and cakes to the rest of us.

I noticed that Ariadne, who was no more damaged than the children, was lying back on a chaise longue, being ministered to by young Rosie. She was making more of her injury than Joan Bennett, who was the most seriously hurt. In fact, seeing the wheelchair beside the older woman on the couch, I realised that she still couldn't stand or walk, and of course she still had the support neck-brace because of her broken collarbone. It was surprising that she'd been discharged from hospital in that condition. But she was very quiet, unlike her sister-in-law, the beautiful drama queen, who was making the most of her situation.

'No, I cannot eat it like thees, Rosie,' Ariadne admonished her daughter, indicating a slice of cake. 'You must help your poor Momma. I am injure,' she explained.

Young Rosie, good as gold, sat on a stool by her melodramatic mother, and fed her with tiny dainty pieces of cake, holding a paper napkin below her chin, and fussing over her as if she were the mother and not the child.

'You are good girl,' Ariadne informed her daughter. 'Ees a peety you not beautiful like your Momma, only looking like poor Poppa.'

Everyone else in the room took no notice of them, so I tried to do the same. It was difficult, though, not to point out that Ariadne and Rosie had identical injuries.

'Your Chief Detective Inspector and my boss are friends, you know,' Jay Bennett said. 'They belong to the same golf club.'

Anxious to show I knew all about the social lives of my superiors, I confirmed, 'Yes, everyone knows that. And our Superintendent, Mr Wood, plays at the same club.'

Jay Bennett seemed to be having trouble in finding the right words. At last he managed to go on, 'That's why I didn't want to speak to any of them.'

'No, er, really? What, er, what's golf got to do with anything?' I stumbled. 'Or, I mean, what exactly are we talking about? Who didn't you want to speak to, about what?'

At last, I'd opened the floodgates. Once Jay Bennett started talking, he couldn't stop. And what with the others joining in from time to time, it took a while to sort out what I was being told. Not that I could believe a word of it.

Apparently, whatever marvellous record HSE Inspectors had, and for however many years, the moment something a bit questionable came up, they were automatically suspended from work. Well, that didn't matter to Jay, because he was on sick leave anyway. But when it was something as fishy as the fairground case, the other automatic system that swung into operation was re-investigating his last inspections over the previous six months. Which was quite a lot, he being a hard-working official of a very busy Executive.

Jay had worked at the HSE since leaving University, and in the fifteen years he'd been there, he'd acquired a reputation second to none. Everyone saw him as a sort of shining example, dedicated and diligent. I'd heard myself from Vera Varney that he was incorruptible, so that wasn't just according to his own family.

So it was a kick in the teeth when the re-investigations of his recent cases started to uncover all sorts of bribery, extortion and other sorts of corruption. It looked as if he'd offered to OK some outstandingly messy situations in return for payments in money or kind. And messy meant endangering life, on an even larger scale than in the fairground case. Presents of designer clothes for Ariadne had been mentioned, for example. And it had been suggested that the one little walk-on part she'd had in *The Bill* was a payment in kind for Jay Bennett overlooking a serious infringement. The investigations were continuing.

'This is a fit-up,' Anthony Bennett shouted, clutching his bandaged head. 'They've got their reasons for wanting Jay out of the way!'

'Oh, now, just a minute—' I started to protest, but my voice was drowned out in the general uproar.

When the noise died down a little, we could all hear Ariadne whingeing away to her daughter, 'Rosie, darleeng, is no more hot, the tea. Get me a better cup, eh, sweetheart.'

I thought the others would say something about her not worrying about her husband, but it seemed as if they were used to beautiful Ariadne only being interested in beautiful Ariadne, because again they all went on as if she hadn't said a word. Except, of course, for little Rosie, who trotted off to the kitchen to get her mother a hotter cup of tea.

'Can we please start from the beginning,' I said to Jay. 'Why did you ask me to come here? What do you think I can do? I'm the latest rookie, I've just been promoted from the uniformed branch, I'm just a beginner Detective Constable, nobody in the department talks to me, I don't know anything about the investigation. I was only sent to the hospital to talk to you all because we thought you were just the victims of an accident. If my guv'nor had known you had anything to do with the HSE or the fairground inspection, he would have interviewed you himself.'

'Yes,' he said grimly, 'and wasn't that lucky for me. If your boss and his friend my boss had got their heads together, I wouldn't just be looking to lose my job, I'd be awaiting trial by now.'

There was a silence, obviously a novelty in that household. Then Mr Bennett senior spoke for the first time.

'I told you, Jay, it's senseless asking this young lady to help you. As she said herself, she's in no position—'

'Who's going to do anything, then?' Anthony Bennett interrupted.

'Not me,' I said firmly. 'I don't know what you want me to do, but whatever it is, I can't help. I can only suggest you get yourself a good solicitor, Mr Bennett – I mean Mr Jonathan Bennett, and do as he advises you.'

Cycling home, I thought hard about what I'd heard. Maybe it was true that there was corruption throughout the branch of the HSE that Jay Bennett worked for, and they wanted him out of the way in case he ruined all their nice little rackets. It didn't seem likely, but just suppose he really was the shining incorruptible, and his simply being there was a danger to all the rest of the gang.

A whole department? Surely not. Of course, I didn't even know how many people we were talking about, or how many investigations, or even what size area they covered. But anyway, the thing was, even if all that was true, what could it possibly have to do with the fact that his boss and my boss and my boss's boss all played golf together? Absolutely nothing! All this upset had obviously turned the whole Bennett family into a bunch of raving paranoids. Forget it, I told myself, pedalling harder to encourage me and the bike up a hill. But then, freewheeling down the other side, and therefore thinking of the other side of the argument, I remembered Alfie's unsupported suspicions. Shut up! Rubbish! I told myself.

So what with all this internal argument and dithering, I shouldn't have been surprised a week later to see Jay Bennett hopping in to the Shady Lane cop shop on his crutches between two uniforms.

'We got a result on the fairground case,' DI Gerald Graves told us. 'The owner finally coughed.'

'What happened, Guv?' Dusty Miller asked in her smarmy way.

'He admitted he bribed Jonathan Bennett to certify all the mechanisms were safe and in perfect order. He never looked at one of them! What a berk, risking his own family on a ride nobody had ever inspected!'

I looked round the office to see how Alfie was reacting. He wasn't there.

Chapter 4

Trudging slowly out of the back door of Shady Lane, I was nearly mowed down by Dusty Miller charging past me like a whirlwind. As I staggered to keep my balance, she shouted back at me, 'Sorree! Things to do, people to see, in a rush!'

Then, just to amaze me more, she spun round and came back to face me, even faster than she'd gone the other way.

'Want to come with me? I suppose you *can* drive? You can be my driver, if you like. You might learn something.'

I hated to admit it, but she was right. If I went with her, I'd certainly learn something, even if it wasn't to my advantage. I actually had my mouth open to accept her sneery invitation, when on the other side of the wire fence I saw Carole Partridge, with her brother's dog Freda. Carole was waving to me. Freda was peeing. Good thing it wasn't the other way round.

But this put me in a quandary. On the one hand, if I went with Dusty, I might find out something useful. On the other hand, if I went with Carole, I might find something out about Alfie. Like what was biting him these days. And I had about five seconds to make up my mind. I decided.

'Sure,' I said to Dusty. 'I'll be your driver. Which car? Where to?'

And as we swept past Carole and Freda (still peeing – there was something wrong with that dog, I thought), I leaned out of the window and shouted to Carole, 'Come back in a couple of hours and I'll meet you here.'

I hoped she'd heard, but I couldn't tell.

Dusty said, 'Listen, Greta, I know we're not friends, but I'm going to give you a friendly word of advice. Don't get too chummy with suspects or their families.'

'Don't know what you mean,' I muttered between clenched teeth.

'Yes you do. And you know I mean friends as well. You arrested that Trulove woman, and then you've got all thick with her two mates and the wife of the murdered man. Then you started getting matey with the Bennett family, and God alone knows where that mess is going to stop unravelling.'

'Where are we going now?' I tried to change the subject. I didn't want to ask her how she knew so many details of everything I did and everyone I spoke to. I had a feeling I wouldn't like the answer.

'The building site where they've just got planning permission for a ten-storey block of flats, out towards Elstree. We're going to talk to the site manager. But Greta, really, what I'm telling you is honestly for your own good. You're just a rookie, and you don't know what trouble you can get yourself into.'

Then she laughed, like water going down a plughole in Australia.

'I don't know why I'm bothering, anyway. Specially if you're not going to take any notice. Turn left here. Robson's the name of our man today.'

It turned out I didn't learn a thing from Dusty. I should have known she only wanted me to drive her so as she could look more important. Anyway, Mr Robson didn't seem very impressed. All she had to do was ask him a couple of questions. The answers didn't mean much, anyway.

No, he hadn't had a visit from the HSE. Yes, he'd been in contact with them. Yes, he expected a visit from their inspectors any day now. No, he didn't know how many or what their names were. End of interview.

Dusty was very quiet on the way back to Watford.

Carole and Freda were waiting for me.

Freda was ecstatic to see me. Anyone would think we were old friends. She slobbered all over my jeans and then sat on my foot.

'I must talk to you, Greta,' Carole said. 'I can't seem to talk to Dad these days, he's gone so moody, even Mum can't work out what's wrong.'

'Well, I hope you're not going to ask me about him,' I started, but Carole interrupted.

'It's not about Dad, it's about my friend Sharon, she's my best friend and I've known her all our lives and she's like a sister to me, and she's in such a state, I don't know what to do. What it is, she thinks her father's going to kill himself!'

'What! Why on earth would a girl think that? Is she inclined to be, er, over... er... imaginative...?'

I didn't want to hurt Carole's feelings by suggesting her friend was a bit potty, so that was the most tactful way I could think of putting it. Well, according to Carole, Sharon was the most down-to-earth, sensible, intelligent girl in the world.

'...a bit like a younger version of you,' Carole concluded flatteringly. Well, if she wanted to get my attention, that was a sure way of doing it.

She went rambling on with her story about her poor demented friend Sharon and her father who was usually even more sensible, etc. than she was, but he was behaving so out of character and sort of despairing, that she didn't know what to do. So of course she had confided in her friend Carole Partridge, who had decided that I was the one to go to for advice. I got the feeling that ever since I'd introduced Carole to karate, I'd become a sort of hero figure to her. Well, she was going on and on, and probably she'd still be standing there gabbing away to this day, if I hadn't had one of my inspirations.

'What does Sharon's father do?' I asked.

'Oh, he's just got some boring old business. He's an accountant, or a solicitor or something like that. Course, he is a Councillor as well, so she thinks he's really important. Her Mum loves it, swanning around being lady muck. Sharon's tried talking to her, but her idea of a tragedy is not having matching shoes for the right clothes for the right occasion, so it's a waste of time asking her to take an interest.'

'Leave it with me, Carole. I'll see if I can think of some way to reassure your friend that her Dad is OK. What's their surname, by the way?'

'Bennett. Why?'

'Oh, I don't know,' I managed to say in a reasonably ordinary voice, though I got that strangling feeling coming on. 'Just thought it would be handy to know. Must go now, Carole. See you later.'

Oh no, I said to myself as I staggered back into the cop shop. It must be a coincidence. It's a common enough name, as I noted when I first went to interview them in the hospital.

What was going on in there put the Bennett puzzle out of my mind for a while.

It's a funny thing that although I'd been at Shady Lane for years, I'd hardly ever seen our Superintendent. Well, at the so-called jollifications for Christmas and the like, he'd been visible at a distance, hobnobbing with the senior officers and their wives. And naturally I'd seen him sort of coming and going. But I'd never had a really good look at him, close enough as you might say for identification purposes.

And now, here he was, Superintendent Wood in person, present in the flesh in our own CID office! Although in the flesh was a bit of an exaggeration, because he hardly seemed to have any. He was a tall skinny man, and until you got closer to him, he looked a bit like one of those gaunt trees in winter with nothing to hide the bare branches, or in his case, the bones. Naturally he was in the full fig uniform, as he would be, coming to talk to the common mob. But it didn't seem as smart as it should. Either the sleeves were too short, or it wasn't his own jacket, but his knobbly wrists seem to stick out for miles before they ended in hands and fingers like bundles of sticks. Altogether, he reminded me of the Scarecrow in *The Wizard of Oz*. (I used to love watching that video with my Gran when I was a kid.)

And there was Dusty Miller, ogling up at him like the Wicked Witch of the West, too. She was nearly my height, so he must have been nearing seven foot for her to have to tilt her head back to gaze at him like that. Oh yes, and there was Alfie, at last, and even he looked a tich next to Mr Wood. And Alfie was a good six four. When I'd seen the Super from afar, so to speak, he'd never struck me as so enormously tall.

Anyway, after all these ruminations, I finally turned on to what the Old Man was saying. Apparently he'd come down from his office Up Top to congratulate us all on our fine work in apprehending that dangerous villain from the Health and Safety Executive, Jonathan Bennett.

'Who knows,' he waffled on, 'how many lives could have been lost, how many innocents injured, if this team of dedicated officers hadn't ferreted out this menace, who had deceived so many people into believing him to be an honest and trustworthy citizen…'

I tuned out. It must be true, it had to be true. This whole branch of the Hertfordshire Police couldn't be mistaken. Everybody from the Super on down must know what was what. I was just a beginner, a rookie who knew nothing. How could I be right in thinking Jay Bennett was innocent? I looked across at Alfie, standing looking almost reverently at Mr Wood as he blethered on. Even Alfie seemed to agree that Jay Bennett was a wicked con man. I must be the one who was out of step.

And Sharon Bennett, Carole Partridge's friend, was right to be worried about her father. Because he must be related to Jay Bennett, and possibly involved in his graft and extortion – maybe even using his position as a Councillor! So naturally he'd be worried at Jay being arrested.

At last Mr Wood had droned to a halt, and pausing only to shake hands with Chief Inspector Chester and Inspector Graves, he ambled out.

I rushed over to Alfie and practically dragged him out of the office.

'Alfie, you've got to stop avoiding me! We must talk!' I yipped at him.

'What's up with you then, girl?' he rumbled, but it was unconvincing. Alfie wasn't cut out to be a liar, even by omission. He knew very well what was up. And he knew we couldn't talk about it in Shady Lane, or anywhere near it.

'Come round to my place for a drink after work!' I hissed at him, but not quietly enough. Dusty Miller was just going past, and she gave us both such a knowing leer that I felt like demonstrating my latest karate move on her, then and there.

Alfie burst out laughing.

'Now you've done it, girl,' he guffawed. 'Our names will be mud from now on. Wonder what my Betty will make of that!'

He came, just the same, and I hardly gave him time to get inside the front door before I burst out at him.

'What's bloody-well going on, Alfie? Come on, don't start—'

He plodded past me, sat down and said, dead-pan, 'Thought you invited me for a drink, girl. Manners to offer that before you begin shouting, innit? *And*, furthermore, I might remind you that you're speaking to a senior officer here. Just because me and my Betty been nice and friendly towards you, don't mean you can't be polite and speak to me according to my rank.'

I was flabbergasted. I'd thought that, although Alfie was my senior and mentor, we were really mates. If he was going to pull this stuff on me, there was no point in trying to talk to him off the record. But I'd have to give it a try, because I had nobody else. If Alfie wasn't going to be my rock and my salvation, then only religion was left. That would have made my old Gran laugh.

In silence, I emptied a large packet of crisps into a bowl and put it at his elbow, got out a bottle of Guinness and waved it at him enquiringly. He gave a gracious nod and accepted it, tucking into the crisps.

I waited.

Finally, spraying crisp crumbs into the air and down his ginger beard, he asked, in a more reasonable way, 'What was it you wanted to ask me about, Greta?'

This time, I tried to keep it low-key and mind my language.

'I want to remind you, Alfie – or would you like me to call you Sarge or sir? — that first you gave me a gypsy's warning about graft and corruption, then you phoned me in the middle of the night to tell me to forget every word you'd said. And ever since then, you've been so keen on avoiding me that you even rushed out without your supper one evening – that gave Betty the fright of her life, I might tell you.'

During this, which I'd only meant as an introduction to what I really wanted to talk about, Alfie had gradually stopped chewing and slurping, and now sat quietly holding his Guinness in one large paw and a few crisps in the other. That part of his face which his beard left visible was slowly going dark red.

'Alright, that was stupid,' he muttered. 'I shouldn't never have talked to you like that. That was why I told you to forget it.'

'Well, I might have done if you hadn't started acting so daft. But really, none of that is what I wanted to talk to you about. It's the Bennett case. How can anyone honestly believe that Jay Bennett would have extorted money from a fairground owner to certify that his machinery was all safe, and THEN TAKEN HIS OWN FAMILY ON ONE OF HIS RIDES? Look at all those umpteen people who are willing to swear that Jay Bennett is the most honest incorruptible to walk the earth since the last saint died. Even if they're all barmy or crooks themselves, it still doesn't make sense. He just wouldn't do it.'

'None of your business, girl,' Alfie rumbled glumly, still not noticing that he'd stopped eating and drinking. This could only be a sign of a very worried Alfie, I knew.

'Not your case, not my case, nothing to do with us,' he went on, absent-mindedly dropping his handful of salt and vinegar flavour on my white goatskin rug, a present Jim had brought me from his last trip to somewhere in Spain. How do you get crisp crumbs out of long white silky fur, I wondered. And what would Jim say if I had to throw it away? I gave a mental shrug. I'd never liked that rug much, anyway, and I didn't give much of a toot about Jim, either. This was all to stop myself thinking about what Alfie was saying.

'But why should anyone take any notice of the fairground man who said Bennett was a crook? What sort of case can there be? Anyone listening to Bennett's defence would be bound to believe that he wouldn't risk his family's lives,' I argued. 'It's obvious the CPS will throw the case out, or if they don't, the magistrates will, or if they don't—'

'Then you've got nothing to worry about, right, girl?' Alfie interrupted. 'Anyway, what about all the investigations of Bennett's previous activities? That's come out all fishy, as well. I'm telling you, Greta, it's not your business. Nor mine. Let the law take its course,' he instructed me, reinforcing this with a loud burp. 'Beg pardon,' he added politely.

'Another Guinness?' I offered. He nodded, and finished off the one in his hand. There was another silence.

'So there's no connection between what you said that you told me to forget you'd said, and this case, and your daughter's best friend Sharon's father suffering from a serious depression, then?' I asked.

Alfie actually jumped to his feet, adding a splash of Guinness to the mess on the goatskin rug. It was beyond help now.

'What? Roddy Bennett suffering from depression? How do you know that? Did my Carole tell you that? Why didn't she talk to me about it?'

'Why are you so excited? Do you know Rodney Bennett?'

'Course I do, and so should you. He's a Councillor, and he's the Chairman of the Planning Committee. And they gave planning permission for the block of flats that Jonathan Bennett is supposed to have given a fraudulent HSE certificate to the builder for on his scaffolding which has now been condemned as dangerous!'

While I was still trying to pick the bones out of this jumble, Alfie added, 'And Rodney Bennett is Jonathan Bennett's cousin.'

Ouch.

Chapter 5

By luck I'd been put on nights when Jay Bennett's case came up at the Magistrates' Court, so I could sneak in and see what happened. The whole Bennett clan turned up, too, including Ariadne leaning heavily on little Rosie, and Joan Bennett still in her wheelchair.

The case didn't get chucked out. It was going to Crown Court.

Ariadne stood up, a dramatic figure in a beautiful genuine original pashmina, and declared, 'You cannot do thees! 'E ees a good pure man! 'E never would do so wrong a theeng!'

Still ranting on like a full Greek chorus, she was escorted out, followed by little Rosie. I watched them, thinking hard. Those original pashminas were very pricey till the shops started being full of cheap ones. How could Jay afford this expensive wife? Her perfume alone would have cost me a week's wages, not to speak of her pricey hairdo and perfect manicure and make-up.

Outside, Joan Bennett called to me.

'Can't you persuade her she'll do Jay more harm than good by going on like that in public?' she asked. 'She won't take any notice of us, but if one of the police tell her…'

'Well, people from other countries don't always understand…' I started, but Mrs Bennett made such a face of pain that I had to stop what I was saying to ask her if she needed help.

'No, it's just that I keep forgetting not to shake my head,' she explained. 'It's you who doesn't understand. Ariadne isn't what you think. She was born in Camden Town, and she's never even been to Cyprus.'

'But your father-in-law said – I thought she was – what about her accent?'

'She puts it on to make herself more interesting. And all that drama, as well. She was educated in this country, and she talks just like the rest of us. Well, maybe a bit cockney, but not like a Greek.'

'You mean she's not really a foreigner?'

'No, just a hammy actress. Anyway, you might like to know that she's decided to hire a private detective.'

'That seems like a good idea. I expect Jay's solicitor can recommend one.'

'No, she's got a relative in Camden Town who's in the investigation business, and she's decided to ask you to help him. I thought I'd better warn you.'

'But I can't, I'm a detective constable, that would be, I mean, I'd get into trouble,' I started gabbling.

Joan patted my hand.

'Don't worry,' she said. 'We all understand your position. And none of the family takes any notice of Ariadne. We just hope she doesn't make things worse for poor Jay.'

'I don't think she can, really. Do you know Councillor Rodney Bennett?' I suddenly asked, on impulse.

'I have to go now,' she said, and sure enough, before I could say another word, Ariadne came sailing along, grabbed the wheelchair handles and whisked her off, just as if Joan had signalled to her.

So even Joan, seemingly the most sensible and straightforward member of the Bennett clan, didn't want to admit their relationship with Councillor Bennett. It looked as if he was about to join his cousin Jay in the warm and nasty.

I strolled back next door to the nick, deep in thought.

Early next morning, while I was still at the sleep-walking stage and fumbling with teabags, somebody came thundering on my front door. It had to be Alfie. Nobody else, except maybe the postman, would arrive at that unearthly hour with so much noise. And after I'd explained a few facts to him a couple of weeks ago, I'd be surprised if even he would be that cheeky again. Well, it turned out all that guesswork, while I wandered dreamily to answer the door, was just a waste of brainpower. It was a complete stranger.

Tall, dark, bright-eyed, he stood on my doorstep flashing a hundred-watt smile at me. Handsome he certainly wasn't, but if good clothes and a cheerful manner at crack of dawn counted for anything, he was certainly somebody's cup of tea. But not mine. I reacted in character.

'No,' I said, starting to close the door, 'whatever it is, I don't want any, and you've got the wrong address anyway.'

He leaned heavily against the closing door, his smile undiminished.

'Greta Pusey?' he grinned. 'It's the right address, innit?'

I peered at him more closely. No, I definitely didn't know him. But I had to admit to a certain curiosity. My private address is very private, and the only men who ever came there – apart from that damn postman – were Jim and Alfie. So who was this?

He tried to come in, but I wasn't having any of that. Feeble as I am on waking, I'm hefty enough to stop tricks like that.

'Aristotle Anapolis,' he announced, apparently not a bit embarrassed by his failed attempt to shove his way into my home. 'You can call me Ari,' he added, thrusting a card at me, 'seeing we'll be working together.'

I focused on the card. Sure enough, it said, in Greek-looking lettering,

ARISTOTLE ANAPOLIS, PRIVATE INVESTIGATOR
YOU CAN TRUST ME WITH YOUR MOST PRIVATE PROBLEMS

My first thought was: not another Ari! Ariadne Bennett was enough to cope with, but a male Ari was one too many. Then the rest of his statement sunk in. What did he mean, seeing we'll be working together?

'You'd better come in,' I opened the door wider and stepped back, only remembering how little I was wearing when I saw his beaming smile change to something a bit more lecherous. Well, how was I to know that some strange man was going to see me in my usual sleeping outfit of a pair of fraying old cotton shorts and a halter top I'd long ago grown out of? I mean, who bothers about glamorous nighties and matching negligées these days? Anyway, however he felt, he managed to keep his feelings in check, and followed me in at a respectful distance.

Before I had a chance to ask him what he meant about working together, he threw himself into an obviously prepared spiel about how he'd known Ariadne all his life, and they'd grown up together, so when her husband was in trouble who else should she turn to, besides him being the best private investigator in London and the Home Counties, etc. etc. Incidentally, his English was just the same as mine, so it seemed that Joan Bennett had been telling the truth when she said that Ariadne put on the accent to make herself more interesting.

Probably he'd have gone on like that for another half hour if I hadn't cut in with a terse, 'Very likely, Ari. But that's got nothing to do with me.'

'But of course I understand your situation, being in the police and all, Greta. You don't mind if I call you Greta, do you?' he swept on. 'I know you can't take an active position to defend poor Ariadne's husband. That's why she needs me to clear his name. But you can tell me the case against him, for a start, can't you?'

'I don't see why I should tell you anything. I'm not even sure I should be talking to you at all. Jay and his solicitor can tell you whatever you need to know,' I said, waking up more by the minute. 'Come to think of it, my best plan is to ask you to leave, now. Otherwise I'll be late for work.'

This wasn't absolutely true. I always get up hours before I need to, because I have to re-adjust to the world very, very slowly after waking. I actually had plenty of time to chat to Aristotle Anapolis and have a leisurely breakfast and walk quite calmly to the cop shop. I just didn't think it was a good idea. But Aristotle made it clear that he didn't agree with me. And short of physically chucking him out, there wasn't much I could do about it. After all, I'd let him in freely enough.

'You'll be making your tea now, won't you? How about offering me a cup,' Aristotle coaxed. 'There's no harm in us having a cuppa together, is there?'

Tea. Teatime. Of course, I was on nights. It wasn't crack of dawn at all, it was teatime. Just because I'd woken up in my usual haze when the alarm went off, and was still staggering about trying to remember my name when the doorbell rang, I'd thought it was first thing in the morning. Then my mind had gone wandering off about the postman, and I'd assumed it was about six o'clock in the morning. No wonder Aristotle was so bright and breezy. He'd had most of the day to get used to being awake. Naturally, I didn't let on any of this discovery to him. I just made out I'd known all along it was late afternoon.

'Sure, right, no harm at all in us having a cup together. Then you can go,' I added. 'I'm sure I shouldn't have anything to do with you or your investigations. Sit down, and I'll put the kettle on.'

And throw a few more clothes on while it's boiling, I added silently to myself. Aristotle was looking altogether too interested in my legs – in all the parts of me that were visible, actually.

I made up my mind to keep the conversation away from the Bennett case.

'So how long have you been a private investigator?' I asked Aristotle chattily, plonking a mug of the dark brown stuff at his elbow.

'I knew you were a rare one as soon as I set eyes on you!' he hollered out enthusiastically. 'You're the first woman I ever met who can make a decent cup of tea, instead of that pee-water they usually give you. Yes, four sugars, please.'

And with his mouth full of toast, he proceeded to give me a short history of his detecting career. He must have been older than he looked, because he said he'd been a regular copper for five years before he decided to branch out on his own. He got a job with an old Greek geezer in Camden Town who specialised in finding out which of their employees were robbing local bosses in various businesses, retail and manufacturing. Seemed there was enough of that sort of thing going on in the area to keep the firm ticking over on a regular basis. It was quite a paying outfit, but when the old boy retired and Ari kept on the premises, he decided to branch out into more varied and exciting types of investigation.

'So have you had a lot of interesting cases since then?' I asked him, and he shuffled his feet and looked uncomfortable.

'Not really,' he blurted out. 'Well, tell you the truth, this case about Ariadne's husband is my first one.'

'And how are you going to set about it?'

My waking-up process was in full swing now, and I was beginning to realise that this poor sod had no idea how to get started on what was virtually his first case. It was a lot different from his experience of catching sweat-shop machinists smuggling rolls of material out of the factory under their maternity clothes.

Lucky for me I had a good excuse not to help him. I wouldn't have a clue how to set about it, myself.

*

When I got into work, everyone was rushing around in a great lather, barking unfathomable syllables at each other. I couldn't catch what was going on at all, so it was a great relief when Alfie got hold of me and pulled me out into the corridor.

'Come on,' he said, 'no time to hang about.'

I was thrilled. It didn't matter what it was, if I was going to be doing something, and not just watching everyone else being busy, that was good enough for me.

'What's up?' I gasped as Alfie hustled me downstairs and out into the car park.

He shoved me into a squad car and started to drive off.

Did I mention that Alfie is the world's worst driver? He is also that rare thing among men, a rotten driver who doesn't think he's that old champ, Graham Hill. (More like his son Damien, who'd had to give it up.) We'd only gone a few yards down the road when Alfie gave me the keys and got out to swap seats. That made me feel even more the cat's pyjamas.

'Where to?'

'The Bennett family house in Radlett. You know the address better than I do,' he added with a bit of a stern look.

As we zipped out of Watford, I asked him again what had happened.

'You'll have to ask your friend Jonathan Bennett,' Alfie answered, still not a bit friendly. 'He claims his wife's been kidnapped. You might believe that. Nobody else does. He's lucky it's us going to interview him, otherwise he'd be in for a rough time.'

I decided to keep my lip buttoned for the rest of the short journey. When Alfie had the hump, it was best to keep quiet. And anyway, what could I say at this stage? Certainly this wasn't a good time to tell him about Aristotle.

We drew up in a burst of flying gravel in front of the Bennett house, and I noticed that Alfie was in no great hurry to get out of the car. He sat there looking glum and sighing a lot. Finally he shook his head, and said, more like his usual chummy self, 'Come on then, girl, let's get to it. See what the silly buggers have got to say for themselves this time.'

'Before that, Alfie, can you tell me what's happened up until now?'

'I don't know, do I?' he countered irritably. 'Your man Jonathan Bennett phoned to say his wife's been kidnapped, and we got elected to come and find out more. But you say nothing about his own case, right? Not having you getting into trouble with Cheerful Charlie.'

This was encouraging, although delivered snappily. Translated, it meant that Alfie was still looking out for me, and didn't want me getting into Chief Inspector Chester's bad books.

I didn't feel better for long, though. Even though I was sympathetic to Jay Bennett, I simply couldn't swallow his story.

After we'd gone over it a few times, Alfie said in his most stolid old-timer's voice, 'I'm sorry, Mr Bennett, I can't understand how you conclude that your wife has been kidnapped just because nobody's seen her since yesterday. There must be a hundred explanations more feasible than abduction. I understand that you've contacted all her family and such friends as you know of, but that still doesn't mean that she didn't leave of her own accord.'

Almost wringing his hands in his despair, Jay said, 'But I told you, she never goes anywhere on her own, and she never goes away for more than a few hours without her overnight bag and her model's case with all her cosmetics. And since the accident, she wouldn't move out of the house without Rosie – our daughter.'

Alfie stuck to his guns.

'I'll report her as a missing person. Rightly speaking, it's too soon even to do that, but since you're so sure, we can make an exception.'

And Jay had to be satisfied with that.

I wanted a quick word with his sister-in-law Joan, to ask how she was getting on – and maybe get an opinion from her about Ariadne being missing, but Alfie said we had to get back to the station. So apart from a caring smile and nod to Jay, I wasn't able to say or do anything helpful.

And on the way back to Shady Lane, all I could get out of Alfie was the remark that he thought it was all very fishy. I was wondering when I'd get a chance to contact Aristotle to see what he had to say about his missing client.

Back at the nick, Dusty Miller was full of herself. Puffed up with her own importance, she told me she was on a kidnapping case. Misinterpreting my dropped jaw and crossed eyes, she crowed, 'Yes, the first kidnapping case in Watford in fifty years, and I'm on the team!'

'Who... who...' I couldn't seem to stop myself sounding like a lost owl.

'Councillor Rodney Bennett! And his wife's had a ransom note already! Oh, just a minute, I don't think I was supposed to tell you that. Keep it to yourself, OK, Greta?'

'Come on, you two, don't stand there nattering,' DS Freddy Forbes interrupted before I had a chance to ask Dusty any more. 'It's all hands in the incident room for this one.'

Dusty looked choked. She'd thought she had an exclusive on this, and now we were all in on it.

A neatly typed message was being thrown on to the screen when we went in. Originally it must have looked like something a typist would have been proud to give to her boss, but it had been torn into bits and then pieced and stuck together. That made it reasonably readable. But it seemed to have so little to do with this case – or any sort of police work at all – that for the moment I thought I'd got myself into the wrong shop. Sudden thoughts of trying to get some vocational guidance came into my mind. If this was part of being a detective, I wasn't suited to it. The message read:

THE DELIVERY OF SERVICES TO THE PEOPLE OF WATFORD AT A REASONABLE COST REMAINS THE AIM OF THIS COUNCIL. TO DO THIS WE WILL NEED TO BECOME MORE EFFICIENT. THERE IS SO MUCH THAT WE

DO WELL, BUT EQUALLY THERE IS MUCH THAT NEEDS
IMPROVEMENT. I AM LOOKING FORWARD TO WORKING
WITH FELLOW COUNCILLORS, OFFICERS AND THE
RESIDENTS OF WATFORD TO BRING THESE
IMPROVEMENTS ABOUT AND MAKE WATFORD AN EVEN
BETTER PLACE TO LIVE.

Before I had a chance to put my foot in it by asking the
nearest person what this speechifying had to do with us, DI
Graves said, 'OK, we've all seen that, but the important thing
is what was on the back of it.'

After a little tussle at the back of the room, the message
was replaced with a hand-scrawled one which read:

> *I'll let you know the price for the return*
> *of Roddy Bennett.*

If that was Dusty's idea of a ransom note, it certainly wasn't
mine.

'Fingerprints on both sides seem to be Councillor
Bennett's and his secretary's,' said DS Forbes, 'and she
confirms that she typed that extract for him last thing before
she left. Then the Councillor was working alone in his office
until quite late. That was the last anyone saw of him. No sign
of a struggle. No clothes, toiletries or personal effects
missing from his home. No suggestions from his wife.'

Dusty piped up, 'We found the ransom note torn up in his
wastepaper basket. It looks as if the kidnappers changed their
minds about it.'

That was the opposite of help. All it did was baffle us all
even more. That Dusty! It probably wasn't even a ransom
note in the first place.

Anyway, after that there was a long silence, broken by
Alfie clearing his throat in what could only be described as a
meaningful manner. All eyes swivelled to him. What a relief.
Someone was going to say something, however useless.

'The Health and Safety Officer awaiting trial, Jonathan Bennett, says his wife has been kidnapped,' he rumbled. 'We could see no reason to believe this. No ransom note. She's only been gone for a matter of hours. He's just panicking because he doesn't know where she is, and he says she never goes anywhere on her own. But could there be a connection? Can we establish how well she and Councillor Bennett knew each other?'

I plucked up all my courage. I'd probably get jumped on from a great height for opening my beginner's mouth, but I just had to say my bit.

'Does anyone know, I mean, have there been any reports, is anyone else missing?'

I should have expected it. A great guffaw of laughter came at me like a tidal wave. Even Alfie was laughing at me.

But when it died down, DI Graves said, in quite a kindly way, 'No, Greta, there hasn't been an epidemic of missing persons from the Bennett family, nor any family in Watford so far as we know. Or did you have a theory of mass migration?'

Later on, when I was still feeling mortified, Alfie said to me, 'Never mind, girl, we've all got to begin somewhere, and if you can't laugh sometimes, you'll never laugh.'

Alfie had a great collection of meaningless sayings like that, which didn't tell you anything except that his voice was still working.

But much later still, when it turned out that two officers of Watford Town Council had also disappeared, nobody was laughing. These couldn't all be kidnaps. Obviously, people were running away from something. What did these people know that we didn't?

I was just relieved that neither of the missing officers was called Bennett. Nor Rodney. On the other hand, it turned out that there was a more puzzling link. They were both also members of the golf club used by Jay Bennett's boss, and Councillor Rodney Bennett, as well as many of my own superior officers. Was this golf club a sort of Masonic connection? Now that there was so much fuss about the Masons and their influence in the police, maybe a golf club was the latest secret handshake centre?

Even I could see that was just rubbish, so I didn't bother to suggest it to Alfie. What seemed a more significant connection was that Rodney Bennett was the Chairman of the Watford Council Planning Committee, and the two missing officers worked in the Planning Department.

'Make of that what you will,' as DI Graves remarked in a knowing voice to DS Forbes.

When I got home next morning, Aristotle Anapolis was waiting on my doorstep. I was not a bit glad to see him, especially when he told me he'd rung my bell and a very rude man had opened the door, told him to bugger off, and slammed it in his face before he could say a word. So Jim was back.

'Come on,' I said wearily, 'let's go somewhere for a cup of coffee.'

'Why can't we go in your place?'

'Because I don't want my boyfriend to hear what we've got to say.'

Aristotle looked pleased.

'Intimate, is it going to be?' he leered.

'No,' I grumped, 'it's all bad news. And you can forget the other stuff. Our connection is business only, and don't you forget it.'

I could see he was disappointed, and in a way I was, too. He was fair to middling fanciable. But I had enough on my plate with Jim.

Anyway, I told Aristotle about all the missing people, and he was as blank about it as I was.

'Group kidnap, innit?' was his only offering.

'Not much good for you,' I pointed out, 'losing your client so early in the case.'

'Werl,' he said, 'she's not so much a client, more an old friend, innit?'

Whereupon he produced his mobile, got a number, and had a rapid-fire conversation in what I guessed must be Greek. Sounded like Greek to me, anyway. I was tired and hoped Jim would have gone by the time I got to bed.

'It's OK,' said Aristotle, disconnecting his phone, 'Ariadne's with my Ma.'

Chapter 6

I was too hopped up and excited to sleep after making sure that Aristotle was telling the truth and that we did actually know Ariadne's whereabouts. Which was just as well, since Jim was still there, waiting for me to join him in bed.

'What are you doing,' I protested, pretty daftly I have to admit, as it was perfectly obvious what he was doing. 'I mean, shouldn't you be off delivering or collecting something, or going off to the Continent or back home to your wife and kids up North?'

'Shut up,' he explained, 'and come here. I thought I'd give you a bit of a treat and take the day off. Don't start telling me the tale about a hard night's work and needing your sleep. Come on, give us a nibble.'

But I didn't half have a good sleep afterwards. I never even heard him go. Lucky I set the alarm for hours earlier than I needed to get up, otherwise I'd have got it in the neck for being late for the night shift.

When I came out of my usual waking-up fog, I started to think about Ariadne and what I should do about her. And her friend Aristotle. Tell Alfie? That seemed the safest thing, then he could help me decide who else to tell. No, maybe I ought to talk to her first to try to find out why she sloped off like that. But I couldn't do that without asking Aristotle where to find her. And that meant that I was working with him, and putting him before my own department. Surely my first loyalty was to them and to Alfie? Then again, what about poor Jay Bennett, doing his conkers about his missing wife?

By the time I trudged into the nick in Shady Lane, I still hadn't come to any firm conclusion. So this was why detectives went around frowning all the time. It doesn't half make your brain hurt, all that thinking.

They'd made a bit of progress on the case during the day, but it was no big deal. Roddy Bennett's secretary gave them some samples of his writing and printing, and with these, our tame hand-writing expert said that the Councillor had written the 'ransom note' himself. The conclusion was that he'd tried to make it seem as if he'd been kidnapped by writing that message on the back of a bit of one of his speeches, then thought better of it and torn it up and dumped it. And then, by the looks of things, done a runner.

That left us no wiser where he'd gone, or why. Or if there was a connection between him and the two missing Council officers. Dusty Miller was of the opinion that he'd run off with his cousin Jay's tasty wife, Ariadne. I wasn't even slightly tempted to explain that this wasn't the case, or how I knew. It would have been fun to see Dusty's face when I scored one off her, but it wasn't worth the risk of getting myself in the poo.

'So what have we got on our plates tonight, Sarge?' I asked Alfie, who shook his head glumly.

'Nothing what I can see, girl. Why, you got any ideas?'

'Well,' I dithered, but Alfie gave me such an encouraging smile, I plucked up courage and suggested, 'how about going to see Vera Varney?'

'What, the widow of that poor old lover-boy what got done in by your Gladys Trulove? What would we want to do that for? I saw her that night,' he grinned, 'the night of your first murder.'

'Yes, but since then I found out that the late Julius Varney worked with Jay Bennett at the HSE. And Mrs Varney told me that her husband mentioned some funny goings-on there.'

Alfie's look darkened. 'I told you, Greta,' he began, but I butted in with, 'I know we mustn't interfere in the Jay Bennett case, but we could just have a chat with her about her husband, couldn't we? Wouldn't that be OK, Alfie? I mean, if we've got nothing else to do…'

Vera Varney was even more of a picture than when I'd seen her before. She was wearing what could only be called a gown. It was constructed – that was the only word for it – of some filmy material in the colour I'd learned from her to call apricot. It had lots of ruffles and flounces, and she had a matching bow in her – almost apricot-coloured – hair of bubbly curls. I was amazed to see a look of admiration on Alfie's face. I could hardly believe my eyes. In fact, I have to say it was more than appreciation. It was downright lechery.

The Widow Varney saw this, and didn't seem to mind.

'Oh, it's the sergeant. How nice of you to call,' she simpered, and then, noticing me, added, 'oh, hallo, er…'

'Not too late to have a chat, then,' Alfie boomed, sticking his chest out and almost strutting into the house as she stood aside for him.

This was a side to Alfie that I'd never suspected. I'm far from naïve myself, but I thought I had him pegged as a devoted family man and faithful husband. But there was no mistaking the flavour of the unspoken between these two. She was willing and he was keen, and if I hadn't been there, they would have been at it like rabbits in five minutes.

I'd made a serious mistake in suggesting this call. I had to find a way to get him out of there before he found an errand to send me on, to give him a clear field to do what it was they both wanted to do. The atmosphere was thick with it. It wasn't just that I was shocked at Alfie. After all, I suppose he had to be as human as the next man. But we were meant to be on duty, and I was disappointed at my own lack of judgement. If I was wrong about Alfie, who else might I have been wrong about?

With growing gloom I watched them settle down for a cosy chat over coffee and little cakies with apricot jam in them.

Looking soppy but pretending to be still all business, Alfie said, 'About your late husband…'

Putting her little apricot-tipped paw on his arm, the Widow Varney batted her eyelashes at him and twittered confidentially, 'It wasn't that my Julius was a bad man, you know, Sergeant. Actually, apart from his – er – you know, sexual peculiarities, he was the soul of honour.'

'Go on,' Alfie urged, his naturally ruddy colour deepening, maybe with passion. Certainly not embarrassment. 'Do you mean by that, Mrs Varney, that if he told you something about his suspicions concerning his work, you could be sure it was his honest opinion? I mean, he wouldn't just spin you a line?'

Vera edged another inch along the couch. I wouldn't have thought she could get any closer without actually sitting on his lap. This was awful.

Inspired by anxiety, I burst into their comfortable chat with, 'Er, excuse me, Sergeant, but is your mobile switched on? I'm afraid I forgot to leave word at the station where we were going…'

Sure enough, it wasn't, and thank heavens, the moment he did switch it on, it rang. Even across the room I could hear the bark of DI Graves informing DS Partridge that he was wanted back at the office, pronto. Didn't even waste time asking where he was. That was a bit of luck, too.

On the way back, I asked Alfie if he felt he'd learned anything about the late Julius Varney's opinion of matters at the HSE.

'We didn't really get time to go into it, though, did we?' I added. 'And anyway, like you said…'

'…course, like I already told you,' he said, 'even if we was on the case, it wouldn't be evidence, hearing what a dead man said to his wife before he got killed.'

I decided not to point out that it *could* only have been before he got killed. Unless his widow was into speaking to the dead as well as being a bit funny about apricot. I made an enquiring sort of noise instead, like, 'Mmm?'

'But seems like you was right,' Alfie went on, 'obvious there was a lot of hanky-panky going on there in that HSE, and that there Jonathan Bennett was the fly in the ointment stopping the wheels going round smooth. What I can't make out,' he added in a much more lively voice, 'is why that Julius Varney carried on with all those women when he had a lovely wife like that waiting for him at home.'

Luckily by that time we'd got back to the cop shop, so I didn't have to censor the obvious answer off the tip of my tongue.

But one of these days, Alfie, I thought to myself, you're going to hear some home truths from me. You criticising Julius Varney for straying round the neighbourhood like the local tomcat seems like a case of pots and kettles. The only difference was that probably Alfie Partridge hadn't yet had the opportunity to be another one the same. And now thanks to my stupidity, the offer, in the shape of the bereaved Mrs Varney, was plonking itself under his nose.

I've got to admit at the time it didn't even cross my mind to think of my Jim in the same way. But looking back, I can see there was nothing to choose between the lot of us.

DI Gerald Graves was literally hopping from foot to foot when we went into the office he shared with DCI Cheerful Charlie. I was afraid he'd ask where we'd been, but he was in too much of a hurry to get on to bother about that.

'Come on, Alfie, you've got a train to catch, and you can take young Greta with you. Here you are, here's your travel warrant for the two of you, buck up, you can just catch the ten to midnight from the Junction. Here's all the background,' and he shoved a pocket tape recorder into Alfie's hand and absolutely bulldozed us both out of the door. Don't know what the panic was about. We had plenty of time, it was only just gone eleven o'clock and it couldn't take us more than five minutes to get to Watford Junction

Station. So Alfie had time to phone Betty to tell her not to keep his supper hot.

We had a cup of tea and a snack at the café by the station. Well, I say a snack, but Alfie as usual managed to tuck away quite a mountain of food while we were looking at our travel warrant and listening to the instructions and background on the tape. And of course he managed to get greasy fingermarks on the warrant and a few crumbs into the tape machine. Didn't stop us hearing what it was all about, though.

Anderson and Gustafson, the two missing employees of our local Town Council, had been in a car crash somewhere up North. Anderson, who'd been driving, was in hospital, and Gustafson was dead. Someone from the local cop shop was going to meet us off the train at Durham and take us to the local hospital. We were to interview Anderson, and if he was fit enough, escort him back to Watford. Simple enough, it seemed to me.

'So what was all the fuss and excitement, then, Alfie?' I asked.

I should have been ready by this time for the usual answer.

'Buggered if I know, girl,' he said.

I decided that the hours on the train would be the ideal chance for me to come clean to him about Aristotle and Ariadne.

I should have known better. The moment we took our seats, he shut his eyes and was gone off with the fairies for the whole journey. So I was still stuck with this piece of information on my chest like indigestion. I was brooding about it all the way to Birmingham, where we had to change trains for Durham.

And we had to run like hell to get our connection, too. So then I had to listen to a long moan from Alfie about how he'd hoped to have a cup of coffee and a bit of cake between trains, and he hated waking up all in a rush, and he wondered if our train was late or the other one was early. I wondered if he was always like that when he first woke up. Poor Betty, if he was.

Anyway, I couldn't get a word in there, either.

Chapter 7

Whatever message had gone ahead of us, the locals must have decided it was all quite important. The DC who whipped us from the station to the hospital, all sirens and lights flashing, was unexpectedly respectful. Asked no questions, and called Alfie 'sir' all the time. Didn't speak to me at all, of course.

Then at the hospital, our man Anderson was in a private room with a uniformed plod sitting at his bedside, notebook at the ready.

I must say, this Anderson didn't look like a man who'd just survived a serious car crash in which his passenger had been killed. True, he was lying back on his pillows looking about the same colour as they were, but he didn't have a scratch or a bruise visible, and none of those nasty tubes and wires and machinery and stuff you might have expected.

After hearing about the accident, I'd been trying to get myself ready for one of those scenes, like you see on TV, where things are going bleep and you're scared stiff in case they stop, which means everyone runs about like hell, shouting baffling things which are probably to do with resuscitation.

No, nothing like that, he was just lying there looking not exactly grand, but not even groaning a bit. I don't want you to think I was disappointed, but it was a bit of a let-down.

'What's he say so far?' Alfie questioned the uniform without even a 'Hallo there' to start with.

The PC shook his head.

'Not a word so far,' he admitted, closing his notebook and looking apologetic, as if it was his fault.

'What does the doc say?' Alfie asked.

'He can go tomorrow,' said the plod, even more unhappily. 'No injuries, just shock. No treatment required. Will you be taking him back with you?' he asked, brightening. 'Sir,' he added as an afterthought.

Alfie ignored this and plonking his meaty hand on Anderson's shoulder, gave him an unfriendly shake. Anderson's eyes opened very slightly. He squinted through this narrow slit at Alfie, then shut them firmly with a deep sigh.

'Mister Anderson!' Alfie boomed, making us all jump.

'Yes, what now,' Anderson whispered.

'Can you tell us what happened?' Alfie continued at the same volume.

Anderson opened his eyes. They were the brightest blue I had ever seen. I've never seen eyes that colour, even in touched-up photographs. I noticed then, for the first time, that his hair was so fair that it was almost white. Anderson, I thought. Gustafson. Were they some kind of Scandinavians?

'We were going to the port to get the ferry to Stavanger,' Anderson mumbled. Alfie signalled to the uniform to make notes. Good thing he hadn't picked on me – I couldn't remember for the moment what I'd done with my notebook. 'Gus was navigating, and he changed his mind at the last minute about the directions he'd been giving me, and I slammed on the brakes. It was his car. I thought it was quite old, so I didn't know it had a driver's airbag. He went through the windscreen. No passenger airbag. I'm OK. It's not right.'

'What's not right, young feller?' Alfie asked in a much gentler voice. Almost fatherly, he sounded.

Anderson started to cry without a sound, no sobbing, just tears running down his cheeks. The young PC looked as if he was going to join in. Even Alfie looked sympathetic.

'It's not fair,' Anderson muttered. 'It was his car, it was his idea, he shouldn't be dead, he should have been driving, he shouldn't be dead.'

'Why were you going to Stavanger?' Alfie asked.

'We were going to get another ferry from there to Iceland.'

Up until this I'd managed to hold my tongue and leave it all to Alfie, but hearing this, I couldn't help myself.

'Iceland?' I burst out. 'What on earth would anyone want to go to Iceland for?'

If the whole thing hadn't been so sad, I might have made a few cracks about shopping somewhere nearer, but it wouldn't have been right in the circumstances. I could see – we could all see – the young feller was seriously upset about what happened to his friend. Remarks about frozen food would not have been suitable.

'Gustafson's family came from Iceland,' Anderson said. 'He said we could stay with his uncle and we'd be safe there. For as long as we liked. No problems, no questions asked. Poor Gus. What can I tell his family now?'

'Why were you going to Iceland?' Alfie asked. 'You weren't taking a holiday. Neither of you had applied for leave. You hadn't told anyone you were going. What was it all about? What do you mean, you'd be safe there? What were you both running away from?'

Anderson gave a deep sigh. It seemed to come from his toes.

'You'd better ask Rodney Bennett that,' he said sorrowfully, and shut his eyes again.

Alfie wasn't about to give up at this stage, just when things had started to get interesting.

'And can you tell us where we can find Mister Rodney Bennett?' he asked, going back to his original unsympathetic manner. 'I expect you know he went missing at the same time as you and your friend Mr Gustafson bunked off out of Watford. I suppose he wasn't going to meet you in Iceland, by any chance?'

Anderson showed his first signs of life. Those surprising blue eyes flew wide open and he looked straight at Alfie for the first time.

'Who did you say you are?' he asked. 'You're not one of the local police, are you?'

So now we had to start right at the beginning, where Alfie introduced me and himself and we showed him our warrant cards and explained where we'd come from and why, and all the stuff we should have done when we walked into the hospital room. I'd been wondering all along why we hadn't done it all by the book in the first place, but I knew better than to go against anything Alfie did, even if he wasn't following his own hard and fast rules. But if I'd behaved like that, I wouldn't half have got it in the neck from him.

The result was that Anderson couldn't or wouldn't tell us any more, and we'd have to go to the local nick to arrange to take him back to Watford with us in the morning. Well, I say in the morning. It was nearly that by that time. So the first thing Alfie mentioned when we got back in the squad car was breakfast.

Turned out their canteen was a sight better than ours. And while Alfie was tucking in and I was indulging in a mouthful or two myself, their local DI came to talk to us.

And he practically took my mind right off everything – the case, the breakfast, my career ambitions – the lot. It wasn't just that he was so handsome, but as well as that there was some special something about him that made my toes curl and tingle.

Oh, wow, that DI Derek Michaelson! And I should point out that I'm not usually all that susceptible. Up until then, all the running in my so-called love life had been done by the men, and as far as I was concerned, I could take it or leave it. I mean, not that I'm a cold fish. I enjoy a bit of a tumble as much as the next woman, but there was no romance in it. So this was a new feeling. And I wasn't sure I liked it all that much.

Anyway, he sat and talked to Alfie while Alfie went on shovelling food into his gob as if he hadn't eaten for a fortnight, and I sat with egg dripping off my fork and my eyes riveted to his face. He told us he'd just been made up from Sergeant to Inspector, though I could see he wasn't all that much older than me. He was one of those Fast Track types who'd come into the Service from University, the lucky devil. I'd started to wonder if I could get a transfer up here, when I heard him mention to Alfie that he was looking for a posting nearer to London.

'Don't look in our direction,' Alfie mumbled through a mouthful of bacon, sausage and egg, and then washing it all down with a hearty swig of tea, added more plainly, 'we've got more DI's than we know what to do with.'

The DI looked disappointed, but not a patch like I felt. To think I might never see this tasty detective again! The first man I'd ever met who made me feel so squiggly!

Well, I've got to admit that when we all got up to go – even Alfie having eaten himself to a standstill – I did get a bit of a shock. Not only did Alfie look nearly a foot taller than DI Michaelson, but we could all see he was a good few inches shorter than me, too. But I wouldn't have cared, tall or short, if I could have had a crack at him. Still, he showed no such interest in me, so I suppose it was just as well that we weren't likely to meet again. Except in my dreams.

At the railway station, I went to get us some papers to read while Alfie looked after Anderson, who seemed a bit wobbly. When I saw the photograph on the front pages of most of the tabloids and even a couple of the posh papers, I felt a bit weak myself.

Ariadne Bennett smouldered out at me, under headlines like 'SAFETY SUSPECT'S WIFE MISSING' AND 'TWIST IN SAFETY CASE'. I could see at a glance that they all had the same photograph, but I gathered up an armful of different papers, to see if they all had the same story.

It looked as if I'd have no choice about when to tell Alfie about Ariadne and Aristotle. I'd have to tell him now. But could I do that in front of Anderson? Anyway, I'd give him the papers first. I gave one to Anderson, too, and watched him carefully to see if he reacted to the picture of Ariadne. He didn't even glance at it, just took it, laid it down, shut his eyes and went fast off to sleep the moment the train started.

Accounting for the usual trimmings that journalists add, specially when they've got hardly any facts to go on, the story was the same in all the papers. Ariadne had disappeared, and she was the wife of an HSE officer who was awaiting trial in a corruption case. Nothing could be written about Jay Bennett's case, of course, it being *sub judice*. So they concentrated on Ariadne, her beauty, her acting and modelling ambitions, and the fact that she was a devoted wife and mother. The more I read, the more I wondered who had given this story to the papers. It was so rapturous about Ariadne, it was like the sort of press release that studios put out when they give a build-up to a new 'discovery'.

Knowing that Ariadne hadn't been kidnapped, and putting two and two together, I came to the conclusion that she'd sent this story to all the news media herself, complete with her best publicity photograph. Surely she wasn't trying to use her husband's troubles just to get herself in the public eye? Could she be so desperate for fame that she'd stoop to such a low trick? Judging from the opinion I'd picked up from her sister-in-law Joan, the answer was: probably.

I hoicked Alfie out of earshot but still near enough to keep an eye on Anderson. He seemed to be asleep, but you never knew. Not that I had any reason to think he was pulling a blinder, but I'd got to the point where I didn't believe anything was what it seemed. So I thought we'd better make sure he didn't just disappear.

'Well, girl,' said Alfie, 'and what's up with you? Not going to ask me why that DI took no notice of you making eyes at him, are you?'

I gave him a light friendly punch on the arm. I felt comfortable enough with Alfie these days to be able to do that and know he wouldn't take offence. Also, I didn't know how to answer without giving away that he was smack on target. Sometimes Alfie could be very shrewd.

'It's about Ariadne,' I started breathlessly, and was glad to see his expression change from heavy teasing to genuine interest. But as I went on about Aristotle and knowing Ariadne's whereabouts and suspecting she was using her husband's misfortune for her own selfish publicity, Alfie went from a puzzled frown to a dark look of definite reprimand.

'And you're supposed to feel sorry for this Jonathan Bennett?' he said. 'But you never had the heart to tell him his wife is safe and not kidnapped? Greta, I'm disappointed in you.'

So by the time we got back to Watford, I was still under the cloud of Alfie's disapproval. And in an atmosphere of cold silence we delivered Anderson back to Shady Lane and went to our separate homes without another word.

I was tired and fed up and smarting from Alfie's criticism, partly because I knew he was right. So the last thing I wanted to see when I got home that morning was that bloody Greek on my doorstep, with a woman. If she'd been the semi-missing Ariadne Bennett, I might have forgiven him. I had a quick mental flash of myself restoring her to a grateful husband, and all the scenes of rejoicing...

No, it was some little scruffy redhead in a dirty mac and too much make-up. And just to make things worse, before they saw me, they were laughing together. I'd give them something to laugh at, I thought grimly, marching up the path with my fists clenched.

Then Aristotle saw me and turned on his hundred-watt Greek smile.

'Greta!' he exclaimed. 'So lovely to see you at last—'

I didn't give him a chance to go on with his shmoozing.

'Listen, Mister Onassis or whatever you call yourself,' I interrupted, 'get off my doorstep and out of my life.'

This might have been very successful if I hadn't remembered something in the nick of time.

'But before you go,' I added quickly, 'give me your mother's address so that I can go and see Ariadne.'

His scruffy friend chimed in at this point.

'Ms Pusey,' she started, 'I'm an investigative journalist—'

'And I'm a Detective Constable…'

'…from the *News of the World*,' she went on as if I hadn't interrupted, 'and I believe there has been some serious corruption amongst the Councillors and officers of Watford Town Council.'

She paused to see the result so far (like I was going to be impressed), so I took the chance to barge between her and Aristotle, open my door and hop straight in, slamming it in their faces before they realised what was going on. I pushed up the letterbox flap and shouted through it, 'Write down your mother's address and stick it through here, Ari. And take your snoopy friend off my doorstep.'

Before I'd done the few strides it took to get into the bedroom, the phone started ringing. Of course it was going to be Aristotle, who else?

'Greta,' he purred in his most charming voice, 'please give us a chance to talk to you. It might be as important to your career as to mine.'

'Piss off!' I shouted and banged the phone down. I was tired and irritable and probably not thinking straight. Ari soon put that right.

When he phoned the next time, he came to straight to the point without bothering about getting round to it.

'If you won't co-operate with us, I won't be able to give you my Ma's address,' he explained.

I plodded back to the front door and opened it.

'I'll make us all some coffee,' Ari said, bustling past me into the kitchen as if he was a regular visitor or part of the household. 'You two sit down and get to know each other.'

'My name's Joan Smith,' said my new manky-looking friend. 'Can I call you Greta?'

'OK. Do you really work for the *News of the World*?'

'Well, I have done. I'm more of a freelance, really. But they do take stuff from me sometimes,' she insisted.

I thought this was probably an exaggerated claim, but I was too tired to argue the toss. Anyway, I wanted to know what she and Ari were up to.

'You probably want to know how I got on to this,' Joan Smith smiled, showing some nasty ferrety looking teeth and puffing out a pong of stale cigarettes. 'It was pure luck. If I didn't live in Camden Town I wouldn't have seen Ari's advert. Mind you, it was more brain than luck that I jumped to a connection between him and Ariadne when I saw the papers this morning. So when he told me what he knew about Ariadne's husband and everything, it came to me that this is a case worth investigating.'

'Right,' said Aristotle, banging down a tray of coffee mugs and a plate of my best Belgian chocolate biscuits that I usually saved for special visitors. I gave him a sour look which he didn't notice, but he went on, 'See Greta, we've got the perfect team here, with Joan's press connection and me working for Ariadne and you being in the police—'

'Forget it,' I interrupted. 'There's not going to be any teamwork here. I can't stop you and your friend snooping around wherever you like, but I'm having nothing to do with it.'

Joan laid a grubby little claw on my hand.

'Of course we couldn't ask you to do anything that would interfere with your police duties,' she said, 'but it's obvious that Jay Bennett is being framed somehow or other, and we all know you don't want to see an innocent man go down because he's in the way of the real villains.'

'What real villains?'

During this conversation, even though I was having trouble staying awake, I'd been behaving like a real detective and closely observing this woman. The more I looked at her the less I believed she was who she said she was. For one thing, she was unusually dirty-looking, even for a journalist. She looked as if she never washed, and was a complete stranger to showers or baths. Also, her red hair had black roots and was a ridiculous colour – a sort of London bus red, which was a bad choice. There was nothing wrong with dyeing hair. I'd thought of doing mine from time to time when I got fed up with it being a sort of nondescript lightish brown, like weak school gravy. But there's red and red. And her filthy nails were badly painted a bruised-looking blue, which didn't go with the hair or the dirty raincoat. All in all, she looked like someone who'd been sleeping rough and was trying to cover it up.

She gave a sort of laugh which didn't sound genuine.

'Well, I'm an investigative journalist, aren't I? So it's my business to find out who the real villains are. But if you'd help, with Ari here backing us up…'

'OK,' I said, giving her a big surprise. She'd clearly thought she was on to a loser, but give her her due, she was a tryer. What I meant was that I'd made up my mind, but not in the way she wanted.

'Tell you what,' I went on, 'I'm dead knackered now. Give me a few hours to catch up on some sleep, then we'll get together and talk things over. I've got Ari's phone number, but give me yours as well and I'll give you both a call when I've had a good kip.'

'Well, er, tell you the truth, my mobile's on the blink at the moment,' she said uneasily. She meant she didn't have one. What! A journalist without a mobile! Come on, she must think I'm daft, I thought.

'OK, I'll try your home number. Just jot it down here,' I gave her a notepad, and watched her squirming some more.

'No, er, I don't suppose I'll be at home for a bit. Why don't you just give Ari a call, and he'll find me if we're not already together,' she simpered.

I was quite surprised at how well I'd hit the jackpot there. She must be living in a squat, and she was no more a journalist than I was.

Anyway, like most of my colleagues, I hated journalists. Apart from always getting things wrong and distorting everything they're told, they've got this rotten way of asking people questions. Like when somebody's relative has been run over, they'll say, 'And so how gutted do you feel, Mrs Brown?' or 'How anxious are you for the police to find the culprit, Mr Jones?' or saying to the police 'What are your chances of finding this child alive, Chief Inspector?' Heartless buggers, all of them. This Joan Smith certainly seemed to match the photofit there, alright.

Very likely what happened was that Ari couldn't afford real advertising, so he'd been following the example of the local tarts and putting his business card in phone boxes. His new little friend must have picked one up and got struck by the resemblance between his name and the one in the headlines. Then she'd probably thought she could row herself into the situation somehow.

Maybe she was just a wannabe journalist. Who could tell. My poor tired little brain couldn't work out any more possibilities. All I wanted to do was get rid of the pair of them until I was fully functioning again. And before they finished off my best biscuits.

*

It seemed to me I'd only been asleep for half an hour when the phone woke me.

I'd been having a wonderful dream about that handsome DI Michaelson. He'd come to work at Shady Lane, and he'd asked for me to be on his team. He hadn't really made any advances to me, but it was a start. And it gave me plenty of opportunity to admire his sturdy little body and to gaze into his chocolatey brown eyes. Just as I was trying to work out how to get him to visit me at home one evening, there was this terrible noise like all the sirens in the world going off together.

As usual, I tried to turn off the alarm and then the radio before I worked out what the noise was, picked up the phone and grunted into the wrong end of the damn thing. I squinted at the clock. I'd been asleep for eight hours! It certainly didn't feel like it. Not at all refreshed, I tried to take in what was coming out at me. It was Alfie booming away.

'Greta, can you hear me? What's the matter with you, girl? Are you ill? Wake up!'

'What, what, hallo,' I mumbled. 'Alfie, I thought we were having two days off now.'

Then a thought crept into my fuddled brain. Had I slept the whole two days off? Maybe I should have been at work by now. I tried to focus on the calendar, but it stayed obstinately blurred.

'What day is it, Alfie?'

His answer reassured me. It was OK, I'd only slept the eight hours I'd thought I needed. So why was Alfie phoning me on one of our days off?

'Can you hear me now, Greta?' he bellowed. 'I know we're supposed to be off today and tomorrow, but I thought you'd want to know the latest. Rodney Bennett has been found!'

Abruptly I came fully awake. It was the fastest transition I'd ever made from being dead to the world through to firing on all cylinders. So Alfie's next words reached me loud and clear. I wasn't dreaming. He actually said, 'His body was shoved behind some pipes in the basement of the Town Hall!'

Then he added, in typical Alfie fashion, 'So it wasn't suicide.'

There was a pause while I tried not to laugh. It wouldn't have been fitting, on hearing of a death, but Alfie's talent for the obvious sometimes made it difficult to stay serious. His next remark was not quite so clear.

He said, 'My girl will be very upset.'

His girl? Who could he mean? I thought I was his girl. He couldn't mean Betty. Oh, of course, he meant his daughter, Carole.

By the time I'd worked this out, he was going on, 'Best friends with his daughter she's been, since they were little nippers. You wouldn't like to come round and help me tell her, would you, Greta?'

Chapter 8

I slouched along moodily, kicking stones out of my way. That hadn't been one of Alfie's best ideas. Carole had just refused to speak to me, though I couldn't for the life of me see why or how she could possibly have blamed me for her friend's misery at the tragic loss of her father. Just because she'd asked me to help when Sharon Bennett had been so worried, she seemed to think it was all down to me how things turned out. Still, I suppose it was pretty stupid of me to expect logical thinking from any offspring of Alfie's.

And that was another thing. Bad enough that Dusty Miller should have decided it was important to phone Alfie on his day off to tell him that they'd found Rodney Bennett's body. Why Alfie? And why Dusty? But what I most wanted to know was, how did she know Alfie's home number? What kind of relationship had there been between Alfie and Dusty before I came on the scene? Maybe this was why she disliked me from the off, and not what I'd thought in the first place. Perhaps it had been vain of me to think it was because I looked like a model (well, from the neck down, anyway) and she looked like a get-together between two ironing boards.

Just to round off an ideal free day, I absent-mindedly kicked a pebble that turned out to be a large dog-turd and got shit all over my best boots. That was it. I decided to go to the pictures. Another mistake. The film was *Fargo*, where a pregnant slow-talking Minnesotan cop solved crimes and came out on top. Great. I couldn't even match up to a dumbo like that. I stamped home in a worse mood.

So of course I shouldn't have been surprised to find Aristotle and Joan Smith waiting on my doorstep again. A perfect end to a perfect day.

But I had an idea.

I invited them in so sweetly that they exchanged puzzled and suspicious looks as they trooped in behind me, and they both became positively uneasy as I graciously offered them refreshments. The perfect hostess, me. This wasn't the Greta they'd met before. Good. I had them worried.

'Now Joan,' I said, 'I'm really sorry that I can't tell you anything just now that will help you. Not about corruption, anyway. But you being an investigative journalist,' I went on, trying to keep the sarcasm out of my voice, 'I can put you in line for something else. A terrific feature story. I'm sure it'll help you get your foot in the door with any leading newspaper. It's about a very unusual murder case.'

Her pink little eyes lit up and she edged forward in her seat. I told her all about Gladys Trulove sticking a knife in Julius Varney.

'The thing is, you see,' I explained, 'you can't write up the actual case yet, but what you can do is interview all the leading characters. You've never met anyone like this lot. I can tell you they're all just made to order for a really fascinating piece for any of the Sundays – even a quality broadsheet might accept it if you do it right.'

She got doubtful all over again.

'Why, what's so special? Don't people stick knives in each other all the time, even in Watford?'

So I told her all the details about Gladys and her friend Vera and Julius's other two lady friends. And about Gladys being so concerned about Vera having nobody to go with to the bingo... and about Gladys getting so confused about names, even her best friend and her best friend's husband, the deceased.

'That's the thing, you see, that's what the case will hinge on,' I told her. 'They've been granted adjournments twice now, because her lawyers can't decide whether to plead diminished responsibility or provocation. She's no help. All she'll tell them is that she did it and she's sorry. See, what I think you should do is interview all the people, so that when you come to write up the actual case when it does get to court, you'll have a marvellous detailed story. Nobody else will, so you'll come out on top.'

All this while Aristotle had been slouching back on the couch, munching his way through every biscuit in sight. His eyes were glazed with boredom, and I thought he'd either nod off or march out any minute. I should have known better. A. Anapolis didn't give up so easily. He'd decided to talk to me, and he'd wait out any scruffy little journalist, however persistently she hung around.

Joan Smith whipped out a dog-eared notebook and a chewed biro from her raincoat pocket.

'Can you give me all their names and addresses?'

I obliged, and she was off like a shot without even finishing her lager.

As the front door banged behind her, Aristotle came to life.

'That worked OK, Greta, didn't it?' he beamed, as if he'd done the whole thing himself. 'Now we can have a proper talk, just the two of us.'

'Right, and you can start off by telling me what Ariadne thinks she's up to, sending that stuff to all the papers. And don't say she thinks it's going to help her husband's case, that won't wash.'

If I'd doubted Aristotle's story that he'd been a cop, his next words made it clear that he'd told the truth.

'Buggered if I know,' he said, in true time-honoured police style.

We sat and looked at each other blankly for a while, and it was then that he made his move. I've got to admit, it's possible I might have been sending him the wrong signals. I could see all along that he fancied me, and in different circumstances I might possibly have felt the same about him. But that was before I'd met my dreamboat, DI Michaelson, and nobody else measured up. And then of course there was

Jim. Not that he was important, but he did exist, and he was in my life, in a way. No, it wouldn't do to get involved with Ari. I gave him a hearty shove.

'Well, you can't blame a guy for trying,' he said good-naturedly, picking himself up off the floor. I must say, he had a lovely temperament.

'Anyway,' I said, 'about Ariadne. Can't you persuade her to go back to her husband, or at least give him a call? The poor sod's in a bad enough state, without her mucking about and giving him a nervous breakdown. Or maybe I should talk to her? I've asked you enough times for your Ma's address and phone number so that I can have a word with her.'

'No, forget it,' he said firmly. 'She's made up her mind she's not going back until I find a way to clear his name. Any ideas, Greta? It's a tough one, innit.'

'But you said that if I co-operated with you and your scruffy friend, you'd give me your Ma's address.'

He gave me his beaming smile again, but his words weren't so friendly.

'If that's your idea of co-operation I wouldn't like to see what you'd do if you thought I was the enemy,' he said. 'What I need to know from you is how do we set about trying to clear Ari's husband's name, not some guff about an old lady who stuck a knife in her geezer's gut. You might palm some reporter off with that but it won't wash with me. Come on, Greta, what about some help here?'

I didn't know what to say.

'I don't know what to say,' I said. 'It's obvious to me that Jay Bennett has been fitted up, but I can't think why. And as for proving it, you need a lot more inside knowledge than I've got.'

'Inside! That's it! You've got it!' Aristotle positively yelled, rushing up and down my sitting room like a demented greyhound. I watched him racing about, my mind a blank. All I could do was wait for him to calm down and tell me what he was on about.

'That's what we need, Greta. Someone inside the HSE. First thing I'll do is hang about outside Jay's office and see where the people go for a drink at the end of the day. Then I'll get chatting to a likely-looking one and see if I can get him talking about things. Or maybe I could even get a job there myself. That's brilliant, Greta!' and in his excitement he put his arms round me and gave me a hearty kiss.

It wasn't at all bad. Not like his idea, which I thought was a stinker. Still, it gave him something to do which seemed useful to him, and in return he gave me his mother's address and phone number, before rushing off to put his theory into practice. The poor silly lad.

Thinking it over, I decided I didn't want to talk to Ariadne myself, so I phoned Jay Bennett and told him where she was. The pathetic blighter was absolutely blithering with gratitude. Of course, whether he'd be able to persuade her to come back to him was another matter, but at least he'd know she was safe and stop imagining all that rubbish about kidnapping. I tried to ask him about his cousin Rodney, but he was in such a hurry to tear off and see his beloved, I couldn't get any sense out of him.

I was just sitting there brooding on the disappointing events of the day when my doorbell went again. If that was bloody Joan Smith or beaming Aristotle Anapolis, I said to myself, they'd get their toes crushed in the slamming front door. Surprise. It was neither of them. It was Alfie and his daughter Carole.

'Carole wants to apologise to you,' said Alfie, grabbing her by her collar and hauling her into my hall. 'She didn't mean to be rude, did you Carole' – he gave her a gentle shake – 'and she knew you couldn't have done anything to save her friend's father, didn't you Carole.'

'That's right,' she said in a small voice. 'I was just upset. I'm sorry, Greta.'

Alfie let her go. I gave her a bit of a hug. Nothing too loving, a bit friendly. Just one karate champ to another.

'It's alright, Carole,' I said. 'I'm sorry I couldn't help your friend.'

'Right then,' she said. 'See you.'

And she was gone. Alfie hovered, and I tugged him into the sitting room. To my mind, we had a lot to talk about. First off, I asked him what was really sticking in my head. About him and Dusty. Turned out it was obvious, if I'd used my brain.

'I always get the new ones to look after for a bit, being the oldest-serving officer in the Department,' Alfie explained. 'Then once they're settled in, we can work together or not, depending if we hit it off. The young feller before Dusty, he couldn't stick it at all, and he left the Job altogether. Then I got Dusty into the way of things, but I didn't really want her for a partner. Then you came, and I reckon you're the likeliest youngster I've had on my hands for a long time. Promising, I'd say you are.'

'Have a Guinness, Alfie?'

I would have given him more than that if I'd had anything better. I felt absolutely radiant. Words of praise from Alfie! What more could I want? (Apart from the fantastic DI Derek Michaelson, and I knew he was out of reach.)

'Course, we won't know what Roddy Bennett died of,' Alfie said, 'until they do the autopsy, and you know they can take their time over that. But what we do know, because some bright spark spotted it, is that he had track marks all up his arms.'

'Track marks! You mean he was on the hard stuff?'

'Well, I suppose he could have been a diabetic, but if not, what else could it have been?'

This made me feel a whole lot different about this case. Alfie couldn't have known that I had a serious hang-up about drugs. Not just the usual police dislike of the whole business, but a really personal hatred. It was only natural, since my mother, who'd given birth to me at fourteen, had died from an amphetamine overdose when I was only two years old.

My Gran had brought me up with the belief that drug-taking was even worse than murder.

And now it seemed as if we had a case that involved both.

'Has Anderson been questioned yet, Alfie? Do they think he knows something about Bennett's death?'

'Hold on a minute, girl. Haven't I told you to think things through logically? You're asking the questions in the wrong order. You're getting a bit over-excited, by the looks of you. Calm down. It's not even our case.'

'What do you mean, the wrong order?'

'First question: is Anderson on anything himself? Second question: what about Gustafson? Is drugs the link between those three? Was those two running away because they done Roddy Bennett in, or because they knew he was dead? Or some other reason?'

I pulled myself together. Alfie was right. I mustn't let my personal feelings affect my view of this case, whether we were involved in the investigation or not.

'Do you know the answers to any of those questions, Alfie?' I asked more calmly.

'No, but I can tell you we're in for a lot of leg-work. While we're waiting for the autopsy report on Gustafson and the hospital notes on Anderson, there's their three families to be interviewed, and all their friends, and all their workmates at the Town Hall, too.'

'What, are Anderson's and Gustafson's families here, then? I thought they lived in Iceland or Norway or somewhere like that. And that's another thing. How did it come about that we've got these Scandinavians working on our local Council?'

'Yes,' Alfie confirmed, 'there's a whole lot of questions. So do you want to give up your second day off and come back on the Job tomorrow?'

Without giving a flicker of thought to all the domestic chores I'd planned to catch up with the next day (the hell with cleaning and washing!), I told him, 'Not half! If we don't, we might miss something.'

Chapter 9

My teeth were chattering. I was ashamed of myself, but I couldn't help it. I'd never had a gun held to my head before, and it was amazing how much more terrifying it was than it seems when you see it happening on TV. On those cop shows, people go on talking and behaving as if it's the most natural thing in the world to be on the brink of death. Believe me, that's not how it feels. It feels as if nothing worse could ever happen.

And the awful thing was, I didn't know why he was threatening to blow my brains out. Or how he'd got into my bedroom.

'Listen, Anderson,' I said, trying to keep my voice steady, 'what good do you think this is going to do you?'

Without a word, he gave me a violent shove and I fell. I kept on falling, and even in my terror, I couldn't help wondering how far I could drop before he took aim and fired.

I woke on the floor beside the bed in a tangle of bedclothes, sweating and whimpering. I'd thought I was screaming, but it actually came out very quietly. I lay there panting for a while, getting myself together. It was unusual for me to have such a vivid dream, and I hadn't suffered from nightmares since I was a little kid. So what set this off? While I was trying to work out the significance of it all, I actually went back to sleep where I was on the floor.

But later, when my brain got into gear, I decided that my subconscious had been telling me something about Anderson. I just wasn't sure what the message was. But I decided to keep alert for anything about him that came up.

The briefing that morning was the most fascinating event in my entire police career.

Anderson had been charged under the 1861 Accessories and Abettors Act, which I've got to admit I'd never heard of, for helping to conceal Rodney Bennett's body. Apparently this wouldn't prevent a further charge being made against him, depending on what Bennett had died of. Perhaps he and Gustafson together had murdered Bennett. Was this what my dream meant? Anyway, this more minor allegation was enough to hold him on, until the autopsy results came through.

Meanwhile, liaison with Durham had revealed that Gustafson's body had the same track marks as one of our bright sparks had spotted on Bennett's arms. But Anderson was as clean as a whistle, according to the medical report from the hospital. They'd even tested his blood and urine. We were told that this thoroughness was due to the alertness of a certain DI Michaelson of Durham. That just added to the thrill of the whole thing for me. I'd known at first sight that he wasn't just a sexpot, but a brain as well. If only I could find a way to see him again!

No, but, back to the case. There was now a suspicion that Anderson wasn't such an innocent in the accident which killed Gustafson. So I wasn't the only one who was doubtful about him. Maybe he'd planned to get rid of both Bennett and Gustafson, because all three of them had been in some scam together, and with the other two out of the way, he'd get out of the whole thing. And what might that scam have been? Drugs? Something to do with planning permissions, perhaps? There could be a lot of money involved in getting go-aheads for developers to build where they shouldn't.

So, DCI Chester concluded, we had a lot of work to do, digging out all the background. And close liaison would continue between us and the Durham lot, in the person of DI Michaelson. I looked hopefully at Alfie. We were the first to make contact with DI Michaelson, so maybe we would be assigned this little task? No such luck. DI Graves was to maintain communication on a daily basis. It then emerged that while Anderson was still in hospital, but before we'd arrived, he had already been charged with dangerous driving causing death. Now it was a question of which case would come up first in which Crown Court.

As for the rest of us, well, we'd be given our duties of interviewing all families, friends and work colleagues of the three men. And with a final warning to get on with it and look sharp, Cheerful Charlie marched out, looking nothing like his nickname.

'Looks like a long day for us, girl,' was Alfie's only comment, when DI Graves gave us our assignment. 'Thought we might get the Town Hall job, all on one spot, like. But Freddy Forbes and Dusty Miller drew that one, so we're off on the family interview trail. Might as well do the Gustafson lot first, get the miserable one out of the way.'

'But we're not breaking the news, are we?' I asked. I've always hated that job, telling people somebody's died. 'They do already know he's a goner, don't they?'

'Oh, sure, they've been told that, alright. But we've got to give condolences and speak gently and all that, like you always have to with the bereaved,' he directed me.

I didn't really need to be told that, and as it turned out, it wasn't necessary anyway. Mr and Mrs Gustafson were far from weeping and wailing about the loss of their son. If it wouldn't be too difficult to believe, I might have said they weren't really even upset. I mean, it would be stupid to say they didn't care at all about young Gus (whose real name, it turned out, was Albertus) popping his clogs. Of course anyone with any feelings at all would be sorry to hear about such a violent death as crashing through a windscreen and head-on into a hundred-year-old oak tree. But it was like this:

After the usual mutters of 'Sorry for your loss' from us both, Mrs Gustafson said, 'We have feared a bad end for Albertus for some time. Please sit down and I will bring some coffee. Then we can tell you about our son.'

Alfie and I exchanged uneasy glances. This wasn't a bit what we'd expected. I sat down and produced my notebook, but Alfie stood in front of the fireplace, rocking heel to toe in the way that cops used to do in old movies. He'd told me once that doing that, and an occasional slight knees-bend, saved you getting stiff and aching feet and legs if you had to stand for a long time. But I couldn't see why he was doing it now.

His wooden expression told me nothing. I decided not to wait for his lead.

'Can we start now, Mr Gustafson?' I asked. 'Or do you want to wait for your wife to come in?'

'No, I will tell you one thing first,' he said. 'We made the mistake of our lives in leaving Iceland to come to live here. I was offered a position at the Biochemical Laboratories in Hatfield when Albertus was just a small boy, and we thought it would be a good thing for his education if we lived in England. And at first it seemed we were right. I even became a British subject five years ago. I am sorry for it all, now.'

What was so weird was that he made all these surprising statements in a completely flat voice, with no sign of emotion. I glanced at Alfie, who was still inscrutable, so I went on.

'Excuse me for asking, Mr Gustafson, but you don't look like a typical Icelander to me. Are you actually an Inuit?'

'No, of course not,' he said with his first hint of feeling. 'We are originally a Danish family, from when Iceland was a Danish possession. You must see from my appearance, and you would have seen from my son if you had met him, that we are not Inuit at all. It was partly to prevent him mixing with those people that we came here. Very undesirable.'

'But then,' Mrs Gustafson picked up, coming in with a loaded tray, 'the people he chose to mix with here were even worse than the Inuit. Can you believe that, even worse than the Inuit.'

As I didn't know what was supposed to be wrong with the Inuit, I had no idea what they could mean by very undesirable and even worse.

Alfie came to life.

'Let me help you with that tray, Mrs Gustafson,' he said with heavy old-world charm. I suspected that this was because he'd spotted a heaped plate of delicious-looking goodies in amongst the coffee things. But maybe I was misjudging him, because he went on, 'What sort of people were they that you disapproved of, that your son chose to mix with?'

Mrs Gustafson showed a lot more emotion than her husband, but it wasn't grief at the loss of a son that she seemed to be feeling. We could see she was very angry, and had no idea what a common story it was that she had to tell. Her son had chummed up with the lowest element at his school. His parents, older sister and teachers had put their best efforts into giving him proper guidance, but he'd gone from heavy drinking and clubbing to pill-popping. If only they'd known how familiar that story was to me!

'But what worried us most was, where was he getting the money for all this,' Mr Gustafson took over the story from his wife. 'And this we were never able to find out. It all went on after he left school, and we thought he wouldn't be able to get a job. However, his sister was engaged to be married by this time, and her fiancé had an uncle who worked in the Town Hall, and he suggested that if he could get a job for Albertus, maybe this would settle him down.'

'And that was in the Planning Department?' Alfie asked, daintily brushing crumbs out of his beard, all genteel-like. 'Where he met young Anderson? And Councillor Rodney Bennett?'

Both Gustafsons nodded, and Alfie went on, 'And did your son's behaviour improve from that time?'

'Improve, no,' said Mr Gustafson. 'Changed, yes. He changed. He became a different person completely. Not better. Just different. Quieter. Moody. Secretive. No more clubs and drinking. Going out for meetings late at night. Itching a lot. Always seeming to have a slight cold. His breath was often bad. Sometimes he had body-odour. His health was not good in general.'

Alfie and I both knew this was all classic stuff, but it was clear that the Gustafsons didn't.

'Did you meet Anderson?' I asked. 'Did he ever come here?'

'Oh yes, at first we hoped he would be a good influence on Albertus,' Mrs Gustafson said. 'He seemed such a nice quiet well-behaved boy. But then we found that he was always the one who phoned about these mystery meetings, and we realised that he wasn't so much quiet, as sly.'

Oho, I thought. There you are. Sly. Not violent like in my dream. But certainly not the little angel he seemed.

'So it wouldn't surprise you to know that your son was injecting himself with illegal substances?' Alfie asked. Again they shook their heads silently, sadly. 'And do you think it possible that he was paying for this habit by falsifying planning permissions? That he was in league with his colleague Anderson and Councillor Rodney Bennett in this practice?'

'Ah, I see what you are thinking, Sergeant Partridge,' Mr Gustafson said with perfect courtesy and no hint of irony. 'But of course you have difficulties because there is no proof of these activities, am I right? Well, I suggest you might want to look a little further before you make such decisions about our son. He was a wild and foolish young man, but perhaps it would be better if you would question Councillor Bennett on this subject.'

Alfie looked surprised, as well he might. One minute these people seemed more aggrieved than grieving about the death of their son, and then they were springing to his defence. It was a bit of a switch. But then on the other hand,

Alfie had been pushing it. And maybe parents were always like that.

Mr Gustafson rose and opened the door. 'I'm sure you would like to pursue your enquiries, Sergeant,' he said politely. 'And no doubt you are already aware that young Anders Anderson is a qualified draughtsman. You were talking about blueprints, were you not?'

On the way to interview Anderson's parents, Alfie said, 'What do you think he meant, Greta? I don't remember saying anything about blueprints.'

Instead of answering him, I burst out, 'Listen Alfie, I think that Anderson is the villain of the whole affair. I had a terrible nightmare about him last night…'

'Oh, woman's intuition, is it,' said Alfie with heavy sarcasm. 'I thought we'd be going on facts, not whether you had some cheese before you went to bed. What's that got to do with blueprints, anyway? I don't even know what a blueprint is, except a copy of a porn video. I suppose you're going to tell me now that they were making blue films at the Town Hall, starring Anderson, Gustafson and Councillor Bennett?'

Breathing hard and trying not to lose my temper, I explained to him as calmly as I could, 'It's like this, Alfie. Anderson was a draughtsman. They make blueprints which are plans of buildings. If Anderson made false ones it might have helped to get developers permission to build when they wouldn't have got planning permission if the Planning Committee had seen the real plans.'

Alfie burst out laughing.

In a very bad impersonation of a Gestapo officer in a fifth-rate nineteen-forties black and white British film, he said, 'So, ve haf to find zee plans, no? You vill talk, or it vill be the verse for you!'

Sometimes, I thought, it was hopeless trying to talk sense to Alfie.

*

A car, a car, how could I get a car? If I confided in Alfie, he might have offered to come with me, but I didn't think he'd let me just borrow his car on my own. And anyway, that would have meant I'd have to tell him what it was about, and he'd have scoffed at me for having another outbreak of woman's intuition, instead of paying proper attention to my brilliant new idea. And hadn't I just decided it was hopeless trying to talk sense to him?

I could probably have hired a car, but I wasn't keen. The only one I could think of was Aristotle. I knew he'd be only too pleased to drive me anywhere, and if I told him I wanted to park in an unlit carpark at midnight, he'd jump at the chance. Especially if he thought it would help him professionally as well as in a more personal way. Yes, I decided, he was my only chance.

As I expected, when I phoned and told him what I was after, he was so keen to say yes that I didn't have time to explain, even if I'd wanted to. So that was how the two of us came to be scuffling about in the front seat of his dirty smelly scruffy old Alpine. Finally I had to bat him pretty hard round the head to make him stop mucking about and pay attention.

'Bit much, innit,' he moaned, holding a cold can of lager to his ear. 'Good thing I brought some supplies in a cold bag, though. Come in right handy, this did.'

'Well, Ari, if you'd only listened to me in the first place on the way here,' I told him, 'you'd have known I didn't ask you to bring me here for fun and games. If you'd used a bit of common sense, you'd have realised if that was what I was after, I'd have invited you to my flat.'

'Well, you said there was a boyfriend, see,' he explained, peering at the lager can, probably to see if there was any blood on it, 'so I thought it was going to be awkward like, at home.'

He sighed, opened the lager and drank deeply and noisily.

'You better tell me what it's all about, then,' he said gloomily.

'Right then, for the third time,' I gritted. The fact was that I'd been regretting the whole idea for quite a while now, and was in two minds whether to chuck it and give up.

'This carpark is in the Borough of Harrow, so it's nothing to do with us at Watford,' I explained, 'so I can't be here officially. And anyway, even if I could, I haven't got the authority. But it used to be a good trading spot for dealers, and a lot of their customers came from Watford. So when I heard that those two dead men were both users, I thought I might find something out by staking out here.'

'But you said couples came here for snogs, too,' Ari grumbled, 'and I thought all the rest was just moody to cover up that you really fancied me. What do you think you'd find out, anyway?'

'Oh I don't know, Ari,' I burst out, suddenly fed up and irritated, with myself, with him, with everything. 'You're right. I'm sorry I hit you. Let's go home and I'll make you a nice cup of coffee and give you an aspirin for your head.'

I was damned if I was going to tell him how I knew about this place. He certainly wasn't a close enough friend to be told about my Gran following my teenage mother and finding out that this was where she scored. Nor how she'd tried to tell the police about it, with no result. Anyway, that was long ago. It was stupid of me to think they still used the same meeting place. And that was amphetamines, but Councillor Rodney Bennett and young Albertus Gustafson had been injecting the hard stuff. By this time I was glad I hadn't said anything to Alfie about this mad idea, the link was too feeble and my reasoning was out by a mile.

'Just a minute,' Ari said, 'what's going on over there? In that far corner?'

He pointed, I squinted, but I couldn't see what he meant.

'What, what did you see?' I asked him, but he just shook his head, started up the motor and switched on the lights.

As he swung the car round towards the exit, I got a glimpse of the driver of one of the cars parked right up in the corner. I couldn't believe it. I must have been mistaken. After all, it was only a quick glance. But it did look remarkably like Detective Chief Inspector 'Cheerful Charlie' Chester. So what, I argued with myself. Even if it had been Cheerful Charlie, what did that mean? Absolutely nothing.

'Are you going to tell me what you thought you saw?' I nagged at Ari. 'I don't care if you were right or wrong, just give me a hint.'

'Well, it's very dark there, innit. And I could have been wrong. All right, all right,' he added hastily, ducking as I made a threatening gesture towards his ear again. 'It looked like two people leaning out of car windows next to each other, and one of them give something to the other one. That's all. It don't mean nothing, right.'

'Which car, Ari? Was one of them the one you caught in your lights as we were leaving?'

'Right, that was the one it looked like was taking the parcel. Nice car it looked like, too. Could have been a Lexus or sunnink like that. Why, did you know him?'

'No, of course not, how could I? No, forget it, Ari. I'm sorry I wasted your time. It was very nice of you to help me with such a wild idea. Come home and I'll make you a nice cup of cocoa and some hot buttered toast,' I offered, although it was pretty late and I was a bit worried about being able to get up in only a few hours.

'I'd rather have a wild idea of my own,' he laughed, and ducked again, although I hadn't threatened him that time.

He was really a nice guy, that Aristotle – kind, good-natured and quite fanciable. If I hadn't happened to have met the man of my dreams recently in Durham, I might have taken him on and given Jim the Long-Distance Lorry Driver the boot. But I was used to Jim, he was like an old doormat, and I stood no chance with the handsome DI Michaelson, so I thought I might as well leave things as they were. And at least I only had to put up with Jim once a fortnight. Any more would have been too much interference with normal life.

Anyway, I managed to convince Ari that our stake-out at the carpark had been a waste of time, although I had some private doubts about it myself. And I got him talking about Ariadne. I shouldn't have been surprised, but I couldn't help laughing a bit when he told me her single name. It was Adamantus. It was so right for her, somehow. I had to explain to Ari that adamant meant hard as steel or diamond.

'Right, that's her. Like a diamond. Beautiful but resistant,' he surprised me by saying. 'Well, when we was young and like at school and that together, I had a right royal crush on her,' he admitted. 'But she wanted something better than me, I was alright for mucking about with, wasn't I, but not for serious. Soon as she set eyes on that Jay Bennett, though, she decided he was the step on the ladder she was looking for, and he stood no chance, the poor silly bugger. Seventeen she was, and carrying on alarming because her mum thought she was too young. So Mr and Mrs Adamantus give in, didn't they, and no sooner was the wedding over than she found she was expecting.'

'She was only eighteen when Rosie was born?' I asked. 'Is that why she's so desperate for publicity now? Because she's thirty and she's afraid she won't make it?'

'Right, but that didn't work neither, did it? Getting herself in the papers about being kidnapped and not being kidnapped,' he sighed. 'Poor Ariadne, all she did was a storm in a eggcup. The papers've forgot all about her already, innit. Didn't help her with her stupid career, didn't help her daft husband neither. Still,' he brightened, 'I might be able to help Jay. I got a job at the HSE HQ at Luton, starting next Monday.'

'Oh, Ari, how clever! Why didn't you tell me? What's the job? How did you get it?'

He smirked. I could see he was dead chuffed at a bit of praise from me. It made me realise that I might have been a bit unkind to him up till now. But then I had to listen to a long boring account of how they took up his references and he had to take a test, and what his job would be. Far as I could tell, it was the vacancy caused by the departure of the late Julius Varney. Small world.

*

I was right to be worried. Getting up for work later that morning was even tougher than usual. After all, I'd only had about three hours' sleep, and I was usually a bit of a sleep-walker at the beginning of the morning after a good eight or ten hours. And all this switching from day-shift to night-shift and back again wasn't doing my internal clock much good, either. Still, I managed to stagger in on time, and luckily Alfie made none of his frequent remarks about the weight of my eyelids, so I gradually managed to wind myself up into being something like a normal human.

Not that much alertness seemed to be called for. We were going to interview Mr and Mrs Anderson, parents of Anders Anderson the draughtsman. Of course all we could expect were protestations of what a law-abiding hardworking boy he was, good to his parents and kind to the budgerigar.

What I hadn't expected was the likenesses. Apparently Grandfather Anderson had been living with them since the recent death of his wife, and when I looked at him, it was as if I could see straight into young Anders' future. Mr Anders Anderson senior was an older version of Anders, with those same amazing blue eyes, and the old man was a washed-out likeness of both. Physically faded he might have been, but in personality he overshadowed the lot of them. Nobody could get a word in when Grandpa was at it. You could see where the Vikings came from. Tall, blond, blue-eyed and fierce, Grandpa was.

'I came to this country during the war,' he boomed, 'and fought alongside your countrymen. I married an English girl, I settled here, I've been a good citizen all these years and brought up my son here to be the same. And this is what I get for it! My grandson is led astray by a Danish Icelander and an English Councillor, and now he is getting the blame for everything!'

'Excuse me, sir,' said Alfie, looking more uncomfortable than I'd ever seen him, 'but if I might just ask—'

Grandpa Anderson was having none of it.

'I'm still speaking, officer,' he thundered, 'and you may speak when I've finished. I'm stating facts, and you may take note of them or not, as you wish. Now, where was I? Oh yes, this boy Gustafson, he was a bad lot. Probably his own parents will tell you that, even if they are Danish Icelanders. He was always in trouble, and my grandson was always trying to get him on to the straight and narrow.'

And so it went on, just as I'd expected. When Grandpa Anderson had finished, Mr and Mrs Anderson took up the tale, and all we got was the usual blah about the sweet innocent Anders Anderson being used and gulled by the wicked druggie crook, Gustafson.

'Personally, I don't believe a word of it,' I said to Alfie on the way back to Shady Lane. 'That Anderson is just too good to be true. Nobody who looks that innocent can possibly *be* that virtuous. I think he's sly.'

Alfie laughed. 'There you go again, Greta. Have you got any evidence, any actual facts, to go on? Or is it just that instinct again? Come on, girl, just type up all the notes and go home and get some shut-eye. You look as if you could do with it.'

What I actually wanted was time to do some hard thinking. Rolling around in my head were a lot of bits and pieces of fact, half-fact, theory and – I had to admit Alfie was right – instinct again. I needed to try to get my thoughts into some sort of order.

Of course, no such luck. When I got home, Jim was there again. It seemed a bit soon. Surely it wasn't a fortnight since I'd seen him? But there was no chance to question him, because he was entertaining a visitor. In *my* home! What a cheek. And what made it worse was who it was.

As I walked in, he was handing a glass of lager and a beaming smile to my least favourite scruffy red-headed journalist, Joan Smith.

Chapter 10

At the briefing next morning, I had trouble getting my head together. When I was at home, dealing with Jim and that pseudo-journo grubby scruff Joan Smith, I was trying to think about work. And now that I was actually at the cop shop, I couldn't get my mind off the previous evening, coming home from work to find Jim behaving as if he lived there.

Not to speak of the night before that. What with spending half that particular night peering round an unlighted carpark in Old Redding, and nearly all the rest of it listening to Aristotle Anapolis telling me about his early life with Ariadne Adamantus, I'd gone to work only half my usual self.

Then after Alfie coming over all chauvinistic and scornful about women, finding my least favourite person of my own sex in my home had been the last straw. And Jim explaining that he'd thought, by the way she spoke about me, that she was a close friend, just made me even more fed up. I'd even prefer Dusty Miller to that grubby Joan Smith. At least Dusty looked clean and proper in her shapeless way, and she was in a decent job. It just showed what little Jim knew about me, to think I'd have a journalist for a friend!

So now at the briefing, with all this churning round in my head, I wasn't listening with as much attention as I should have. Alfie reported on our interviews with the two lots of parents, then there was a lot of stuff about people who worked in the Planning Department in the Town Hall, and it was all a bit dull, and the voices buzzed on and I could feel myself drifting off...

Until DCI Chester stood up. My eyes flew open, and I looked at him, hard. Was he the man I'd seen in the carpark? And if he was, what did it mean? Absolutely nothing, I told myself. Pointless getting uptight about it.

Still, I listened to what he had to say with much more concentration than I'd put into anything up till now. He'd taken Councillor Bennett's widow to the morgue for the formal identification, taken her home, pacified her, then asked her a few questions.

'It's no surprise that she knew nothing about his drug-taking, nor any hanky-panky in the Planning Department,' he said.

Hanky-panky? I thought. What kind of a word was that for a senior police officer to use? I always thought the public laughed at us for being too formal in our language. What did he mean? Corruption? Fun and games with the female employees? Bribery?

'She is a very naïve woman, innocent of the ways of the world,' Cheerful Charlie went on, 'and she is still of the opinion that her husband was kidnapped when he first disappeared. Apparently he didn't confide in her.'

I don't know what got into me. One minute I was sitting there, staring at the DCI and paying almost feverish attention to him, and the next I was on my feet, interrupting him with a question. And what a question!

'Is Mrs Councillor Rodney Bennett a member of the golf club that he *and you* belong to, sir?'

There was a terrible silence. Out of the corner of my eye I saw Alfie going a nasty shade of dark red. But that was nothing compared to the colour that DCI Chester went. I thought he would explode.

'DC Pusey,' he said in a voice that dripped icicles, 'what exactly is the inference of that question? Perhaps you'd like to explain yourself fully to me in my office immediately after this briefing.'

I could feel myself going all hot and shrivelling, like a bit of overdone pizza. It was bad enough when they were all staring at me, but now it was even worse, when everyone was avoiding looking my way. I sat there with flaming ears, and eyes down, and wished I'd never been born. Alfie probably wished the same. If I'd ever been capable of thinking myself out of a hole, now was the time to prove it to myself.

In the meantime, in an atmosphere you could cut holes in with a blunt instrument, the briefing went on. They hadn't found a cause of death for Rodney Bennett, was the next piece of news. None of the obvious, like OD on drugs, violence to the person or poison, or even just plain heart failure.

'Not shot either, Guv,' called out Dusty Miller, I suppose to try and lighten things up a bit, but it hardly raised a titter.

She shot me a bit of a look. I couldn't read it. Was it sympathy or gloating? In my confused state I couldn't tell the difference.

Anyway, the big news came at the end. There was nothing to link Anderson to Bennett's death. Even if it turned out that he died of neither natural nor accidental causes, it was odds on that Gustafson was the villain. And if Anderson was involved, there was no way it could be proved. Nor could it be shown that he had anything to do with any shenanigans in the Planning Department at the Town Hall. So he was being sent back to Durham to face charges of causing death by dangerous driving, and that was going to be the last we'd see of him.

That put the tin lid on everything. On top of being in deep shit with the boss of my department, now I realised that dreamy DI Michaelson wouldn't be coming to Watford, and my life wasn't worth a biscuit.

So much for my imaginary problem, of choosing between a brilliant career and a love life with the man of my dreams. At the rate I was going, I'd be lucky if I was sent back to being a uniformed plod and having a bunk-up once a fortnight with a long-distance lorry driver who didn't even know I hated journalists.

*

'Well, DC Pusey,' said Cheerful Charlie, not laughing even slightly, 'would you like to explain the question you hurled at me at the briefing this morning? Were you suggesting that there was a friendship between myself and Councillor Rodney Bennett of an unethical nature?'

'N-n-no, s-s-sir,' I stammered, 'I don't really know what I meant, sir. I think I might have had in mind that if you knew Mrs Bennett in any kind of social way, even only playing golf at the same club, perhaps that might explain how you could tell what kind of woman she is.'

Into the continuing icy silence, I blundered on, 'I mean, sir, if you'd only just met her when you took her to identify her husband's body, somebody might wonder how you knew how innocent and naïve she is…'

My voice trailed off under his glare, and I remembered, at this worst possible moment, an old black and white film where the villain, probably Sidney Greenstreet, said in a menacing voice, 'Go on. With every word you are digging your grave with your tongue.'

It wouldn't have surprised me if DCI Chester had spoken those very words at this moment. I wished I could sink down in a girlish swoon. Then maybe he'd relent and I'd come round with him chafing my hands, or something.

As it happened, it was nearly that good. Still looking very stern but not so empurpled, he just said, 'Well, Greta, think before you speak in future. Off you go.'

Wow! I'd got away with it! Still alive and still a Detective Constable! Now all I had to do was make my peace with Alfie. That shouldn't be too tough. After all, if I could get by with Cheerful Charlie, it was odds on that Alfie would be even more understanding. He'd made it obvious he had a soft spot for me.

All wrong. When I walked into the canteen, he was sitting next to Dusty Miller at the round table, and all the other fellers were there, but there wasn't a chair for me. And nobody moved round to make space for me, either. They all avoided my eye, and pretended to be absorbed in a joke Dusty was telling.

'So God answers Eve in the Garden of Eden, "What's the prob, Eve?" and Eve goes, "I'm lonely," and God says "Don't worry, kid, I'll create a man for you." "What's that?" says Eve. "This is a flawed creature, with many bad habits, he'll lie, cheat and be vain, and give you a bad time. But he'll be bigger, faster and will like to hunt and kill things. He'll look silly when he's aroused, but he'll satisfy your physical needs. He'll like childish things like fighting and kicking a ball about, and he won't be too smart, so he'll also need your advice to think properly." Eve says, "Sounds OK, so what's the catch?" And God tells her, "There's one condition. Because he'll be proud, arrogant and self-admiring, you'll have to let him believe that I made him first. Just remember, it's our little secret – you know, woman to woman".'

A great howl of laughter went up, so they hadn't heard it before, old as it was. The men were all looking at each other and shaking their heads, and they were all ribbing her and saying things like, 'Dream on, kid', and 'Feminists live, KO!' But the most hurtful thing was Alfie saying, quite quietly for him, 'Tell it to Greta, Dusty, why don't you?'

And I felt absolutely crushed. I'd fucked up big time, and no mistake. How was I ever going to get right with Alfie again?

It was even worse when he did speak to me.

'Come on, Pusey,' he said, 'we've got to look into a suspicious prowling.'

I couldn't very well say anything about him calling me Pusey – he'd never called me that before, even when I was first assigned to him – so I just said, 'Why us, Sarge? Isn't that usually a job for uniforms?'

'Still asking questions, eh?' he said, almost but not quite cracking a smile. 'The reason it's us, if you must know, is because it's Jonathan Bennett's house, and it's empty because he's still staying with his parents in Radlett, and you know better than anyone where his wife is. Neighbours called in with a worry about seeing strangers round the house. Come on, then, look sharp.'

We drove to the Bennett's house without a word. Of course, not a sign of anything suspicious when we got there, so we had to talk to the neighbours. When I say neighbours, I mean the nearest house, which is not like a side-by-side on the lines of where I live. No, there was about a hundred metres of garden and trees and bushes and stuff in between, so it was hard to see how they could have spotted anything going on, unless they had very powerful binoculars. It was all so posh, the houses didn't even have numbers, just names. So we called in at The Garth and spoke to Mr and Mrs Hayley-Jones, who turned out to be quite nice, bright ordinary people, not like you might expect from the name.

She said, 'What caught my attention was that it didn't seem possible that they were burglars. The woman was wearing a light-coloured raincoat, high heels and she had bright red hair, and the man seemed to be wearing some sort of uniform.'

Mr Hayley-Jones and Alfie were both laughing quite openly. I wasn't. I had a gloomy suspicion.

'You see, officer,' Mr Hayley-Jones said to Alfie, 'why we thought it was worth phoning to report it. I mean, people looking like that, prowling round an empty house in broad daylight! Whatever they were up to, we didn't think it was breaking and entering, so it didn't seem a situation that called for dialling 999. Sorry to have dragged you here, too late to catch them of course, but it's a bit strange, isn't it?'

'Got all that noted down, Pusey?' Alfie asked me, and on my nod, he added to Mr and Mrs, 'probably reporters, I shouldn't be surprised. Maybe don't know Mr and Mrs Bennett aren't in residence at the moment. But thank you for letting us know.'

And with broad grins from all three of them, hands were shaken, goodbyes made, and we drove off. I decided not to say anything to Alfie about Joan Smith. I was in enough trouble with him already.

'Betty wanted me to ask you to come to us for Christmas,' Alfie suddenly said, 'but I'm not sure if I want to. Are you going to volunteer for extra duty in Trafalgar Square on New Year's Eve?' And before I could answer, he added, 'You know, if you do, you'll have to go back into uniform. Might be good practice for you.'

What did that mean? That I was in danger of being sent back to being a plod? Was he giving me a warning? I suddenly decided that whatever I said now, I couldn't make things worse, so I might as well take the plunge.

'DCI Chester hardly told me off at all, Alfie,' I said. 'Why do you think that was? He never seemed a soft-hearted man to me. He just sort of told me to think before I speak in future. I thought he'd give me a really hard time, didn't you?'

I didn't get much out of that. Alfie just stroked his beard a lot and said 'Hm' a few times. But I could tell he was thinking. Just as I was parking the car – very neatly, I might say – he said, 'Well, shall I tell Betty you'll come to us for Christmas dinner, or what?' and I knew he'd stopped being angry with me. He still wasn't calling me 'Greta' or 'girl', so we weren't quite back on the old footing, but things were on the up. So I wouldn't spoil it all by telling him about Joan Smith.

*

I might have mentioned my feelings about those women detectives in fiction, who always seem to need to spend several hours every day working out at the gym or going for five-mile runs or weird stuff like that. I love to read those books, it's so encouraging to have women as heroes these days instead of those Sherlocks and Lord Peters and Poirots of the past.

But I don't understand why they have to be so physical, specially the ones who leap out of bed before dawn after a heavy night fighting villains or rumpling the sheets with a handsome suspect, and get fit for another exciting day by exercising! True, I do enjoy my karate, but I don't have to go every day, and I certainly don't feel my life isn't complete without exercise to help me think.

What's wrong with a pizza and a beer in front of the TV for a little relaxation, anyway?

Just the same, and regardless of all that, on that particular evening I felt that a little rollerblading round the emptier streets of Watford would help to clear my head before I hit the pillow. So I donned the trusty blades and off I went. Not too much, I told myself, just about a half-hour of crisp cold fresh air, and that would be it.

So who could have known beforehand what I was going to do? My rollerblading was a close secret. I hadn't even told Jim or Alfie about it. Always kept the blades hidden in my backpack. It must have been just a random mugging, not an ambush waiting for me.

Lucky in a way that when I got in to the nick the next morning, there was such interest in the latest bit of news that people hardly glanced at me. I'd tried to cover up the scratches and bruises with make-up, but I'm not much of a hand with that stuff, and the general effect was a bit blotchy. I need not have bothered, though, if nobody was going to notice anything different about me anyway.

I couldn't seem to find Alfie, so I finally located Dusty Miller and asked her what was going on.

'Nothing much really,' she said, very offhand. 'Don't know what they're all getting so excited about. Just an accidental death. I suppose it's because it's where that fairground accident was, you know, with the HSE man and his family. But it's just a coincidence, nothing to do with the fair.'

I didn't see it that way at all. Coincidence? There was no such thing. Only Dusty could think that.

'Who? What? How?' I started to gabble, but now Dusty was peering at me and smirking a bit.

'What happened to your face?' she grinned. 'Not much good at the cover-up, are you. Been having a bit of a scrap with the boyfriend, have you?'

'Never mind that, Dusty, tell me about the accidental death. Who was it?'

'Oh, they came back to put up the Christmas fair, you know, like always,' she said, 'and this feller got in the way when a caravan wasn't properly wedged still or whatever it is they do with them to keep them still, and it rolled over him. Didn't stand a chance, did he.'

As usual when death was mentioned, Dusty's eyes were bright and she was practically drooling with ecstasy. She really ought to work in a mortuary, not in the police. She'd make a marvellous undertaker's assistant, Dusty would.

'So what's it got to do with us? Why's everyone in such a state this morning?'

'Oh, well,' she said all casual and offhand, 'I suppose it's because he was the one, you know, Danny Robbins, who first blew the whistle on that HSE man. About him being on the take.'

And seeing my dropped jaw and popping eyes, she went on, 'You must remember, Greta, it was through him coughing his part in it that they started looking at the previous cases that HSE man had handled. What you looking so gobsmacked about, then?'

I took a few deep breaths. I couldn't believe even Dusty could be so thick as not to see there must be some link between this death and the case against Jay Bennett. And if there was a connection, then maybe Danny Robbins' death was not an accident at all.

'Where's Alfie?' I asked Dusty, but she just shrugged and started trying again to get me going about the state of my face.

'I was mugged,' I snapped at her as I turned to run up to the canteen, the most likely place for Alfie to be at any time of day or night.

And I heard her noisy laugh going on behind me as I raced out of our office. Just my luck, I ran full tilt into DCI Chester and nearly knocked him flying down the stairs. With a flukey quick reaction I managed to grab him and set him on his feet almost before he seemed to realise who I was or what I'd done.

'Now then, young Pusey,' he greeted me not at all cheerfully, 'what's up with you? In urgent need of a boost from our canteen coffee, are you? What's that stuff on your face? Have you been fighting?'

It was no good snarling a few words at him the way I had with Dusty.

'I was mugged last night, sir,' I muttered. 'I saw them off alright, but they managed to do me a bit of damage first. Three fellers and a girl, and the girl scratched me all down the side of my face, as you see. I tried to hide it with some make-up...'

He laughed in a sarcastic kind of way.

'Well, let's hope you're better at detecting than you are at hiding injuries, Greta. Did they get anything off you?'

'No, sir, I didn't have any money on me at the time.'

I wasn't going to tell him that because I'd been on my rollerblades it had been difficult to balance long enough to use my karate moves on them. And by the time I'd picked myself up, it was too late to blade after them. He looked me up and down thoughtfully but asked no more questions.

He just said, 'Well, you'd better go on to the canteen, then,' and went on his way. I didn't like to ask him if Alfie was there. Stringing out any discussion about anything with Cheerful Charlie was the last thing I'd want to do at any time, particularly after our previous day's meeting.

Alfie was up there all right, deep in conversation with his fellow-sergeant, Freddy Forbes. Neither of them noticed as I went in, so I just sat down at a nearby table and waited for them to surface from what looked like a serious discussion. I was dying to know what they were talking about, but they kept their voices very low, and all I could hear was the rumble of Alfie's bass and the low mutter of Freddy's. It had to be to do with the 'accidental' death of Danny Robbins, I was sure.

So I was pretty chuffed when Alfie saw me and beckoned me over to join them. This meant I was going to be on the inside of what was going on, for once. That would make a welcome change.

'You'll be interested in this, girl,' Alfie said, ignoring my pleased grin as well as my damaged face. 'We was just talking about the change that's come over the job since the CPS came on the scene. Probly before you joined the Force, there was a time when we give our evidence straight to the magistrates and they decided what to do. But now since we have to take everything to the CPS, they tell us if we've got a case or not. And if they say not, it's goodbye Charlie and the magistrates never get to hear a word of it. *And* there's all this extra paperwork, and all,' he finished glumly.

I couldn't see the point of this little speech. Of course I already knew everything that Alfie said, and I knew too that lots of the old-timers were fed up about it. But things change and new systems replace old ones, and so what? Surely this wasn't all that Alfie and Freddie had to talk about? What was the good of sitting in the canteen beating their gums about the fact that they didn't like things being different?

And why weren't they talking about something really interesting, like the death of a material witness in a really baffling case? After a respectful silence, because I didn't want Alfie to think I was unsympathetic about his belly-aching, by changing the subject too quickly, I asked him.

'What do you make of this business about the fairground feller, Alfie? You know, Danny Robbins, the one who fingered Jay Bennett the first time.'

This got him to give a proper look at me for the first time. I should have known I wouldn't get the kind of answer I was looking for.

'What happened to your face, girl?' he asked, and Freddy leaned forward to get a better look at it, too.

'It's all scratched and grazed,' Freddy stated after a careful inspection.

'Yes, I know,' I said impatiently, 'just a few thugs tried to mug me last night, that's all. But what about Danny—'

'I hope you apprehended them,' Freddy interrupted. 'Can't let these little buggers get away with it, you know, even if the CPS doesn't think we've got a case.'

I just managed to swallow the groan that bubbled up. I really didn't want to antagonise these two sergeants, specially my own dear Alfie, but there were times when it was difficult to appear as respectful as a rookie Detective Constable is supposed to be. I explained as briefly as I could about how they got away, and because I didn't mention the rollerblades, they could see it would have been difficult for me to catch them after I picked myself up.

'But she's a champion runner, our Greta,' Alfie informed Freddie, 'and if anyone could catch them, she'd be the one.'

'Do a lot of running, then, do you, Greta?' Freddie asked, and I said yes just to save time, although the fact is that I run as little as possible, as it's always seemed a pointless occupation to me.

So then blow me down if he didn't start going on about how I should join in the Watford Marathon organised by the Rotary Club. And I couldn't shut him up until I'd agreed to put my name down. If there's anything that seems dafter to me than racing round a track, it's running for charity. Why can't people just *give* the money without someone doing something like running for miles or climbing a mountain to wheedle the cash out of them? But I suppose I needed the goodwill in my new department, even after the time I'd been there by then.

Then finally I got these two silly blighters to talk about this fairground death which I believed was suspicious. Naturally they refused to agree with me. Wouldn't hear a word of it.

'Come on, Greta,' Alfie grinned, 'you don't have to make a case out of every accident that's reported, even if we had already had contact with the deceased on another matter. I know what you're up to, you're looking for a loophole for that Bennett feller from the HSE, just because you've got a soft spot for the family.'

'No, go on, Alfie, is that right?' asked Freddy, interested in the subject at last. 'What does our Greta think, then, this feller Jonathan Bennett never took all those bribes and that?'

I hate it when people talk past me like that. If he wanted to know what I thought, why did he have to ask Alfie? I know he's my mentor, but that doesn't mean he's my mouthpiece as well.

'No, as a matter of fact, Sergeant,' I said politely but coldly, 'I can't believe that any man would take a bribe to say that a fairground ride was safe for use if it wasn't, and then take his whole family on it and risk their lives. I think the whole thing is a put-up job to get him out of the way.'

A big grin now formed on Detective Sergeant Freddy Forbes's face, even wider than the one already splitting open Alfie's beard.

'Read many detective novels, then, do you, Greta?' he guffawed.

I felt like banging their heads together, but I just offered them both another cup of tea instead.

At least I still had Aristotle on my side, and even, at a pinch and if absolutely necessary, that mucky little journo, Joan Smith.

So it turned out that this frustrating beginning set the pattern for the rest of the day, and it was all so maddening that I almost wondered what I was doing in this joke factory in the first place. Not a single soul thought that Danny Robbins' death was the least bit suspicious, and it was obvious that it was going to be put in the 'forget-it' files along with the mysterious passing of Councillor Rodney Bennett.

As for any idea that there'd been any conspiracy anywhere in the whole of Hertfordshire, except what could be laid at Jay Bennett's door, well, do me a favour, and call me over-imaginative. It was clear that was the kindest thing they were all calling me these days. Even that second cousin to my Gran's old washboard, Dusty Miller, was referring to me as 'poor Greta'.

By the time I got home, I was so fed up that I phoned Aristotle. Of course, I wasn't looking for company or anything like that. I just wanted to know how he was getting along in his new job at the HSE, and whether this meant he'd absolutely given up the detective business. But he was so full of news and so bubbling keen to talk it over with me, that I agreed when he said could he come round to my place and have a beer with me.

'How about if I bring a pizza, Greta? What do you like on yours?'

Well, I couldn't refuse an offer like that, could I. And it was a pretty good pizza, with everything on it, which is my favourite. The black olives and anchovies don't half give you a thirst, though, so it was just as well he was bright enough to bring a six-pack with him, too.

'Turns out the geezer whose job I got was murdered, Greta,' Ari mumbled with his mouth full of pizza.

'Go on,' I laughed, 'I suppose his name wasn't Julius Varney, by any chance?'

'How did you know that?'

'Because it was my first murder after I got out of uniform,' and I gave him a quick run-down on the Gladys Trulove case.

'But you know what, Greta,' he said, 'one of the security guards told me he wasn't surprised Julius went and got himself killed, only he didn't expect it to be done by no girlfriend. Because Julius was getting a bit too nosy about some of the files and reports, and that kind of snooping could be dangerous. That's a turn-up, innit?'

Chapter 11

When the alarm woke me next morning, I kept still with my eyes shut, hoping I'd just had one of those Freudian sex-dreams. But when I finally plucked up courage to open them and turn my head a little bit, I saw it was not a dream. Real life was what it was. What could I have been thinking of? Or not thinking at all, just turning the brain off and letting the rest of me take over. Just as I was sinking into complete self-loathing and disgust, Ari opened his eyes and gave me that lovely beaming smile.

'Hallo gorgeous,' he said, and kissed me. He couldn't know that I hate being kissed first thing in the morning before either of us has had a chance to clean our teeth. As a matter of fact, it was such a sweet gentle childish little kiss that I didn't mind it at all.

What was happening to me? I had a semi-permanent lover who had the key to my front door, I was madly in love with a Detective Inspector in Durham who hardly knew I existed, and here I was having it away with some dopey Greek who'd won his way into my bed with a pizza and a couple of beers! I'd heard that the plain-clothes lot had looser morals than the rest of the police, but I hadn't expected to sink to their level so quickly.

While all this muddle was spinning round in my head, Ari jumped out of bed and turned off the alarm. His nakedness showed a reason why he'd rather have stayed where he was.

'Come on, Greta,' he said, quickly popping on his pants to hide the state he was in, 'jump about, we've both got work to do. I'll put the kettle on,' he added, taking pity on my dazed condition.

He didn't hang around, either. Put a mug of strong tea in front of me and soon sloped off. My usual morning fog cleared in record time, which helped me turn over all the tricky possibilities until I got dizzy.

First, what had made me tumble into bed with Ari? After several seconds of deep thought, I decided it was a mixture of his pheromones and my hormonal surge. Not that I was turning into what my Gran called a loose woman. One that slept around. Certainly not. But the other question was, what did it mean to him? Did he think I was an easy one-night stander? Was that all he'd been after all along? Or was he expecting some sort of regular relationship? His offhand departure, without even a kiss or a kind word, would seem to mean that I'd seen the last of him. So why did I have mixed feelings about that? Did I want to give Jim the push? And if I did, was it because of Ari or my new passion for DI Derek Michaelson of Durham?

I gave up and went to work. Career first, I reminded myself. That didn't stop me putting on my shortest sexiest skirt, fishnet tights and heels. It wasn't really the weather for it, but I thought it was time I gave the boys a look at my legs. They'd only seen me in jeans until now. And I put on proper make-up, too.

Even Alfie noticed the difference. I still wasn't up to his height of about six four, but I wasn't much short of it.

'Hope you don't have to chase any villains today, girl,' was his only comment.

But the other fellers were more outspoken, and I couldn't help wondering why I felt so pleased and flirty about it. This wasn't my usual style at all. What had one sexy night with Ari done to change me? And why couldn't I remember all of it?

Anyway, it all turned out to the good, because our job that day was to escort Anderson back to Durham. So if I saw my heart-throb, he might actually notice me this time!

He did, and we had a proper conversation. Nothing much, but we did speak. He told us that he'd had no luck in getting transferred to a London posting, or anywhere near. And he casually mentioned that his main reason for wanting the move was that his girlfriend lived in Highgate, and he wanted to be able to spend more time with her! Ouch. End of all my dreams.

Did that mean back to Jim or Ari for me? Or both? Or neither?

Career first, I had to remind myself again.

That didn't stop my heart giving a little extra thump when I got home that night and found Ari waiting on my doorstep.

'What do you want?' I greeted him sternly. 'I hope you're not jumping to any conclusions, just because—'

He gave me his lovely beaming smile again.

'Thought you'd want to know the latest news,' he said. 'About the HSE and Joan Smith, too. Best to keep up, innit?'

And before I could so much as nod and open the door, he added, 'You look extra smashing tonight, Greta. Hope you haven't got a hot date or anything?'

Ari took me out to dinner that night. Not a pizza, not a McDonald's, not even fish and chips. A proper Greek meal, in a restaurant I didn't even know existed. I'd lived in Watford all my life, too, and thought I knew every shop and restaurant. It was lovely, with taramasalata and humous and wine and everything, and he made a big fuss of me and I was glad I was wearing a skirt and heels instead of my usual stuff.

'Listen, sweetheart,' he said, and that was the first time anyone had called me that except in sarcasm, but he didn't notice my reaction because he was getting all serious, 'I didn't want to say anything last night about all your bruises and scratches, because we was having such a smashing time and everything. But I've got to ask you, did you recognise any of them what jumped you that night? And if I know you, Greta, you give them a few what-fors and all before they run off, right?'

I couldn't see where he was going with this, but it was clear that he'd paid attention when I'd told him about what happened the other night.

'Of course,' I said, 'there were three of them, and I could tell one was a woman by her outline and the way she scratched instead of hitting, but I couldn't see any of their faces. I gave them all a bit of a thumping, but she got the worst of it, and judging by the blood on my hands and some of the noises, I'd say she might have got a broken nose. Why?'

By this time, Ari wasn't just looking serious, he was grim.

'Joan Smith,' he said tersely.

'Oh, don't spoil a nice evening by talking about her,' I said. 'What about her? I suppose she's found my attackers single-handed, or some other marvellous investigative thing, has she?'

Then the penny dropped. I couldn't believe he meant what he meant.

'You mean, you can't mean, how can you—' I started, but he was nodding.

'Yes, I saw her today,' he said, 'and if you think it's a coincidence that she's got a broken nose, two black eyes and a big bruise on her jaw, I don't.'

I still couldn't believe it. Why should she?

'Why should she?' I said. 'Maybe she doesn't like me any more than I like her, but that's ridiculous.'

'Who is she?' Ari said. 'Do you know who she is? I don't, she just turned up and said she'd got my phone number off a card in a phone box.'

'But this is silly,' I said.

Then I thought about it more carefully. I started to form a theory. It seemed really far-fetched, but by now I felt I could say anything to Ari and not feel a fool.

'Do you think somebody put her on to you because you might find out something that would clear Jay Bennett?' I asked. 'Like maybe she's not even a wannabe journalist. Or they just want to know how you're doing, and if you might be a real help to Jay and a threat to them?'

'They? Who? We don't even know who we're up against here,' Ari said, and for once I didn't pick him up on taking for granted that we were working together. In fact it sounded rather good to me, him talking about 'us' and 'we'.

There was something about Ari that made me feel all warm and friendly. I don't mean just the sex, though he certainly was a sight better at it than Jim, who should have stuck to lorry driving. And what I felt towards Ari wasn't love, either, not like the thunderbolt of it that struck me when I met DI Derek Michaelson. No, it was more the sort of comfortable feeling I had with Alfie and Betty, or the way I used to feel with my Gran. I decided not to tell Ari any of this.

Instead I told him about the description we'd got of one of the prowlers round Jay and Ariadne's empty house.

'Right, that's her again, innit,' Ari said. 'Like we thought, she's up to some no good alright, and you can bet someone's paying her to snoop around. Looks like I'd better cosy up to her and see if I can pump some facts out of her. If not, you'll have to knock her about a bit more. Try that.'

I actually felt a sort of twinge of something – not jealousy, nothing like that, it might have been indigestion – when Ari said he'd cosy up to Joan Smith. It put a nasty unhealthy picture in my mind, that was all. So that had nothing to do with the fact that when he asked if he could come in when we got back to my place, I gave him a firm No. It was just that I didn't want him to think it was a standard thing between us.

After all, I still had Jim to think of. An occasional one-night event would be no skin off his nose, especially as he wouldn't know anything about it. And anyway, he had a wife of his own somewhere up North, wherever it was he came from. But I didn't want the complications of two regular – er, well, two regulars.

So I told Ari I thought it was a good idea for him to get close to Joan Smith (if he could bear it) to see if he could find out anything about what she was up to. And I gave him a few friendly kisses and a pretty thank-you for the dinner, said goodnight and went to bed on my own.

I'd just got my head down when the phone rang. I was beginning to get used to being woken up at unusual times, so with hardly a groan I answered, 'Yes, Alfie?' But it wasn't Alfie this time, it was Ari, all excited because he'd been struck by an idea, and couldn't wait to tell it to me.

'I don't care what time it is, I'm on my way to wake Ariadne up now,' he shouted. 'Mr and Mrs Adamantus will have the needle, but that's tough, innit. When she was all pleased with herself getting her picture in the papers, she must have talked too much about getting me to try to clear Jay's name. I'll find out who she spoke to about me, then we'll be able to track back and see who that Joan Smith is working for.'

'But what's that got to do with her trying to do me a mischief in the middle of the night? It doesn't make sense...'

'Listen, I'm a detective, I'll work it out. I'll teach that little scruff not to take us on. Sleep well, sweetheart.'

And he was gone, leaving me to think it over. Had he told me that Ariadne was back with her parents now? Probably. Why did he keep calling me sweetheart? As he would likely say himself, just a way of talking, innit.

What complicated plot would have Joan Smith, whoever she really was, nosing around Aristotle and Ariadne and me, and then joining a small mob trying to do me harm? Were they only trying to damage me, or something worse?

I let go all these questions and snuggled down with the nice thought that Ari had referred to Joan Smith as a little scruff. So he certainly didn't fancy her, I thought cheerfully as I dozed off.

Chapter 12

I was a bit surprised when Alfie told me next morning that
we were going to the inquest on Councillor Rodney Bennett,
but I was a lot more amazed when we got there and I saw that
the whole of our department had turned up. Even Dusty
Miller. Surely that was a bit unusual, the whole shower, I
muttered to Alfie, who just told me to keep my lip buttoned.
If I'd thought that was strange, I was positively mystified
when I saw that Superintendent Wood was there, too.

And what was it all for? The coroner concluded that the
medical evidence showed that the late Councillor had died of
a massive heart attack, and it appeared that for reasons
unknown, a person had tried to hide his body in the basement
of the Town Hall. Indications were, he added, that this person
was an employee in the Planning Department who had
subsequently died in a car crash. It was all very smooth, with
no references to drugs or suggestions of foul play, and
certainly not a word about possible irregularities in the
Planning Department.

On the way out, I raised my eyebrows enquiringly at
Alfie, but before I could say a word, he gave me a hard shove
and a grim look. Then I saw that the Super was right behind
us, waving his bony hands about and talking to DCI Chester.

'That's all tickety-boo, then, Charlie,' he said, almost
smiling.

Tickety-boo? I thought. What can that possibly mean? I
didn't get a chance to talk to Alfie properly until we went to
the canteen for coffee later that morning. And even then, he
didn't give me much chance.

'Now then, young Greta,' he said, puffing himself out to
appear his most impressive, 'you were lucky enough to

overhear what Mister Wood said to Cheerful Charlie. Everything's turned out very neat and shipshape, that's what he meant by that expression you never heard before. It's an old army word, and it means it's all satisfactory, see? So I don't want to hear no more of your daft ideas and theories, about coincidences and innocent people being accused and all that. No more about corruption or drugs, right?'

And he managed to make himself look positively menacing. I could see he meant every word. He couldn't know that he was really forcing me to take up a sort of partnership with Aristotle Anapolis in the pursuit of justice.

'OK, Alfie,' I said meekly, 'I'll take your advice and forget the whole thing. Specially as it's nearly Christmas,' I hinted.

'Well, course you'll come to us Christmas Day, girl, that's all fixed,' he beamed, thawing visibly and dropping the heavy sergeant act. 'Then you've got yourself on the rota for joining up with the Met for New Year's Eve duty on Trafalgar Square, haven't you? I expect you'll want me to come with you, eh?'

That was the last thing I wanted. It took all the tact and diplomacy I could manage to get him to think it was his own idea that it would be better experience for me without him looking after me. After all, I'd done that bit of service for the last three years without an Alfie nursing me.

*

I've got to admit it was the best Christmas I'd had for years – since Gran died, in fact. Betty did us proud with the grub, so we all felt as if we'd burst after that terrific feed-up. Alfie and she had done up the tree beautifully, and the twins had done a lovely job with all the other decorations, and Freda and Muriel wore pretty satin bows and behaved themselves amazingly well. Freda was too full of turkey to beg for scraps from our plates, and Muriel didn't scratch or bite me even once.

We sat around reading silly riddles from the crackers to each other and making up daft answers, and it was simply great. It was a real family time, and they all made me feel as if I belonged. I was so happy I didn't know how to thank them. But they could see for themselves how much it meant to me.

Of course the great let-down came a week later, in Trafalgar Square. When I saw my dreamboat, DI Derek Michaelson, with *his* dreamboat. She was just stunning. Beautiful, dressed like a model, just his height, laughing, with an air of sophistication I could never hope to manage. No wonder he was smitten. No wonder he wanted to get a London posting. No wonder he didn't even see me, pining after him from a distance like a moon-struck calf. I was just another galumphing great uniformed PC with big feet and mousy hair.

The career, I said to myself. Concentrate on the career.

This didn't stop me waking up late the next day with an entirely new and brilliant idea. Because of the double shift and the days off I'd given up previously, I was entitled to three clear days off-duty. I phoned Durham and persuaded them to give me a London number for DI Michaelson. I thought it might be pushing it a bit to ask for his mobile number. It wasn't my fault that they thought I was phoning from Shady Lane because it was necessary for him to call in there before going back to Durham. Lucky for me they didn't ask what he was wanted at Shady Lane for. I would have been stuck for an answer there, so good thing they didn't think of the question. And they gave me the number right away, so I didn't have to work out what to do if they'd said they'd call me back.

It was a bit painful for me when this high-class female voice answered the phone, even though I knew the number I'd got would be at her place. But I got some satisfaction from hearing her call out to him, 'They'd better not be calling you back on duty, darling', in a really sharp and threatening voice, as if to say, you'll get some stick from me if you spoil my plans, *darling*.

When I heard his voice saying, 'DI Michaelson' I had to take a deep breath and summon up all my nerve.

'I'm really sorry to trouble you, Inspector,' I started, 'I'm sure you won't remember me, DC Greta Pusey, I came up to Durham with DS Partridge in connection with the accident…'

'Oh yes, of course I remember. What can I do for you – Just a minute, how did you get this number? This is a private ex-directory telephone—'

'Yes, well, I'm sorry,' I interrupted quickly, 'but I must have given a wrong impression somehow to your people in Durham, because they said I should phone you at this number. I'm sorry if it's not convenient…' I seemed to be starting every sentence with apologies, but I couldn't stop. If he was going to be angry, I'd never be able to tell him what it was all about, and I didn't know how to get to the point. But he saved me the trouble.

'Well, I suppose it must be something important, Pusey,' he said, obviously through gritted teeth. 'Just tell me what you're phoning about, as briefly as you can, and let's get it over with.'

'I need the advice of a senior officer who isn't attached to Watford or the Met,' I blurted. 'Can you spare some time to meet me somewhere, anywhere in the London area, so that I can talk to you? I promise I won't take too much of your time.'

There was a long, agonising silence, and I heard That Woman calling out in her upper-class voice, 'Derek! Will you be long on the phone, darling?'

Very tersely, he said, 'Meet me at Archway Underground Station at seven-thirty a m, the morning after tomorrow,' and hung up. What! Seven-thirty in the morning at Archway

Station, wherever that was! And he hadn't even waited for me to say I'd be there! Well, I probably should have been grateful he'd agreed to see me at all. Still, he wasn't very friendly about it. I just hoped I could make him understand about the whole thing.

Now all I had to do was fill the forty-five hours until I could see him again. When I've got to use up time like that, I've found the best way is to do stuff that I hate. So I caught up with my washing and ironing and cleaning until everything shone and sparkled, then I went to the Watersplash for a long swim and a session in the gym. I'm not usually much of a one for gym work, so that made me feel really virtuous.

I'd been so good, I rewarded myself after that with an extra go with my karate instructor, followed by a large pizza and a phone call and chat with Ari. Of course, I didn't breathe a word to him about meeting DI Michaelson. None of his business. Ari was settling down so well in his job at the HSE, I wondered if he'd end up forgetting all about the private detective lark, and going in for the Health and Safety game instead.

I'd thought hard about getting to Archway after looking it up on the map, and decided my best way was to cycle there. So as to be on time, I set off at five o'clock, and seeing what a bad early-morning starter I am, I set the alarm for three. Just to be on the safe side. I wore my lycra gear and my helmet, as usual. I wasn't going to try to look snazzy. He wouldn't notice anyway. This was a serious meet, and I needed him to see how I felt about it, as well as listening to what I had to tell him.

He was dead on time. Even at that hour of day, he looked good enough to eat. But very grim. He took one look at me and my bike, and showed me where to park it safely. Then he led the way to a nearby workmen's café. He bought two cups of tea and although I looked longingly at the hot bacon sarnies, he didn't mention food, so I thought I'd better not, either.

'Well, Pusey,' he said, 'what's this all about?'

So I told him everything, even starting with silly old Gladys Trulove, because her victim also worked at the HSE, and who could tell whether he was involved in the whole mess or not.

At that part of my account, I thought he might laugh, because his mouth certainly twitched a bit when I was talking about Jules Verne really being called Julius Varney. But he didn't smile or comment all the way through, until I wound up with Superintendent Wood's comment on the way out of the Coroner's Court.

'And your conclusion about this is what?' he asked, stirring his cold tea.

'I haven't got a conclusion,' I admitted. 'But it seems as if there's some sort of cover-up, and Alfie Partridge is the only one I trust, and he thinks I've got too much imagination, so he's no help. Of course, he doesn't know that stuff about Aristotle Anapolis and Joan Smith.'

'Can we just have a short recap?' he asked. 'You think Jonathan Bennett is being set up by his colleagues at the Health and Safety Executive, you think his cousin Rodney Bennett was murdered by unknown means, and you think that the late Gustafson and his friend Anderson were involved with Rodney in some sort of Planning Department bribery and corruption. Also something to do with drugs. Is that it? Have I got it all?'

I could hear how ridiculous the whole thing sounded. I nodded, too embarrassed to speak. What a good thing I hadn't told him about the car-park incident, when Ari thought he saw DCI Chester either giving or receiving a mysterious package in the middle of the night. Then he might have thought I was completely round the bend.

'Well, you might feel a little encouraged to know that Anderson has gone to jail for six months for causing death by dangerous driving,' he said, getting to his feet and pulling on his coat. 'But apart from that, I don't think you've got anything to worry about except annoying DS Partridge with your theories. Happy New Year, Pusey.'

And he was gone.

I rubbed a little hole in the steam on the café window to watch him. He stood on the kerb, stamping his feet, alternately looking at his watch and up the Hill towards Highgate. After just a few minutes, she drew up beside him, in a Porsche, of course. What else would a drop-dead gorgeous bird have? Oh well, at least it wasn't a Ferrari or a Lamborghini. She didn't drive off right away, so I suppose they stopped for a quick snog first.

Going back to Watford I tried not to do any thinking. Just enjoy the ride, I told myself. True, it was one of those cold clear days, no ice or rain and not much wind, when cycling was a pleasure, and there was just the traffic to think about. And I really didn't want to think about making such a fool of myself. All I could hope for, where Derek Michaelson was concerned, was that he believed that I *did* want his advice because he was a senior officer with no connection to Hertfordshire, and not that I just wanted to see him again. He had no reason to suspect that it was a bit of both, and I certainly hadn't batted my eyelashes at him, or anything like that.

But I still had both problems.

Feeling pretty glum by the time I got home, an amazing surprise waited to cheer me up. Jim had made a quick stop-over and left me masses of goodies. The fridge was packed with my favourite Belgian choccy biscuits, Italian sausages and French cheeses and wine (including champagne!), and cartons of cans of Guinness and lager were stacked neatly in the living room. On the coffee table was a big Dundee cake with a note on it:

'Sory I mised you,' it said, 'will make a longer stop on the way back. Wontid to give you all this for Xmas but cooden get her in tim.'

He hadn't signed it. There was no need. If the international food hadn't been a clue, the spelling certainly was. I felt warmer towards him than I ever had since we'd first met. Good old Jim! Just when I needed something to make me feel better.

But there was more. A message from Ari on the answerphone said: 'You got off to a early start today, innit. See you tonight. I'm bringing Joan Smith. We've got a lot to tell you, so be ready with the drinks, OK? Bye-bye, lovely girl.'

The best bit of all was in the last two words. What a comfort to know that somebody thought I was a lovely girl, even if it was only Aristotle Anapolis, failed detective and would-be HSE Officer. I felt so much better, I didn't even start raiding the Belgian biscuits until after I'd had a long soak in the bath. And then I found myself thinking, ungratefully, that it was a pity Jim hadn't left me some nice smelly bubbly bath stuff, too.

*

From the minute I let them in I was wondering what was different about Joan Smith. It was only when we were sitting down that I realised: she was clean. True, she still wore that awful cheap eyestuff and lipstick, but apart from that her face was clean, and so were her hands, and even her hair! She still had a few faint traces of bruising left from our last get-together, but apart from that she looked almost respectable. Ari was wrong, though, about the nose. I hadn't broken it. It was just a bit swollen and bruised, I was sorry to see.

Then I noticed the way she was looking at Ari. She hardly took her eyes off him for a second, even when I was handing her a drink, and as for her expression – I could only describe it as soppy. When did this happen, I wondered. And how, why, and what?

'Go on, Joan,' Ari prompted, and, avoiding my eye, she obediently started into a long rambling apology for attacking me. From this I was supposed to believe that it was just a spur of the moment thing, and at first she hadn't even realised who it was they'd jumped on.

'Course, when I saw it was you, I already had the needle to you, so I just thought we might as well give you what for, even if there wasn't any money in it,' she finished up.

'Why? What was it about?' I started to ask, then, 'oh, you mean because of sidetracking you on to the Gladys Trulove case?' I added, and she nodded, still not looking at me.

'Right,' Ari said briskly, 'now we've got that out of the way, we can talk about the real business. Tell us from the beginning, Joan.'

It was just what he'd suspected. When Ariadne had sent out her 'press release' about her disappearance and the false accusation against her husband, Joan had been sent to interview her to find out whatever she could. She'd been provided with a press pass to help her convince Ariadne that she was a bona fide reporter who wanted to help Jay Bennett get out of the mess he was in.

'Just a minute,' I interrupted. 'What do you mean, you were sent? Who sent you? And how did you know where to find Ariadne? And who gave you a press pass?'

Joan looked straight at me properly for the first time. Not just a glance, but a long sad stare. No mascara, I noticed, just that dazzling bright blue eyeshadow. We looked at each other for a good twenty seconds, before I saw real tears welling up.

'Come on, it's what we come here for, innit,' Ari roughly broke into this speechless exchange of looks. 'You promised me you'd tell Greta how it all come about, and who got you up to it.'

She shifted her pleading gaze to him, by now the tears trickling down her cheeks, but Ari either didn't notice or didn't care. He just got up and handed her another tin of lager.

'See, I'm a snout,' she finally said, 'and it's the cop I work for. He said it was my big chance to get a proper job, he knew I always wanted to be a writer.'

If it hadn't been so pathetic I would have laughed. Whoever this cop was, he certainly knew how gullible this silly little kid was. Big chance! Proper job!

'What's his name?' I asked, but she shook her head. We could see she'd gone as far as she dared. And we tried everything, but nothing either of us could say, kind or bullying, would shift her any further.

When she went to the loo, I asked Ari, 'How did you get her to spill that much? And why is she looking at you so slushy all the time? What have you done?'

'Easy,' he said, 'all I had to do was be kind and understanding, like you know I am. It's just my nature, innit. Seems like nobody's ever spoken decent to her before, so when I said I didn't want anything off her and I'd be her friend, she went all weak at the knees over me. Could be cos I'm so good-looking, an' all.'

And he looked at me with a sort of doggy-devoted look, a bit like Joan had been looking at him, and it dawned on me that he didn't just fancy me, we had something more serious happening here. Just what I didn't need.

Then we had a bit of a farce, with Joan wanting him to take her home and him wanting to stay with me, and me wanting to see the back of the pair of them.

Naturally, I won. After all, it was my home we were in.

And I needed a long think about what I'd heard. What a pity I hadn't got this information from Joan Smith before I tried to convince Derek Michaelson that there was something fishy going on at Shady Lane.

But no sooner I'd got rid of them than I started to wish I hadn't. Not because of anything about Ari. No, it was just that I realised that there was a ton more questions that I should have asked.

For a start, how had Ari got in touch with Joan? Were they seeing each other regularly? Or did he just know where her squat was? If so, why had she trusted him with that information? Then, less important but still interesting, how had she got so cleaned up? If she had the facilities where she was living, why hadn't she used them before? And, more to the point, if there was no bathroom in that squat, had Ari given her the use of his?

Come to think of it, I didn't even know where Ari lived. Was he still living with his parents? No, he couldn't be, because he'd had to phone his mother in the first place to find out where Ariadne was. But out of all this puzzlement, the outstanding question, which I'd been trying to avoid thinking about, was whether Ari had been the other person snooping around Jay and Ariadne's empty house with Joan Smith. Because if there was the slightest suspicion of that, it could mean that I'd been putting my trust in the wrong person.

Another thing: was Joan Smith her real name? And if she was working for a bent cop, maybe she and Aristotle Anapolis were really buddies, and Ari had been fooling me all along with his story of being a private detective working for his old friend Ariadne to help clear her husband's name. It was possible. It all fitted together, if I wanted to see it that way. Of course I didn't. Sleeping with the enemy was the last thing I'd want to do.

On the other hand, if Ari was the enemy, who could I hope for as a friend? There was only one person I absolutely knew I could trust, and that was Alfie. And Alfie didn't want to know about my doubts and suspicions.

Could I possibly make one last desperate appeal to DI Michaelson? No, he'd made it clear that he thought I was a nutter.

So I was on my own.

*

At last it was time for me and Alfie to go to court to give our evidence on the Gladys Trulove case. Alfie took me through my notes over and over to make sure I was OK about everything. I told him how many times I'd been in court when I was still a uniformed plod, but he said this was different and he wanted me to feel confident. A kind man, Alfie, but sometimes misguided. Still, I did appreciate his motives, even if his method was a pain in the arse.

So we did our bit, and I was surprised what a hard time the defending counsel gave us both. What was the point of that, I wondered.

Another thing I hadn't expected was that Alfie and I stayed in the courtroom after the briefs had finished with us. I was pleased about that, because I had a kind of proprietary interest in poor Gladys, and I was secretly hoping that somehow or other she'd get off scot-free. Naturally I didn't tell Alfie how I felt. He wouldn't approve of such sentiment, any more than I would myself in the ordinary way, but somehow my heart went out to that poor silly woman.

I noticed Mrs Julius Varney in the public area of the court. Evidently she wasn't going to be called. As usual, she was a symphony in apricot, including a breathtaking hat which was such a swirl of apricot veiling, netting or curtain material that it added several inches to her height and must have obscured the view of the proceedings of whoever sat behind her. After a while, Alfie saw me gawping at her, and then he caught her eye and they exchanged a few nods and simpers.

First opportunity when the judge called a lunch break, Alfie made a beeline for the widow.

'This must be a very difficult time for you, Mrs Varney,' he offered.

'Ow, no, sergeant, do call me Vera,' the apricot vision insisted. 'Yes, well, poor Gladys,' she went on, 'she was never a clever girl, you know. I always had to help her when we went to the bingo together. Years it took her to work it out, poor thing.'

Alfie was flummoxed.

'I meant hearing all that about your husband,' he explained. 'I do hope it doesn't cause you too much distress. Perhaps you would prefer to go home to wait for the outcome. Would you like me to escort you…?'

Vera giggled. Not a pretty sound.

'Ow no, sergeant.'

'Alfie,' he corrected.

'I wouldn't miss this for the world,' she went on. 'And I'm sure it's a comfort to Gladys to see me here.'

There was no answer to that, and I was glad Alfie didn't try to think of one.

Anyway, the case went on, pretty run of the mill, for a couple of days, and I was beginning to wonder what might be happening back at our cop shop, when the defending barrister put Gladys on the stand. First there was the usual boring establishing stuff.

Then we got to the nub – at least it was for me, if not for the case. Because he asked her how she found out that the deceased had been seeing other women. He must have known her pretty well. Any normal woman would have sussed that situation out years ago. But perfectly innocently she replied that one of his mates from where he worked had phoned and told her about them, in detail.

The rest of the case passed me by in a blur. My mind had clicked on to something so sinister as to be almost impossible to believe. And yet in a complicated way it made perfect sense.

If Julius Varney had really found out that there was wholesale corruption at the HSE, as his widow had hinted to us a while ago, what a splendid way to get rid of him. Whoever knew enough about his complicated love life to speak to Gladys and tell her the details, must have known what Gladys was like. Of course, nobody could have guessed she'd stick a knife in him, but there was a good chance the result would be that Julius would be damaged in some way. The least they could expect was that she'd dong him with a frying-pan and put him out of the way for a while. It was a bonus for whoever it was that the damage was permanent.

While we were waiting for the jury to deliberate, Alfie had a go at me.

'I saw your face light up,' he boomed at me, 'when the accused said one of her boyfriend's mates phoned and told her about his other women. I know you well enough by now, my girl, to know what you were thinking.'

He was so agitated that one of the court ushers had to ask him to keep it quiet. I tried to bluff it out.

With my most innocent look, I said, 'I don't know what you mean, Sarge. I just thought it was interesting, that's all.'

'Stop that, Greta!' he growled. 'P'raps you think I've never noticed you only call me Sarge when you've got a bad conscience. You must think I'm daft. You're imagining someone at the HSE was trying to mix it for Julius Varney to distract him from nosing about finding out some funny business there, aren't you. Well, I'm telling you, just stop making up theories and stick to routine, you'll do better like that.'

And he turned round and stamped off. When he saw me following him, he deliberately marched into the Gents to get out of my reach. I was confused again. He'd pretty well hit on the nail when he'd worked out my idea, and probably his advice was good and he was entitled to be fed up with me.

But what if I was right? I sat there for ages, waiting for him to reappear or the usher to call us back into court, turning it over in my mind and coming to no conclusion. I did also wonder what Alfie was doing in the Gents all that time. Then I remembered he'd had a newspaper stuck in his pocket, so that was all right.

Well, finally we got called back for the verdict, and Alfie rejoined me, looking serious but not furious.

Poor Gladys broke down when she was sentenced to five years for manslaughter, and Vera, sitting near us by now, also burst into loud sobs. I don't know what they'd both expected, but I thought it was pretty lenient, seeing Gladys had admitted sticking a knife into the deceased.

Anyway, it gave Alfie a perfect excuse to see the Widow Varney home, and clearly that meant I wouldn't see him again until next day.

But I'd made up my mind not to tease him about the apricot widow, so when we met at Shady Lane next morning, we were quite friendly. I think he'd decided not to say any more about me and my theories and inspirations unless I gave him further cause. So we were in a sort of state of armed truce.

'Coming to the farewell bash tonight, then, girl?' he asked me in a fairly jovial way. So much had happened since the whip-round for DS Freddy Forbes' retirement present that the date of his party had come round before I'd noticed.

'He's done his thirty,' Alfie went on, 'and I reckon he deserves a jolly good send-off.'

'Yes, of course, it should be a good do,' I said. 'But what about you, Alfie? When will it be your turn?'

I wasn't sure how old Alfie was, but it was obvious he and Freddy were in the same age bracket.

'No, you're stuck with me for a good long time yet,' Alfie grinned. 'I did my ten in the Army before I joined this lot. I've got about another eighteen before I come up for my thirty.'

Was it my imagination, or was there something threatening in the way he said that?

As expected, it was a pretty good party, with everyone letting their hair down and even Superintendent Wood unbending a bit and actually smiling now and then. I thought I saw him laughing once, but it may have been a trick of the light. It was a strange thing about that man, whatever situation he was in he looked like a slightly animated tree, and his uniform never seemed quite the right size. Those bony wrists always stuck out of his cuffs and his fingers looked like a collection of dried twigs. I must say though, he made a really excellent farewell speech to old Freddy, and the best bit was at the end, after he'd given him his presentation.

'Some of you may know,' he said, after the applause and cheering and shouts of 'good old Freddy' had died down, 'that we shall also be losing another popular officer from our ranks. Detective Inspector Gerald Graves has been waiting for a posting to Wales for some time now, and at last it has come through. So he and his wife will be able to be near her family again! And we may now look forward to another of these merry parties in the near future, when we say farewell to Gerald, just when we have recovered from the loss of DS Forbes!'

He went on for quite a bit after that, but I lost track of the rest, because I'd sunk into a rosy glow. This could easily mean that DI Michaelson would get his transfer to Watford. I'd see him here at Shady Lane, probably every day!

And I would be that much closer to my dream.

Chapter 13

Since my transfer to plain clothes I'd been getting used to being woken up for various reasons, like phone calls, in the middle of the night. But gasping for breath with a large leathery hand clamped over my mouth was a new experience. And I could tell right away it wasn't a dream. Even in my stupefied state, though, I realised it had to be Jim arriving late and feeling playful. So I got a firm grip on his wrist and gave it a sharp twist. Nothing happened, except that I went on choking. Jim was never this silent nor this strong. It dawned on me that something was seriously wrong. So, waking up faster than I'd ever done in my life, I started to struggle in earnest, getting a bit tangled up in the bedclothes by trying to get my feet free for a suitable kick. It was no good. All that happened was that another large leathery hand planted itself firmly round my throat.

Just when it looked like this might be my last moment, and in the back of my mind was the sad thought that I didn't even know what it was all about, a husky whisper in my ear gave me a message.

'Stop asking Joan Smith questions,' it said, breathing hotly and wetly.

Then there was suddenly a lot of shouting and banging, and I realised that at this least useful moment, Jim actually had arrived. Of all the people I'd want to help me out of a dangerous situation, Jim was the last. To say that he was out of condition might give you the idea that he'd ever been *in* condition. One look at him was enough to tell you this was a man who'd been born into flabbiness. And sitting in a lorry for all of his working life, noshing and boozing, didn't improve matters. No, normally, if it came to any kind of a scuffle, he'd look to *me* to defend *him*.

But of course my attacker couldn't have known that. All he could have seen was a large male person coming in roaring 'What's going on here? What are you up to now, Greta?'

So the intruder let go of me to face this new and unexpected danger, which gave me a chance to jump out of bed and give him a good karate throw. Then I sat on his head and shouted to Jim to come and join me. Whatever Jim lacks in the fighting department, he makes up for in weight. Anyone being sat on by Jim would never be quite the same afterwards. So we both sat there on this body, side by side, while our prisoner made muffled noises and tried to get up.

'What's occurring, Greta?' Jim asked again, mildly, after a minute or two while we both got our breath back.

When I told him what little I knew of what was going on, he said he had wondered why the front door was already open when he arrived.

'I thought to myself, that's unusual for Greta, she's usually so security-minded,' he added.

Well, nobody ever said that Jim was top of the intelligence league, but even for him, that was a bit thick.

'You didn't think of a break-in, then?' I asked, and he admitted it hadn't crossed his mind.

'It's late, and I'm tired,' he whinged, and I had to accept this excuse.

I don't know how Jim felt, he having plenty of natural padding all round, but by this time I was finding our seat a bit uncomfortable, so I got up and put the light on. We looked at our prisoner.

'Who are you?' Jim asked him, but I didn't have to.

Even in his crushed and battered condition, I could see it was Detective Inspector Gerald Graves.

My first thought was, how embarrassing. What do I do now?

'You going to phone the cop shop?' Jim asked me, and all I could think of was Alfie's time-honoured favourite reply, 'Buggered if I know.'

I helped DI Graves to his feet, brushed him down a bit and sat him on a chair. I could see that Jim was confused, so I just told them both to stay where they were while I checked the front door. Sure enough, as Jim had said, it was wide open, but the locks had been picked so skilfully that they just looked as if they'd been used normally with keys. No wonder Jim hadn't thought it was a break-in.

I shut the door and re-locked it, then decided to play for time by making us all a cup of tea. In the kitchen I noticed the time: three o'clock – and I was wide awake. Nothing like a few shocks to get the system going, I muttered to myself as I put the kettle on, but I think on the whole I prefer my usual sluggish start to the day. Slow is best for me, specially if the choice is between that and an embarrassing intruder.

I heard them go into the sitting room, so I took the tea in there. DI Graves was still looking not quite in working order, though I could see he was making an effort to shake off his shock. I could see his trouble. He'd expected to scare me off questioning Joan Smith, who must have been his snout. He thought he'd give me a serious fright and get me to keep my nose out and behave myself, and then he'd skip off out, and I'd never know who my threatening visitor had been. But it had all gone wrong for him, and now he didn't know what to do. The fact was, nor did I.

Jim said, 'So who is this feller?'

I was in such a muddle by this time I'd forgotten he didn't even know we'd been sitting on a senior police officer. I knew it would lead to a lot of boring explanations, but I thought the least I could do was introduce them. I was wrong again.

Jim didn't want to know anything more than our victim's name, and after that he said, 'Well, I expect you two have got a lot to talk about, but I'm dead tired, so I'm off to bed. See you in the morning, Greta.'

So there DI Graves and I sat, sipping tea and eyeing each other, both wondering what we could possibly say or do next.

Finally, more to break the silence than anything, I said, 'That was dangerous, what you did. You could have choked me, you know. Matter of fact, you nearly did.'

'Didn't mean to,' he mumbled. 'Just wanted to scare you off.'

'Is Joan Smith your snout?' I asked.

He nodded.

'But you'll be transferred soon,' I argued. 'What does it matter to you if I question her from now till we land on Mars? Did you think I'd get her to give away so much that I'd have to report you? So you'd never get to Wales?'

He nodded again. This wasn't turning out much of a conversation. It got worse. We were both quiet for so long that I nearly dozed off. Then finally he spoke.

'Who is that man?' he asked, nodding in the direction of the bedroom.

What a cheek.

'None of your damn business,' I said, coming suddenly wide awake. 'And I think I'm the one to be asking questions, not you. The first one is, since you must be such a dab hand with the picklocks to have opened my front door so neatly, how about giving me a lesson on how it's done? And while you're about it, you might let me know where I can buy a set for myself.'

I could see he was amazed. This wasn't even slightly the sort of question he'd been expecting. But he agreed soon enough, and we spent the next hour working away at this new craft for me, until I was – well, not quite a pro, but pretty good at it.

Seemed to me this could be an extremely useful skill. Who knew when such a knack might come in handy. And then he kindly gave me his set of picklocks, saying he'd get himself another lot before he left for Wales. He might have thought this generosity would be the end of our discussion, but I had other ideas.

'Tell me what it was all about with Joan Smith,' I asked, and this time he gave more of an answer.

'Somebody thought that private detective friend of Jonathan Bennett's wife might find out things better kept quiet,' he said, 'so I got Joan to find out what was going on, that's all.'

'What somebody? What things better kept quiet?'

He shook his head and stood up, putting his leather gloves back on.

'No more questions,' he said. 'I'm off.'

'Oh no you're not,' I told him. 'This is my home, and you broke into it and assaulted me. I could still turn you in and ruin your career if I wanted to.'

'Forget it,' he said. 'You can't prove a thing. You invited me here and your boyfriend arrived and found us at it, there was a rough-house and now you're making a put-up job of getting me into trouble. How do you like that for a story?'

And while I was still staggering from the shock of this calm twist that he must have thought up while he was teaching me to pick locks, he added, 'And don't forget, I'm off out of it. But if you try your story on, they'll believe me, not you. And you'd have to live with the fall-out at Shady Lane for a good long time. The lads wouldn't let you forget it in a hurry!'

He was right. Dumbly I just sat there and watched him go. He even had the nerve to give me a smile and a wink. I felt a complete prat. Why did I give him time to think up his story? Well, I suppose I could have got Jim to back me up if I told the truth, but it would have got messy, and some people would choose to believe the DI rather than me, whatever the official outcome. I had to let Gerry Graves get away with it.

And on top of that, I saw it was almost time to get up, so I could forget about getting a bit of nerve-restoring sleep before starting another day at Shady Lane. Then when I got home, Jim would probably still be there, and I'd have to put up with him, when all I wanted at this moment was a good long talk about everything with Ari.

After an uplifting cup of tea, I stood under the shower for half-an-hour, running through every expletive I knew.

*

Swearing my way out of my fury turned out to be a big help. After I calmed down, I made a list of outstanding questions to discuss with Ari:

1. Who was Gerry Graves's partner or boss giving orders to Joan Smith? He'd said 'somebody' thought Ari might find out things better kept quiet. Who was that 'somebody'?

2. If that somebody, whoever it was, thought that Ari and I were on to something, what was it?

3. Was there a connection between Gerry Graves getting his transfer just now and the possibility that Ari and I might be on to something?

4. Was Joan Smith her real name? If not, what was it and why wasn't she using it? Because she had a record?

5. Could it really be a coincidence that three people had died who were connected in one way or another to this case? Gustafson and Danny Robbins had died in accidents, and we were reliably informed that Councillor Rodney Bennett had died of natural causes. Did we really believe any of this?

When I got this far I thought I'd better get off to Shady Lane before my rage bubbled up again. It was all so frustrating and meaningless, I couldn't even seem to think up a theory, however farfetched, to cover everything that had happened since the so-called fairground 'accident'.

Also, I could hear loud yawns and groans coming from the bedroom which meant that Jim was about to put in an appearance, wanting breakfast. That would have been the last straw in a day which seemed pretty long already, though the real time was only seven o'clock. I loped off.

'Got the date for the Health and Safety Executive corruption case,' Dusty Miller greeted me with her usual knowing grin. 'Going to go a bit hard with your pal Bennett, looks like.'

That was all I needed. A day that started lousy was rapidly going downhill.

'Cheer up, girl,' Alfie admonished me. 'You look like a dying duck in a wet week.'

Another of Alfie's mysterious sayings.

I tried to smile. Couldn't quite make it.

'Here,' he went on, 'there's something I want to ask you. Freddie told me at the party that when he first came here all those years ago, there was a Sergeant Pusey. He said he was really popular, and the whole Force turned out at his funeral when he died young. Heart, it was. Any relation? Only Freddie said he thought he only had one child, a little girl. That couldn't have been you, could it?'

'No,' I said, 'Sergeant Pusey was my grandpa. The little girl was my mother. She died young, too. My Gran brought me up.'

I could see Alfie's lips moving as he worked this out. Then his face cleared as he realised that my mother hadn't been married, and she must have been pretty young when I was born. But the hard look I gave advised him it wasn't a good idea to ask me any more questions. I'd never told anyone about my mother's death being my reason for my fanatical hatred of drugs, and I wasn't about to start now, even with Alfie.

So we moved on to other things.

I was relieved to learn that though Dusty had told the truth and the date had been set for Jonathan Bennett's trial, it was still two months ahead. That meant that we still had a chance of discovering something, anything, that might help his case.

It wasn't that I cared so much about the Bennett family and their troubles, or even that Ari had taken on the job of clearing his name out of friendship for Ariadne. It was because it seemed so obvious to me that he couldn't possibly be guilty of extortion and corruption, either in the case of the fairground incident, or on the grand scale of which he was now accused. What about justice, was what I wanted to know.

I went to see DI Gerry Graves in his office. He went quite pale when he saw me come in.

'Sir,' I said in a pretending to be respectful voice, 'I wonder if you could help me with a problem. It's about a case which won't come up until after you've gone to Wales, but I thought perhaps you could explain it to me.'

*

I got home that evening in a really lousy mood. It had been a shit of a day, with Alfie so angry with me that he could hardly bear to speak my name, never mind have a conversation with me.

That was after he'd given me a piece of his mind for going over his head to Gerry Graves. The Detective Inspector had called him in to get him to explain to me that if I had any difficulties I should ask him first, and also that I didn't need to understand a case that was absolutely none of my business. As far as Alfie was concerned, that was a pretty putrid start to his day, too.

I didn't want to think how he would have reacted if he'd known how my day had really started. Because of course while he was telling me off, I did think for a moment of telling him how DI Graves had made an entry into my home and what happened after that, just to defend myself. But how could I expect him to believe me? That would only have made matters worse. He was angry enough without thinking I was making things up to justify myself.

Anyhow, we got through the day somehow, and at last it was time to go.

Jim greeted me with beaming smiles.

'Your friend Joan is here already,' he said, 'and she says her boyfriend will be along soon, so I'll go to the chippie and get us all a takeaway, shall I?'

That was all I needed to put the tin lid on everything. Jim and me and Joan Smith and Ari was not my idea of a perfect foursome, whichever way you sliced it. Of course Jim had forgotten the rollicking I gave him about being so hospitable to Joan Smith last time I'd found him dishing out tea and smiles to her. It was no good telling him all over again that she wasn't my friend and anyway I hated journalists. Anyway, now I knew for sure she wasn't one. If that was a pig's dinner of thinking for me, it would probably make Jim need a good lie-down. I'd just have to work my way through the evening, somehow.

Then I saw a possibility. If Jim was going out for fish and chips and Ari hadn't arrived yet, I'd have Joan to myself for about a half hour. Right, I said to myself, let's make the most of it. I started off, the moment Jim had gone out of the door, with my most threatening smile. I knew it was working when I saw her cringing, trying to get out of her chair through the backrest.

'OK,' I barked, rolling up my sleeves, 'let's have it. What's your real name?'

She licked her lips.

'Hayley Huntley?' she tried, on a questioning note.

'Come on, I don't want to hurt you,' I growled. 'All I want is the truth. But quickly, before the others get here.'

'Larissa Lamb,' she offered, her eyes darting round the room looking for an escape route.

'Do you want any teeth left to eat your fish and chips, or not?' I asked, and even though we both knew I wasn't serious, well, not very, it was enough to scare her finally into telling the truth. It came hard to her. She was a natural liar, who'd always prefer not to practise honesty if she could avoid it.

'Glenda Brown,' she muttered. 'Ask DI Graves, he'll tell you it's true. That's my real name, what he's got on my record.'

I tried to hide how triumphant I felt. She had a record! I could look her up on the computer and get her whole history!

'That's how he got me to be his snout,' she went on, 'by getting me off last time they picked me up. He done some sort of deal with the uniforms.'

Trying to seem offhand, I asked, 'What did they get you for?'

'They said it was shoplifting, but it was a fit-up.'

'Why should they take the trouble to fit you up, you're nothing to bother about, you're not worth the trouble—'

But she interrupted with a sneer. Just when I thought we were beginning to get somewhere, blow me if she didn't go off on one of her fairy tales again.

'It's because I'm black, really,' she started, and then stopped when she saw me looking at her dead white skin, her brown hair where the red was growing out, her nearly clean hands and fingernails.

'Well,' she went a lot less confidently, 'you've heard of black people looking white sometimes, haven't you?'

I was beginning to see that there was something seriously wrong with this bird. Telling lies wasn't just a necessity or even a hobby with her. She just couldn't stop. What had I read about pathological liars?

'Oh come on, Joan or Hayley or Larissa or Glenda or whatever the hell your name is,' I said irritably, 'stop mucking about and talk sense. Who else did you work for apart from DI Graves?'

'Nobody, honestly, Greta, I never did anything for the sergeant in uniform who handed me over to Gerry, he just said that made them quits and I never even spoke to him again. I forget his name, but Gerry will tell you, I expect, if you ask him.'

'And what were you doing snooping round Jay and Ariadne Bennett's house? And who was with you?'

'Oh, well, when Gerry told me Jonathan and his wife and kids were staying with his parents, I reckoned it might be worth a look round the house, just to see if there was an easy way in, you know. The guy with me was one of my mates from the squat, Garth he says his name is, but it might not be.'

'But you were seen with someone in uniform…'

She looked a bit more nervous.

'Seen, was I? I never knew that. Who was it? Was it you? You're always around, aren't you!' and she threw me a look of absolute hatred. This was a shock to me. I'd taken for granted that we were never going to be best friends, but I hadn't realised there was so much bad feeling on her side. Right away, just to be contrary, I decided to try to get on better with her.

'No, it was the neighbours. They described you both, and we clocked the bird was you alright, but we couldn't get the feller in uniform. If it was this guy from your squat, why was he in uniform?' I asked, trying to sound kind and more friendly than I'd been before.

Of course it didn't work.

She scowled at me as she answered with her usual sneer, 'Charity shops. You can get any old stuff you want from them, old uniforms, anything. And if you say you're homeless, they won't take much money off you, either.'

This was all working out so useless that I didn't mind when Jim came back shouting, 'Come and get it while it's hot!'

Ari arrived at the same minute – he must have smelled the grub – and with hardly another word we all settled down to shovelling hot fish and chips down our throats. For the next half hour the only conversation was on the lines of 'pass the salt' or 'any more Guinness' or 'I've never tried pickled eggs', until we all stopped for a breather.

'That's better,' Jim said, and he turned to Ari and added, 'did you know some feller broke in here last night and tried to have it away with my girl?'

I couldn't tell whether it was the break-in or the reference to 'my girl' that upset Ari more, but something made him jump to his feet and knock over his half-empty can of Guinness. In the flurry of moving things around and mopping-up and so on, I managed to mutter to him not to ask any questions.

When we'd settled down again, I asked Jim if he'd brought any ice-cream, and of course he hadn't. As I expected, good soul that he was, he offered to go out and get some. I thought best not to mention there was plenty in the freezer, so that way I got myself a necessary ten minutes alone with Ari and Joan Smith. I knew that wasn't really her name, but somehow I couldn't think of her as anything else now.

I told them both about my visit from DI Graves and what transpired.

Then Jim came back.

As he was passing out generous helpings of ice-cream, Joan said to him chattily, 'That was Detective Inspector Graves what broke in here last night. Fancy, just to tell Greta to leave me alone! You wouldn't think an important policeman would think I was worth all that trouble, would you,' she simpered.

Jim just stared at her with his mouth open, showing a large mouthful of unswallowed ice-cream.

Ari said hastily, 'Joan, how many times have I told you to stop making up stories. She can't seem to help it,' he added apologetically to Jim, who was looking absolutely gob smacked by this time.

'Of course it wasn't DI Graves,' I chimed in. 'If he wanted to tell me off, he could do it at the station, couldn't he. And anyway, why should I leave you alone,' I went on to Joan, 'when we're getting on so well together.'

Jim turned to Joan. 'Are you a liar?' he asked in his straightforward way.

She gave him one of her smiles showing those nasty pointy little teeth.

'Course not, Jim,' she said. 'Just kidding. I like a joke, don't you?'

The evening hadn't been what you'd call a roaring social success until then, but after that it was all downhill. Finally Ari dragged Joan off, rolling his eyes at me in a meaningful manner while thanking Jim for the fish and chips. I had no idea what his message was.

But at least he'd managed to find out, in a casual sort of way, how soon Jim would be leaving for foreign parts again. So we both knew when Ari would be calling on me again.

*

I could hardly wait to get in next morning, to have a go at the computer to see what I could find out about Joan Smith. After a struggle, I managed to get something out of it, but it wasn't easy. It turned out she'd been done for shop-lifting and got off with the usual wrist-slap, and then she'd been up on a charge of assault which somehow fell through because the witnesses didn't turn up. After that she'd been copped red-handed trying the shoplifting lark again, and I just couldn't follow what happened next. That was probably when the uniforms did a deal with DI Graves, and whoever entered the records didn't want to be too specific. Most likely they'd owed him a favour – we all knew how those things worked, but it didn't do to spell it out too clearly.

It was quite interesting what a string of names Joan Smith was known by. She was most commonly called Joan or Lily Smith, but hardly ever by her real name, which it turned out wasn't any of the ones she'd told me the previous evening. I couldn't blame her for not liking her given name, though, and wondered who ever decided to call her Barbara Barry. And her buddy from the squat, who'd been up on the first charge with her, was called Garth Powell, but mysteriously was most often known as Worm.

By the time I'd got all that, Alfie had turned up and our real day started. But that little tussle with the computer had made my mind up for me. Even if it meant I'd have to give up going to karate, I was going to take a computer course. I could see how useful it might be to be able to wrestle out some more secrets from that obstinate bugger of a machine.

Apart from Alfie giving me a long boring lecture, it was a routine unexciting sort of day, and I think we were both glad to get to the end of it. I was keen to get home to see if Jim had gone, so that I could have another talk with Ari. And of course I did mean a talk, because I'd absolutely decided that Ari and I would have no more nights of passion. Not that I'd had any complaints about our previous session, but just that I didn't think it was right.

Anyway, apart from wanting to see Ari, I was quite glad to see that Jim had gone when I got home, because he could be a bit of a pain sometimes. And as expected, Ari turned up later on with a pizza and a six-pack and, I was glad to see, without Joan Smith.

He told me he was absolutely sure that the whole staff of that branch of the HSE was on the take, except for Jay Bennett. He'd been poking about, eavesdropping and earwigging as much as he could, and he said it was clear to him that they all regarded Jay as a pain in the arse because he was so straight that it would have been ridiculous to try to row him in to all that was going on.

'But maybe you're just putting two and two together and making six because you'd already made up your mind that Jay was the innocent victim,' I objected. 'I mean, have you got any proof at all? Could you find anything in the files that might support your theory?'

'I'm telling you it's the truth, innit,' Ari explained patiently for the third time. 'I can't find any proof, but if you could hear the way they talk, you'd know it's a fact what I'm telling you.'

'But what are we going to do?' I asked. 'All you've done is confirm what we suspected. But that's no help to Jay and Ariadne. And the case will be coming up soon, and poor Jay will probably be sent down for all the stuff that the others were doing that he didn't know anything about.'

'What about the witness who accidentally got killed?' Ari said. 'Even your lot must see that's suspicious, innit?'

I had to admit that there was a lot about the case that I didn't know, because I'd been well and truly told to keep out of it. We sat and looked at each other in glum silence for a while. I could tell we were both thinking about poor Jay and Ariadne and how we hadn't done anything for them.

Then somehow we had to cheer each other up, and one thing led to another, and there went all my good resolutions about not doing it again with Ari. I've got to admit, though, it was even better than last time. And made me wonder again why I'd been wasting my time with Jim.

But I told him next morning when he woke me up with a mug of tea, 'This has got to stop, Ari. We mustn't make a habit of this. It's not right.'

All he said was, 'Seems more than all right to me, lovely girl. Drink your tea. I'm off. See you soon.'

Chapter 14

Suddenly, my heart-throb was with us. Nobody had told me he would be there, but of course they had no reason to tell me anything. Naturally, Dusty Miller knew all about everything without being told, but I hadn't learned how to acquire that knack yet.

'Have you seen that dishy little new DI?' she asked me. 'He's going to take over from Gerry Graves, and he's come down from up North for a talk with the Super and Cheerful Charlie and to find himself a flat.'

Hateful woman, how did she dare know so much about him! On the other hand, good news that he was going to find himself a flat – that meant he wasn't going to move in with his gorgeous girlfriend in Highgate.

'Oh yes, Alfie and I met him when we went up to Durham,' I said in as offhand a manner as I could manage. 'Nice feller, his name's Derek Michaelson. Got a fantastic girlfriend living in Highgate.'

Dusty's face lived up to her name – it went all greyish.

'How did you find all that out, you nosy bitch,' she hissed. Then she cheered up as a new thought struck her, and she added, 'well, you wouldn't be interested in him, anyway, would you. He's about six inches smaller than you, Lofty.'

If there's one thing I hate, it's people making cracks about my height. Not that I mind being tall, in fact most of the time it's a help, but when I was at school I used to get teased about it a lot, and I still feel a bit sensitive on the subject.

'There's nothing wrong with being tall,' I told her, 'and it's a lot better than being skinny, I can tell you.'

'How would you know from up there,' she sneered.

So I came right back at her with, 'At least people looking at me can tell the difference between the front and the back, unlike some women detective constables around here.'

When I was a kid, I'd come in for a lot of baiting one way and another. About being too tall, and having bony knees. About the public way my mother had died of an overdose before the ambulance could get through the crowd standing watching. And some people seemed to think it was even funnier that my Gran was one of the last of the hospital matrons, as well. That was why Gran had enrolled me for karate lessons when I was eight. That changed my life quite a lot, and taught me not to take any lip from anyone.

My exchange of opinions with Dusty was just developing into a nice little slanging match when Alfie came along and interrupted.

'Now then, you two,' he boomed, 'stop that gossiping and giggling and get cracking. There's work to do around here, you know. Come along, Greta. And you ought to know better at your age, Dusty. Not setting a very good example to the young ones, are you now?'

And not even noticing Dusty going purple in the face with rage at the suggestion that she was much older than me, he swept me off. I didn't mind. I felt I'd got the best of that little rally.

'When's that DI Michaelson coming down from Durham then, Alfie?' I asked in my most innocent voice, but Alfie wasn't a complete fool.

'Don't think I've forgotten how you were looking at him all googly-eyed when we were up in Durham,' he said. 'It's no good you getting any ideas, he's already told DCI Chester about his girlfriend in London being his main reason for wanting this transfer. And anyway, I thought you were all for career and didn't care about men.'

'It's nothing like that,' I protested, 'I'm just interested in when DI Graves is leaving, that's all. That was a good farewell party we had for Freddie, and I was looking forward to the next one.'

It wasn't very convincing, but it was the best I could do. But I made up my mind to be more careful with the way I looked at my heart-throb in future. I didn't want word to get back to Delightful Derek that I fancied him.

I did wonder, though, whether he'd be with us in time for Jay Bennett's trial. I knew he wouldn't let on to anyone about our early morning meeting when I'd blurted all that stuff out to him about bribery and corruption, but it would be interesting to see how he reacted to the situation at first hand.

Anyway, I didn't see him at all on that visit, but I did find out when he'd be joining us, so I could start counting the days.

The previous night, Ari had promised me he'd keep an eye on Joan Smith, to see what she might be up to next. But he'd admitted he wasn't at all hopeful about finding anything at the HSE that would help Jay Bennett's case.

I told him all the stuff on Joan I'd got from the computer, and he was as surprised as I was when I told him I'd discovered she was only eighteen. We'd giggled together when I said I'd thought she was forty-five, but when I came to think about it afterwards, it wasn't so funny. I was beginning to feel sorry for the pathetic little thing. I might have gone to the bad like that myself, if it hadn't been for my Gran. Specially having in mind what my mother was like. And who knew if my father was even worse. She certainly didn't, my stupid mother. She had no more idea who he was than we did.

Anyway, Alfie told me we were being seconded to the Fraud Squad for a few weeks. He wasn't sure how long for.

'They need an experienced hand like me,' he explained, 'and it'll be good training for you, as well. It's to do with benefit fraud.'

I thought, how boring, but all I said was, 'Where do we go for the briefing, then?' and when Alfie said Hatfield, another thought struck me.

'Does that mean we won't be around for Jonathan Bennett's trial?' I asked. 'It's coming up soon now, isn't it?'

Alfie was scornful.

'Don't be silly,' he said. 'We wouldn't be able to go to that, even if we was right here in Watford. What do you think, the whole force could take time off to go to court for weeks? Be a long case, that one,' he added wisely.

So I'd have to rely on Ari giving me day-to-day information, and his facts wouldn't be first-hand, either. I was really choked about that. I was sure a serious miscarriage of justice was taking place, and it seemed as if our efforts to put things right had done poor Jay Bennett no good at all.

'What do you reckon will happen?' I asked Alfie, and felt even worse when he said he thought the accused would get three to five.

'Months?' I asked hopefully, but I knew I was being stupid without Alfie's rude laughter confirming that.

'Come on, girl,' he guffawed, 'you've got to get on with your life. You want a career with the police, don't you. You don't want to turn into one of them do-gooders what's always worrying about whether things are turning out the way you think they should. Forget about this Bennett feller, let the law take its course. You're going to get a whole new lot of experience with the Fraud Squad. Concentrate on that, right?'

I knew he was right, but I also knew that Jay Bennett was not guilty of any crime. Not just in the legal sense, but he was also one of life's innocents who couldn't see all the bribery and corruption that was happening around him at work. That was the irony of the whole thing. Whatever was going on, the real wrong-doers had nothing to fear from him, and so they'd never had any need to fit him up to get him out of the way in the first place. And he was so blinkered, he probably didn't have a clear-eyed view of his own wife, either. Everyone else could see through her, but he couldn't. Silly fellow.

So off we went to Hatfield, with me not knowing if I was more fed up about poor Jay Bennett or the prospect of being bored to death investigating benefit fraud.

No surprise to find out I was wrong again. It's one of the things I seem to be getting good at, being wrong. After a lengthy briefing at Hatfield, we were sent straight back to Watford to interview some squatters. And guess what – one of them was Joan Smith, and another was her chum, Worm. And I always say there's no such thing as coincidence!

No sooner had we started to question Joan Smith than she was squawking away, 'You can't touch me, I've got connections!'

'I don't care if you're connected to an electricity substation,' Alfie said, 'if you're claiming benefit you're not entitled to, you'll pay the penalty, even if your uncle is the Chief Constable.'

Then Worm made the mistake of trying to make a run for it. I don't make a hobby of it, but I'm a great runner myself, and I soon brought him back to Alfie, who hadn't made any attempt to follow him. Alfie just stood there like a hundred-year-old oak tree, solid and brambly, and put one large paw on Worm's shoulder.

'What's your trouble, then, lad?' he asked him, but not in a kindly way at all, and Worm looked like his nickname, except for the military uniform, of course.

Alfie gave him a good hard look, then suddenly ripped Worm's uniform tunic off, popping all the buttons at the same time. Then he turned Worm's bare arm over. Sure enough, there were the tracks, all up his arm. Now perhaps we had two matters to deal with.

But it turned out, even with all Alfie's expert questioning, and searching around the filthy squat, we couldn't find any evidence of benefit fraud, so it was only a case for the Drug Squad, not us at all. While we were waiting for some of their lot to turn up to take Worm in to find out his suppliers and see if there was a trail back to a main dealer, Alfie and I talked to Joan Smith.

It was an awkward conversation, because Alfie didn't know that I knew Joan, and she knew that if she let out more to him than I thought was a good idea, she'd be for it from me.

Finally a couple of DCs from the Drug Squad turned up and took Worm away, and we left.

As usual, I'd underestimated Alfie.

He'd been very quiet on the journey back to Hatfield, until we were nearly there, when he suddenly shot at me, 'So where do you know this scrubber from, calls herself Joan Smith? And what about this playmate of hers, who she calls Worm?'

I gave him a heavily censored version of my acquaintance with Aristotle Anapolis, private detective, and Joan Smith, wannabe journalist. He was looking pretty thunderous until I got to the bit where I'd looked up Joan's record on the computer. Then his expression changed. He looked almost shrewd.

'How did you know she had a record? And what other names she used?'

'See, I got a bit friendly with her,' I explained, hoping it all sounded more convincing to him than it did to me, 'and she told me she was Gerry Graves's snout. Then one thing led to another.'

'Go on,' he said, by now looking quite impressed, 'all these years I've been around Gerry, and he never let on. And I bet if Freddie Forbes had known, he'd have told me. So Gerry kept it really quiet about her. Freddy knew all his others.'

We were quiet for a while and I could almost hear the wheels going round in Alfie's head.

'I wonder,' he said, 'if Cheerful Charlie knows about this.'

Now, I said to myself, now's the time to tell him about my stake-out at the car-park with Ari. And being almost sure DCI Chester was handed a mystery package from another car in the middle of the night. I took a deep breath.

Then I funked it again.

*

When Alfie and I got released from our secondment to the Fraud Squad in Hatfield, the case against Jonathan Bennett was still going on.

That was the bad news.

But the good news was that in the meantime we'd been joined at Shady Lane by DI Derek Michaelson.

Even better was that when we were passing on the stairs one day, he didn't just recognise me, he stopped and spoke to me!

'Well, Pusey,' he said, 'I suppose you'll be interested to know that your man Anderson is out, and back home here in Watford.'

That was pretty cryptic, I thought. Why did he tell me that? Of course he was right, I was extremely interested. But was he referring to the suspicions I'd told him about that morning in the café at the Archway? Was he even hinting in a roundabout way that I wasn't completely off-beam in my vague theories? Or was he just thinking he might as well give this crackpot rookie DC a bit more to crack on about?

'I suppose he's had plenty of time to think about having been the cause of Gustafson's death,' I suggested, 'whether it was really his fault or not. I wonder if he'll get his old job back in the Planning Department at the Town Hall.'

DI Michaelson looked at me thoughtfully.

'There's no reason why you shouldn't pay him a visit at his home,' he said, 'as long as it's clear that it's personal and absolutely nothing to do with the Job. You could just have a friendly chat to ask him how he's getting on, what he's going to do with his life next, all that.'

And with a friendly nod, he walked on, leaving me thinking hard.

I'd been doing a lot of hard thinking in recent weeks, partly because of having enrolled on a computer course at the local evening classes. It wasn't easy, and sometimes it made my head swim. At those times I thought again about how tempted I'd been to sign on for saxophone classes instead. I'd always wanted to learn to play the tenor sax, and if I'd had to buy one to practise on, it would have cost me no more than buying a computer to do my homework on. Also, it would have taken less room in my little home, and been more fun, I reckoned. But the clincher was always that playing the sax wouldn't have furthered my police career, whereas being computer literate might.

I'd been so serious for a while about this choice that I'd asked various people's opinions. Alfie had just stroked his beard and laughed, obviously thinking it was some silly joke. Of course Jim had favoured the sax. Alfie's Betty and the twins all thought the computer was the best idea. Ari was the only one who'd made a whole evening's discussion out of it, finally concluding that the computer should come first, *then* I should take up the sax.

'Sex is better than sax, though, innit?' was his last word on the subject. Typical.

I wondered what DI Michaelson would think, if I'd dared to ask him.

Meanwhile, the Jonathan Bennett case was going on and on. And Ari was doing his best to keep me informed each day.

So anyway, one evening I went to see Anderson at his home. It was too far to walk – of course, when I went the first time with Alfie, we had the blessing of a car – so I rollerbladed.

Just my luck, the fierce old Viking Grandpa Anderson opened the door while I was still stowing my blades in my backpack.

'What—' he started, and then I straightened up and he saw my face. I didn't expect him to recognise me after so long, but he was a sharp old geezer.

'Oh, it's you, Detective Constable,' was all I heard as he started to close the door in my face. My years in uniform came in handy as I leaned against the door apparently casually but actually stopping it shutting completely.

'This is an unofficial visit, Mr Anderson,' I gabbled, 'I've just come for a friendly chat with your grandson. Please will you let me in?'

He humphed and ha'd for a minute before grudgingly opening the door again, saying, 'Well, I'll ask him if he wants to talk to you. But he doesn't have to, does he. He's paid the penalty for his stupidity in letting that Danish Icelander lead him astray.'

I thought that was a bit hard, seeing it was the villainous Danish Icelander, Gustafson, who'd lost his life in that little adventure. I said nothing, though, just stepped meekly into the hall and waited. I heard raised voices behind doors, but couldn't make out what anyone was saying. Perhaps they were talking Norwegian.

After a while, the grandfather came out and said, 'Well, his parents are out, but I take it on myself. If you just want a friendly word with the boy, you can come in and talk to him.'

I don't know why I'd expected young Anders Anderson to look different from when I'd last seen him. After all, he'd only been a few months in a low security prison. But he was still expressionless, white-faced, with those startling blue eyes the only really noticeable thing about him. I started off by asking how he felt, and if it had been tough on the prison farm, and he answered politely. Then we got to it.

'Will you be getting your old job back in the Planning Department?' I asked him, still in that friendly offhand kind of way. It was just good luck that the old grandfather had to leave the room to answer a call of nature at that moment. Otherwise I was sure I would have got a very different answer.

'Not much point with old Rodders gone,' young Anderson said.

'Old Rodders? You mean Councillor Rodney Bennett?' I asked, and when he just nodded, I went on, 'You mean he was the one who made it such a profitable place to work?'

I knew it was a leap in the dark, but I was surprised at what a straightforward answer I got. I'd hardly expected the truth, so it was a bit of a shock when I got it.

'Sure,' he said. 'He and Gus both had an expensive habit to pay for, and I just liked the money. But there's no chance of working it like that any more.'

'Do you realise what you're saying?' I gasped. 'You're admitting to involvement in fraud and corruption on a grand scale.'

Anderson laughed.

'This is a private conversation, right?' he said. 'You can report it all you like, all I've got to do is deny it. Got any proof, have you?'

And like a bung out of a barrel, it all came flooding out. He didn't even glance at the door to see if his grandfather had come back from upstairs. He just talked and talked. I could hardly believe what I was hearing.

'Gus and I met Rodders in the boiler room one night, and old Rods was in a bit of a state. His cousin at the HSE was being investigated, and the daft old bugger thought that meant some nosy cop would start looking into our affairs. God knows what he thought the connection might be. We told him he was off his bonce, but he got more and more worked up, and then he just suddenly dropped. No warning, no grabbing at his chest or anything. Just went. When we realised he was dead, Gus said we'd better hide his body and scarper, so off we went, sharpish.'

'Scarper? What is scarper?' boomed the old man from the doorway. 'What is this you are telling this woman? That you have really been involved in some criminal matters, after all? And we thought such an injustice was done when you were penalised for your driving accident.'

Anderson was so naturally white that he couldn't go any paler, but he did cringe a bit. Strangely enough though, his answer was quite cheeky.

'You've been in this country longer than I have, Papa,' he said, 'you should know some rhyming slang by now. Scarper is like Scapa Flow, go. See?'

'What will your parents say when they hear this?' Grandpapa Anderson said. 'Do you want to break their hearts?'

Anderson had quickly recovered his self-confidence.

'Well, don't tell them anything then,' he said.

While all this was going on I was recalling what the Gustafson parents had said. They had kept on insisting that Anderson was the real villain. Not just that he was responsible for Gustafson's drug habit, but also that he was his supplier. Maybe after all they hadn't just been grieving parents trying to excuse their son's behaviour. Well, I thought, I've got nothing to lose.

'You wouldn't happen to know where Gustafson and Councillor Bennett got their stuff?' I asked Anderson, but before he had a chance of another word, the old grandfather intervened.

'Young woman,' he addressed me, 'you should go now. I have to speak to my grandson before his parents come home. In private. Please go.'

Well I had no choice. Strictly speaking I'd had no right to be there in the first place. But it had certainly been worthwhile. At least I knew more now, even if I couldn't use it.

Rollerblading home, I mulled over what had been said. It seemed to me, though, that what hadn't been said was even more interesting. There was something in Anderson's eyes, just a flicker, when I asked him about the drug supplier, that made me wonder if I'd got near to the truth there. Of course, Alfie would have scoffed and said it was that woman's intuition again. On the other hand, maybe I shouldn't have brought up that question at all. That was what caused the old man to chuck me out, and there was a lot more I would have liked to ask. Particularly, what was Anderson going to do now, if he wasn't going back to his old job in Planning? Blueprint draughtsmen could get jobs easily, as far as I knew. But if he was always after the easy big money, perhaps he'd go in for counterfeiting next?

I couldn't help grinning at where my imagination was taking me. Perhaps Alfie was right and I let it lead me too far sometimes.

It was all quiet when I got home. No Jim, no Ari, not even a lurking Joan Smith. I thought I'd give Ari a ring to chat things over with him, but his mobile was switched off.

None of my business what Ari did when he wasn't with me, but next morning I tried his mobile again, and it was still off. So later on I found a spare moment and rang him at the HSE office. He wasn't in, they said, and hadn't called to say he was ill or anything. That evening, when his mobile was still off, I tried his landline at his flat, then got on to his parents. His mother was very cool with me, but said she thought he was away on business. I was a bit concerned by this time, so I rang Ariadne at her in-laws home in Radlett, where she was still staying while her husband's trial was going on.

'I don't know nothin' about Ari,' she sobbed, 'only 'e say 'e 'elp my Jay, and 'e nevair deed.'

'Oh, come on, Ariadne,' I said impatiently, 'don't keep putting on that phony accent with me, I know where you come from. I'm worried about Ari. He got a job at your husband's office just so that he could try to find out something that might help to clear his name. And now nobody knows where he is.'

'I'm sorry,' she said in an ordinary voice, 'I can't help.'

And she hung up. There was gratitude for you.

I went to Joan Smith's squat. She wasn't there, nor was Ari, nor Worm. Nobody else knew anything about her, or so they said.

Finally, I took the plunge and went to Camden Town to see Ari's parents. When I told them that I thought Ari had disappeared, their reactions were very different.

Mr Anapolis said, with a wink, 'Well, you know what boys are like. He's having a passion session, innit. He'll turn up with bags under his eyes, right, in a few days, no harm done.'

And he laughed in a nudge-nudge sort of way.

But Mrs Anapolis said he'd never done anything like that before, and he always rang her at least once a week, whatever he was doing.

'How long since you heard from him?' I asked.

'Ten days,' she said. I counted in my head. Could it have been that long? No, I'd seen him a week ago. But where was he now? And where was Joan Smith?

Well, life had to go on, and when it came time for DI Gerry Graves's farewell party, of course I had to go.

Superintendent Wood made a long boring speech all about Gerry's hard work and dedication and our loss being some other lot's gain and all that stuff. But then it got interesting when he started talking about Gerry's replacement.

'In the few weeks during which DI Derek Michaelson has been working alongside Gerry Graves,' he brayed like some old vicar giving a sermon, shooting his bony wrists out of his too-short cuffs, as usual, 'our new officer has demonstrated a notable aptitude for picking up the reins and running with them. He will be, I am sure, as great an asset to our Criminal Investigation Department as Gerry Graves has been, and I know you will all join me in welcoming him as we say a not necessarily too sad farewell to DI Graves.'

Boy, I thought, he ought to get himself a better speech-writer. Or else give up making speeches altogether. Still, it was nice to hear words of praise about Delectable Derek, even from that animated stack of firewood, our boss.

After a while I found that I was near enough to Derek to edge alongside him and offer a few words of greeting.

'Ah, Pusey,' he said, to my surprise, 'I was looking for you. Come over to this corner, I want a word.'

I was too thrilled to think, so just followed him dumbly, gazing devotedly at his back. It was a lovely back.

'Listen, Pusey,' he said, 'I've been following that case you were so interested in, you know, the HSE chap, Bennett. I have to agree with you, there are some very strange aspects of that case. No, don't interrupt,' he raised his hand as I opened my mouth. 'All I want to say is, let's meet some time and have another talk about things.'

And there and then, we made a date to meet again, horribly early one morning soon at that café at Archway. That will always be our trysting place, I thought dreamily as I walked back from the party.

My dreams were shattered when I got home. Jim was back again.

Chapter 15

'Jim,' I said crossly, 'what's going on? You seem to be coming back to Watford more often lately. It's only a few days since you were here, and now here you are again,' I went on, getting myself thoroughly wound up. 'When we first got to know each other, you used to get here, regular as clockwork, every two weeks, and I knew where I was with you. And now I don't know where I am.'

'Well, kid,' he said, wrapping his arms round me and giving me a thoroughly sloppy and unnecessary kiss, 'seems to me lately you need more looking after.'

I shoved him off me.

'What!' I yelled. '*You* look after *me*! Have you forgotten I'm a Black Belt in karate! You, you big fat slob, what good would you be to anyone in a scrum? What help were you that night when Graves broke in and nearly strangled me? Anyway, what's that got to do with your regular delivery runs?'

'I changed them, that's all,' he muttered sulkily. 'Come on, kid, we've never had a row before, let's not start now. It just seemed to me, since you changed your department, you're getting into more scraps and scrapes, and every time I see you, there's either some rough stuff going on, or else you're all bruised from the last lot. And I'm all you've got…'

'All right,' I sighed. I could see the stupid lump meant well. 'Just try to let me know when you're coming in future. I might have other arrangements, you know. And as it happens, I was planning to go out again this evening, to see if I can find out where Ari and Joan have got to. They both seem to have disappeared.'

Jim looked as sympathetic as his blobby features would allow.

'That's rotten when you haven't got many friends,' he said, and I only just managed not to flare up at him again. How the hell did he presume to know how many friends I had? And how did he come to the conclusion that he was all I'd got, anyway? I could have had hundreds of caring cousins, for all he knew.

'Anyway,' he went on, 'what do you mean, disappeared? How do you know they haven't just merely gone away somewhere for a few days, for a holiday or something.'

I was so taken by the words of this little speech that I nearly didn't take in the sense of what he was saying.

Merely? Where did Jim ever get hold of a word like 'merely'? Surely he hadn't suddenly taken up reading – apart from the sports pages, of course. I remembered him telling me that he read a book once and didn't think much of it, so he decided not to try another one. Still, I wasn't going to pick him up on his 'merely' – he'd probably just heard someone say it and decided to add it to his vocabulary. In the few seconds it took for me to have these thoughts, he was still talking.

'They don't have to tell you everything they're doing and everywhere they're going, do they?' he argued. 'It's being in the CID, Greta, it's made you look for plots and puzzles everywhere. You never used to get so worried about every little thing. Tell you what, I'll take you to the pictures, it'll take your mind off everything, do you good. Come on, must be something you want to see.'

And off we went to see some stupid action thing, which of course Jim loved and gave me a chance to take no notice of it and have a serious think instead. One of the things I had to decide was how much I wanted to tell DI Derek Michaelson when we had our next meeting. Not looking at the screen or listening to all the bangs and crashes gave me a perfect opportunity to turn things over in my mind.

It was almost as good as if I'd been sitting at home on my own with some of my Gran's old Golden Oldies playing in the background. Then I started to have a little ponder about Ari and Joan. Was there a chance that Jim's theory was right? Very unlikely. Also of course he couldn't know that my new relationship with Ari was a good reason for me to want to know everything he was doing.

These two trains of thought collided. How much should I tell Tasty Derek about Ari, his investigations, his connection with Ariadne, our relationship, his disappearance? And Joan Smith? How important was it to tell him absolutely everything? I was going to have to think out all the angles before I decided.

*

By the time the day dawned and I had to get up long before the sun did, I still hadn't made up my mind, but the long cycle ride to the Archway café helped to clear my head. By the time I got there it was obvious to me that I'd have to tell him every single fact if I wanted him to help.

And there he was, the handsome little darling! So compact, so perfect!

Before we got down to cases, though, he let drop a casual remark that made my heart sink.

'I'll be giving up that temporary flat in Watford and moving to this area soon,' he said in an offhand way. I knew what that meant: he was going to move in with that gorgeous bird. Silly of me to care. It wasn't as if I'd ever stood the slightest chance with him. But it did kind of put the clincher on it.

'Now then,' he said, all businesslike. 'First I want to talk to you about the HSE case. The jury's out, but it's pretty clear from the way the judge directed them that they're going to find that chap Jonathan Bennett not guilty of the first charge, that is, endangering the public by accepting bribes to give safety certificates where they were not warranted.'

By this time I was thinking, can I really be in love with this pompous prat? Does he always talk like this? No, I reassured myself, it's just that he's quoting lumps of law, and we police always get very formal when we do that. Of course I love him, however he talks. And anyway, it's nice to know he's so well educated.

While a part of my mind was sorting this out, he pressed on.

'I'm not sure about the situation on soliciting bribes,' he admitted. 'We'll have to see what the jury makes of that charge. And as you very well know, since you insist that it's suspicious, one of the prime witnesses met with a fatal accident, and his written deposition won't count for as much with the jury as if he'd been able to appear in court. There's also the fact that other witnesses failed to give evidence.'

'What!' I exclaimed. I was absolutely bubbling over by this time. 'You mean there's virtually no case against him, after all these weeks? What about all the documentation his superiors were supposed to have found in his office? Surely the CPS must have seen whether there was a proper case or not?'

He took no notice of this, just went ploughing on, 'Then there was the fact that he took his family on that fairground ride immediately after he was supposed to have accepted a bribe not to inspect it. That will weigh with the jury, too.'

'So is that why we're meeting here?' I tried a different tack.

'No, of course not,' he frowned. I think he suspected me of being frivolous. 'I've been thinking of all that you said to me when we met before, and I've been doing a little digging around on my own account. I do believe that DCI Chester is relieved to be getting rid of DI Graves – not that he was a bad egg, just a personality thing, you know. And of course you're quite right in pointing out that Roger Winters, Superintendent

Wood, DCI Chester and the late Councillor Rodney Bennett all belonged to the same golf club. But I'm not convinced there's any significance at all in that.'

'Roger Winters? Who's he?'

'Oh, I thought you knew. He's the Chief Area Officer of the Health and Safety Executive, based in Luton. Responsible for the whole of Bedfordshire and Hertfordshire, not just Jonathan Bennett's boss. Quite a big cheese, you might say,' and he actually smiled. Oh, he was so handsome, I could have wept. Come along, Greta, I told myself. Pay attention. This is serious business.

So then I poured it all out. I didn't care if I was telling him stuff I'd already told him at our first meeting. I told him every single detail, even managing not to blush when I mentioned how close Ari and I had become. I told him about DI Graves breaking in to threaten me against bullying Joan Smith, that she'd admitted he'd put her on to finding out what Ari and I were up to, and how I'd got her record from the computer. I told him about the night when Ari and I went to the car-park and thought we saw DCI Chester being given a mystery package. I related word for word my conversation with Anders Anderson, which confirmed my belief that there'd been dirty business in the Planning Department at the Town Hall. I even mentioned my suspicion that Councillor Rodney Bennett hadn't died a natural death. I told him about Ari getting a job at the HSE to try to find something to help Jonathan Bennett. And last of all, that Ari had now disappeared. Grudgingly, I added, 'That so-called Joan Smith has gone out of sight, too.'

Derek's eyebrows went up at this.

'So how do you know that the two of them haven't just sloped off for a few days somewhere together?' he suggested. I didn't know how to explain that I just knew Ari was too keen on me to do that. So I just shrugged and tried to look offhand.

'And what conclusion do you come to from all these disparate bits and pieces of information, guesswork and intuition?' he asked, seeing I wasn't about to answer his previous question.

I didn't really want to say what I thought. I knew he'd scoff at me again.

'I don't really want to say what I think,' I admitted. 'You'll say it's too far-fetched, and anyway how dare I make accusations, even in this off-the-record conversation, against my superior officers. After all, I know I'm only a rookie in this department, although I've done my years in uniform...'

'So if you're so sure that you know all my answers, what are you doing here?' he asked, and this time he was really grinning quite openly.

Bugger it! I thought. I might just as well take the plunge.

'I think there's corruption and conspiracy,' I blurted, 'I think some of our superior officers are aware of a great deal of criminal activity which they're helping to cover up.'

I gulped and decided to go the whole hog. 'And I think,' I added, 'they might even be involved in drug-dealing themselves.'

'Well!' he said.

After a long silence, while I started wishing I'd never been born, he added, 'Another cup of tea, Greta?'

That was a first. He'd never called me Greta before. I went all melty. Even if he was a bit self-important sometimes, he'd won my heart. And anyway, he was my only chance of finding out if there was something wrong at Shady Lane, or if I was imagining the whole thing.

Pulling myself together, I tried another tack. 'Look, sir—' I started, but he interrupted.

'You can call me Derek when we're alone,' he said, and I was so thrilled I almost forgot what I was going to say. But I had another go.

'Well, Derek, I approached you at first because you were the only senior officer I'd met who had no connection with

Watford, so I knew you couldn't be involved in anything fishy.'

'Thanks for that vote of confidence,' he laughed.

He was laughing at me! What hope was there that he'd take all this seriously if he kept mocking me like that? But I had no choice but to get on with it. So I did. But I thought I'd try a bit of shmooze this time.

'Also, I was very impressed with you when Alfie Partridge and I came to Durham. You seem the sort of officer that we should all aspire to be.'

He made a face. It wasn't working. Change tactics.

'But now I see the whole thing differently,' I went on. 'Now I think because you're on the spot, you're in an even better position to suss out if there's anything smelly going on than you would have been if you'd tried to help me from a distance. When you were still in Durham, I mean. I feel I can trust you,' I added, giving him my most trusting look.

'Where does that leave your relationship with DS Partridge?' he asked. 'Am I to understand that you don't trust him either, along with all your other superior officers?'

'Oh no,' I assured him, 'I think the world of Alfie. He's a rock-solid hundred per cent honest reliable—'

'OK, OK,' he grinned, 'I get the message. No need to go on. But he doesn't take you seriously, right?'

But now there was something different in his attitude that told me even if he wasn't actually as involved as I was, he was at least a bit interested.

'You seem to attach a lot of importance to that incident in the car-park,' he went on, 'when you and your friend Aristotle *thought* you saw DCI Chester receiving a package from someone in another car. You mentioned it when we met before. Still, I think perhaps we should put that aside for the moment, and concentrate on less vague elements. The Council Planning Department, for example, and our friend Anderson. He's quite right that whatever he said to you isn't evidence. But on the other hand, he's probably given us enough to go on to justify more investigation.'

Worried that he was going to say he'd discuss it with DCI Chester, I blurted, 'What do you mean by more—'

'Leave it with me,' he interrupted. 'I promise I won't discuss it with anyone or take things any further without telling you first. Just give me time to think it all through, OK?'

Then, just as I was beginning to feel a bit pleased with myself, he said, with a big unmistakable grin, 'By the way, you haven't told me any more about Gladys Trulove and Jules Verne this time. What happened about those star-crossed lovers?'

Chapter 16

Ariadne Bennett was doing her favourite thing in the street outside the courts. We all stood round the TV watching, as she put on the performance of her life. Jay Bennett stood in the background, as he had probably done ever since he'd known her. She wasn't about to give up the limelight to him, just because it was his case. She was going to make sure that it attracted even more attention at its closing than it had all the time since Jay's arrest. Even their legal team didn't have a chance to get a word in – not with Ariadne in centre stage.

''E is innocent man, and 'ow 'e suffer,' she declaimed dramatically, 'we all, all 'is family, we all suffer. For months we know 'e is innocent but we 'ave to wait. And now! What 'appen now?'

She paused and struck a different pose for the photographers. The reporters pressed closer. Ariadne put on her tragic look.

''E can no work now!' she mourned. ''Ow can 'e go back to 'is job at 'ealth and safety, when they 'ave done thees to heem. They 'ave accuse 'im of terrible theengs. THEY should be put on trial, THEY did wrong to my innocent 'usban'. What weel become of us all now?' she asked the nearest journalist, who backed away, most likely overpowered by her strong personality as much as her perfume.

'Oh boy,' said Dusty Miller, standing next to me watching the TV, 'what a show she puts on! Not enough for madam that her husband got off more by luck than anything, she's got to make a drama of the whole thing.'

'Well,' I muttered, 'she *is* an actress. And she's got a point, too. I mean, the jury found him innocent, so somebody must have tried to set him up.'

I turned to Alfie.

'Will anyone be investigating what goes on at the HSE now, do you think?' I asked him.

He shook his head.

'Hard to say, girl,' he answered, 'but anyway, none of our business.'

And he gave me a hard meaningful look and walked away. I knew what he meant. He was telling me to stop trying to stick my nose in where it wasn't welcome, and just do as I was told. It was getting more and more difficult to tell him about Ari, but I was going to need to do something soon, if he didn't turn up. I was sure his disappearance was to do with Jay Bennett's case, but I couldn't see how or why.

And Ariadne was right about another thing, too. Jay couldn't go back to work at the HSE, and that was the only job he'd ever had since he left Uni. What could he do now? Maybe Ariadne wasn't just hogging all the media attention because of her hopes for fame, but to draw attention to the real troubles of her husband and family. After all, front page coverage might be one way to get some worthy tycoon to come forward with an offer. Although I would have thought that after Jay had been through so much in the past few months, he wouldn't be fit for any kind of work for a while.

As Alfie said, it was none of my business – hadn't ever been, really, never mind the appeals for help from the Bennett family and Aristotle Anapolis. I was sure the rest of the Bennett family would be looking after Jay and Ariadne and Rosie, their little girl. So all I had to worry about was, where was Ari?

When I got home that evening, as usual there was a pile of rubbishy mail on the doormat – catalogues, appeals, offers, and – *a postcard*! A picture postcard of Cardiff Bay, with a badly scrawled message on the back: *'Im in Wales now and worms with me so dunt look for us in watford. hope arry is ok give him my love if you find him. Joan.'*

What did she mean, 'if you find him'? So she knew he was missing. And he wasn't with her. I knew all along he wouldn't go away anywhere with her, specially without telling me. I'm not so daft that I can't tell when a man's keen on me. The more I read and re-read those few words, the more bothered I got. I was sure somebody had done something terrible to Ari, and that little scrubber, Joan Smith knew all about it. That card was just to gloat over me and to tell me she knew how helpless I was against the people she was tied up with. By this time I was pacing up and down, getting quite frantic. This wasn't just getting ideas and theories about conspiracy and corruption, this was a man's life we were talking about!

There was only one thing I could do. I would have to tell Alfie everything and persuade him to help me look for Ari. I put on my backpack and my roller-blades and set off for the Partridge family residence.

Another shock was waiting for me there. Betty opened the door as I was taking off my blades.

'Greta!' she said. 'What's happened? What's wrong? Something's happened to Alfie, hasn't it?'

This wasn't the calm, capable Betty I'd known. Her usually ruddy face was pale, her lips were trembling, and her eyes were full of fear.

'No, of course not, Betty,' I said, as soothingly as I could. 'What makes you think that? Nothing's happened. Let me in. Let's sit down and talk. Tell me what's the matter.'

'He phoned to say he was on that special job again with you tonight,' she said, 'and I knew it must be dangerous because he wouldn't tell me what it was about. And he told me not to ask you, either.'

I was beginning to suss what was going on, but it was difficult to believe.

'So when you saw me on my own, you thought I'd come to tell you—' I started, but she interrupted agitatedly, 'He's been injured, hasn't he? Where is he? Can I see him?'

Oh Alfie, I thought, you've really dropped me in it this time. What on earth could I say to poor Betty? If I told her the truth it could cause a great rift in their marriage; that had seemed so rock-solid to me. If I lied I might get myself in a mess. I decided to lie.

'No, Betty, Alfie's fine, and I'm sorry if you got a fright when you saw me,' I said, playing for time by fumbling with my backpack to put my blades away. Then I took a deep breath and went on, 'He just sent me to tell you not to wait up for him. He couldn't use his mobile. And I think he wanted me out of the way, because you know I'm still not very experienced, and in these delicate situations…'

I let my voice trail away as a hint that I couldn't tell her any more, and then finished off with, 'But if we'd thought that seeing me on your doorstep would upset you, of course I would have phoned you myself. It was a bit thoughtless of us, but it's not like you, Betty, to get so nervous. After your years of being an army wife and then all Alfie's time in the police, I would have thought…'

'Yes, well, but, he's been so different lately,' she sighed, and got up and put the kettle on. That was a good sign. She'd be OK now. But I'd have to hurry off and catch Alfie before he got home and put his foot in it.

Of course, if he wasn't where I thought he was, then we were all in the warm and nasty. I told Betty I wouldn't wait for tea, and hardly waiting to say another word, off I bladed, as fast as I could, to the Widow Varney.

No need to congratulate myself on my detective powers. It was pretty obvious. She came to the door in a filmy apricot negligée, a velvet apricot band holding back her apricot hair, but the colour she turned when she saw me was not apricot at all. More like plum.

I couldn't possibly spell the first word she said. It was like the sort of sound a cat makes when you tread on its paw.

'****! It's DC Pusey, isn't it!' she squawked. ''Ow lovely to see you, even so late. Wot can I do for you, my dear?' she asked, trying to block the doorway. But she was only a little thing, and it was dead easy for me to push her aside and yell down the hall, 'Alfie! Alfie! If you're there, for goodness sake come out, it's urgent!'

And after a while, so he did, and it was a great relief to me to see that he wasn't coming from upstairs. So things hadn't got that far yet. But he was a bit of a mess, with his ginger hair and beard all ruffled, and blobs of apricot lipstick here and there, and no jacket or tie and his shirt collar all undone. Not at all the spruce Detective Sergeant who was usually such an example to us all.

'Er, hallo, Greta, what a surprise,' he mumbled. 'How did you know I'd called on Missis Varney to... er... see how, er...'

'Never mind, Alfie,' I said kindly, 'just get your things and come along with me, and I'll explain as we go. Sorry to have disturbed you, Mrs Varney,' I added to the apricot widow, who was still standing there with her mouth open.

On the way home I gave Alfie a quick run-down on the situation and told him to sort things out with Betty and tell me what back-up he'd need next day.

'But I warn you,' I warned him, 'there'll be a price to pay. I'm going to need a lot of help from you in the future.'

I knew and he knew and I knew that he knew that this was blackmail. But I didn't care, and I didn't think he did either.

Before I had a chance to cash in on this helpful turn of events, though, something else happened.

When I got home later that night, there was a message on my answering machine from Mrs Anapolis, Ari's mother, telling me to meet her at Watford General Hospital A & E Ward East. Telling me! Not asking. It had to be to do with Ari.

I couldn't get there fast enough on bike or rollerblades. Cursing at not having a car, I phoned for a taxi, and was lucky enough to get one in five minutes. But those five seemed like fifty. What could have happened to poor Ari?

When I saw his mother's face I was partly reassured. She didn't look like a mother who feared for her son. She looked like a mother who was furious with her son and anyone he might have been mixing with. Specially me.

'I only sent for you because he asked me to,' were her first words. 'I don't know why he wants to see you.'

'But is he all right? Is he hurt? What happened to him?' I burst out at her, and I saw that she was softening a bit towards me when she saw I was really scared. 'Dehydration mainly,' she said, and walked back into the ward.

When I looked round the waiting area, I was startled to see Ariadne and Jay Bennett sitting there. What were they doing there? Surely Ari hadn't asked his mother to send for them, too? Judging from Ariadne's attitude in the past, she didn't worry much about Ari's welfare, as long as he did whatever she wanted. And if he was unsuccessful, she lost interest in him altogether.

Jay put me in the picture.

They'd gone back to their own home at last, after staying all those months with Jay's parents in Radlett.

'We thought it would be nice to be home again, just the three of us, to start our lives again after all that trauma,' Jay explained. 'Rosie was specially happy to be back, and she ran up to her room, all excited. A minute later she was back down the stairs again, telling me there was a man in her room. Of course I thought it was a burglar and phoned the police right away, but while they were on the way Rosie explained to me that he was tied up.'

'A man tied in 'er room! Oo would do thees!' Ariadne exclaimed, and I said wearily, 'Stop it, Ariadne, there's no audience now. And we all know it's a phony accent. No need to put it on for us. So what then, Jay?'

'I took my cricket bat and went to have a look,' Jay said. 'There was a man alright, but he certainly wasn't a burglar. He was partly covered by a sack, but I could see the bottom half and it was male. His hands were tied down by the bottom of the sack, his fingers were bleeding, and it looked as if he'd tried to bite a hole in the sack. He'd rolled around the floor quite a bit and made a lot of mess and smell. I untied him and took the sack off his head, and it was Ariadne's friend Aristotle, in a terrible state. We could see he'd been there for some time, poor fellow. So we sent for an ambulance and the police and then Ariadne phoned his parents, and here we all are.'

He sighed. He looked very tired, poor man. It did seem unfair that he should have to suffer this after all he'd already been through. But there was more.

'The extraordinary thing was, the police could find no evidence of a break-in,' he added. 'They said somebody had let themselves in with keys to dump the poor chap in our house. Isn't that strange! The only people with a spare set are my parents. But what luck for Aristotle that we went home when we did. We'd been thinking of going away for a week or so for a little holiday. If we had, he might have died there.'

Spoken in Jay's flat, weary tones, this was even more chilling than it would have been if Ariadne had been declaring it in her usual actressy way. Who could have done this to Ari? And why? And how?

I was allowed to see him for a couple of minutes after that. He couldn't tell me anything, just smiled a shadow of his usual beam, and held my hand for a few seconds. I was so relieved that he was found and alive, I could have wept. But of course I didn't. I was tougher than that.

Next day I was summoned to DCI Chester's office.

'I understand you have a set of picklocks, Pusey,' he came straight to the point.

'Sir,' I gasped, 'how do you understand that? DI Graves—'

'Let me put it another way, Pusey,' he interrupted. 'Do you possess a set of picklocks? Yes or no?'

I thought fast. If Graves had told him he'd given me his set, and I denied it, he could get a warrant and find them. I hadn't particularly hidden them, after all. They'd be easy enough to find. Then things would look worse.

'Yes, sir,' I said, 'they were given to me by—'

'I don't wish to know where you got them, Pusey,' he barked. 'You know very well that it's illegal to possess them, wherever they came from. Just tell me, yes or no, whether you used them to gain entry to the home of Mr and Mrs Jonathan Bennett.'

I couldn't believe what I was hearing.

'No, sir, of course not.'

'I don't believe you,' he countered. 'I have reason to believe that you aided someone to overpower this private detective, Aristotle Anapolis, and left him tied up, possibly to die, on the floor of the bedroom where the little girl found him.'

'But, sir, why should I? He was my friend,' I said, but I could see I was wasting my time.

'You will be suspended from duty pending investigation, DC Pusey,' he said. 'Give me your warrant card. DS Partridge will go with you to your home to take the picklocks from you.'

I stumbled down the stairs in a fog of bewilderment. Dusty Miller was at the bottom.

'What's up, Greta?' she sneered. 'Lost another friend and found another enemy?'

*

Alfie was looking baggy-eyed, and I wasn't feeling too bright myself. Derek, on the other hand, looked as alert and as lovely as a baby squirrel on a spring morning. In the short time I'd known him, I'd never seen him look otherwise. The man never seemed to tire. Or to stop looking wonderful.

'Did we really have to come all this way so early in the morning?' Alfie grumbled, between slurps and munches.

We were back at the Archway café, which was much less romantic with Alfie added to our tête-a-tête.

'Just a precaution,' Derek said. 'I know Greta's place is being watched, and it wouldn't be a good idea to meet at your home, with all your family there. So this seemed the safest to me.'

'Yer,' said Alfie wearily, 'I suppose so. But why so early?'

'Before we go on duty,' Derek explained patiently. 'You do believe that Greta is innocent of any crime, I suppose, er, Alfie?'

We'd decided from the first that when we met privately like this, we'd use first names, but Derek didn't seem comfortable with Alfie's, for some reason.

'Werl,' drawled Alfie, 'I don't know so much about that. She does admit to having the picklocks, and I took them off her and brought them back to DCI Chester myself. So that's one bit of wrong-doing, eh, girl?'

I expected this remark to me to be accompanied by a wink or a nudge, but I was surprised to see Alfie was dead serious.

'But I told you how I came by them,' I said to him for the umpteenth time, 'and why I thought I might need to know how to use them. And if DI Graves could use them to get into my house…'

Alfie drew in a noisy breath and shook his head.

'Not the same thing, girl, not at all the same thing,' he admonished me.

I was really getting pissed off with all this. I turned to Derek.

'You believe me, don't you?' I pleaded, and felt a lot better when he said warmly, 'Of course. We wouldn't be here if I didn't think you were just a victim in this whole thing,' he added, 'and we both know jolly well that's why Alfie's here, too, whatever he says about you breaking the law. What can we do, is the question.'

'What about?' Alfie demanded. 'What exactly do we think Greta is a victim of? What do you think, er, Derek, is going on? And who's doing it?'

'Well, Greta's been telling me her theory for some time now, and if you'd been willing to listen, she'd have been telling you, too,' Derek said, 'She thinks there's conspiracy and corruption in Watford. She thinks that there's been dishonest practice in the HSE and the Planning Department of the Town Hall, and instead of investigating, there's a cover-up by our lot.'

'Our lot,' Alfie echoed, not in a questioning way, but in a blank kind of voice.

'And even if she's right,' he went on, 'what are the three of us supposed to be doing about it?'

'And what about the drug dealing?' I put in, but neither of them took any notice of this.

Derek just answered Alfie's question.

'That's what I've been wondering,' he said, 'and I discussed it with my girlfriend. I must tell you that I have the greatest respect for her powers of analysis. She would have made a marvellous detective,' he added reverently.

'What does she do, then?' Alfie asked, as if that mattered.

'She works in the City,' Derek said, even more fondly. 'She has a very responsible position in a major finance company.'

I was feeling a bit sick. Not only were these two geezers talking over my head and ignoring me, not asking me for any input, but now Derek was going on about his fantastic woman. Of course, he couldn't know that every word was breaking my heart, but it was lousy to hear him going on about how brilliant she was, on top of knowing for myself that she was so beautiful and elegant. I could easily hate this woman.

Sourly I growled, 'And has this paragon made a suggestion?'

'Yes, of course she has,' he replied, looking all glowing-eyed and soppy. 'What Erica thinks is that I should take up golf, and join the club that seems so popular amongst some of the leading lights of Watford. Being a practical woman as well as an ideas person, she has already bought me a set of golf clubs. I'm going to follow her suggestion as soon as possible.'

Alfie's mouth was hanging open.

'What good is that supposed to do?' he asked.

'I think that's where there's a sort of clique which is the centre of the whole shebang,' I explained, 'and if Derek can get himself into that gang, we'll be home and dry. You know how the press is always going on about the influence of the Masons in the police, well I think this is that sort of thing.'

Alfie shook his head sorrowfully.

'I think you're both living in a dream world,' he said, as he got up to go. 'I think you'd be better off getting your friend Ari to work out who kidnapped him, girl,' he advised me.

And he left. Derek and I looked at each other. I knew he was full of confidence at his new ploy, probably because the brilliant Erica had suggested it, but I wasn't so sure myself. I thought that maybe while he was doing his thing, I'd find a thing or two to do on my own account.

When I went to the hospital to see Ari that afternoon, I got another big surprise. He was in a private room with a uniform sitting outside the door.

'Hallo Kevin,' I said, 'what are you supposed to be doing?'

Kevin was a man of a few words.

'Guarding,' he said tersely.

'Guarding? You mean he's in danger?'

'S'pose so,' said Kev. And then added chattily, 'S'posed to take his statement when he's well enough, an' all.'

'Well, I'll see how he is and let you know if he's ready to make a statement,' I said, and made to go into the room, but Kevin stood in my way.

'What's up, Kev?' I asked, puzzled.

'Got to see if you're on the list to go in,' he said, producing a crumpled bit of paper. Neither of us knew the reason, but I actually was on the list, so I finally got to see poor Ari.

Of course I expected him to be on a drip after a few days of dehydration, but when I saw not just that, but the dialysis machine and a nurse sitting by his bed, I was shocked. I hadn't realised before just how serious his condition was. He looked awful. When I'd seen him when he'd been admitted, I was so relieved that he'd been found, and he was alive, that I hadn't looked at him properly. But now I saw his face all yellowish and sunken, and black rings round his eyes. And I really understood for the first time that he'd actually been left to die in that empty house. Someone had wanted to kill him, but didn't have the guts to do it directly. So he'd been left to a slow lingering painful death instead. And if the Bennetts hadn't found him, it would have happened. Who could have done this to poor Ari? And why?

'Ari,' I whispered, 'can you hear me?'

He opened his eyes and the ghost of his old beaming smile flitted across his poor face.

'Hallo, lovely girl,' he mumbled, 'glad to see you. What's happening?'

'What's happening to *you*?' I asked, and the nurse answered for him, 'It's not just severe dehydration, he's suffered kidney damage as well. He'll have more tests when he comes off the dialysis machine, then we'll know more about his condition. There's a good chance it's not permanent damage—'

'But how long had he been tied up there without water?' I interrupted, and she shrugged and turned to Ari.

'Bad news, innit,' he murmured, and seemed to drift off. I sat by the bed and took his hand.

'Ari,' I whispered, 'do you know who did this to you? Ari, you must tell me what you know.'

'Don't know, lovely girl,' he said, opening his eyes and looking at me properly for the first time. 'But I got a clue. Look in my locker.'

And he shut his eyes again.

I looked in the cupboard kindly provided by the hospital management, where I found the toiletries which had obviously been brought by his mother. Apart from them, the only other thing I could find was a solitary button. Some clue!

Then his parents arrived and his mother glared at me with such furious anger, I felt I had to go. I could see she thought I was responsible in some way for what had happened to her darling son. Why me and not Ariadne? She was the one who'd started him on this trail. *He* hooked *me* in. But it was no good telling her that, specially not now, at this delicate time.

I sat at home and looked at this bloody button. I guessed that Ari had managed to pull it off one of his assailants in the struggle when they'd set about him. But what can you learn from a button? It just looked to me like an ordinary button off a man's jacket. What ever made poor Ari think that was a clue? I got my magnifying glass and peered at it closely. It was a brown suit button, four holes, some brown thread hanging off one of them, a bit scratched, no fingerprints as far as I could see. Come on, I said to myself, you want to be a detective. Sherlock Holmes would have got the man's name and address off it by now, not to speak of the colour of his eyes and what he had for breakfast. The button continued not to tell me anything.

I did the only thing I could do. I phoned Derek at his private number and left a message to say that I'd got this button which was a clue as to who attacked Ari, but I couldn't deduce anything from it. I didn't add, as I felt like doing, that probably his brilliant girlfriend would be able to tell us how to work something out from it.

Then I went to my karate class, then I went to my computer class. What else could I do? Damn all. Yes I could. I phoned Betty and asked if I could come and visit her.

'Sure,' she said, as I knew she would, 'come for supper. Alfie told me about your bit of trouble, I expect you could do with a bit of company,' she added.

Funnily enough, that didn't make me feel any better. But I had an idea.

'Alfie,' I said, as we all sat round, full to the brim after one of Betty's generous meals, 'how about us doing a stake-out at that car-park in Harrow? You know, the one I told you about that I went to with Ari.'

'Erm,' said Alfie, and I caught his eye and sent him a silent message about the Widow Varney and her apricot lipstick all over his face. I knew he got it, because he changed his tone right away, and said, 'I expect we could. OK with you, Betty?'

Betty wasn't so keen.

'Won't you get into trouble if they find out you've been working with Greta when she's suspended?' she worried. 'Sorry, Greta, but there's no point in Alfie getting himself suspended as well, is there?'

'No, it's all right, girl,' said Alfie, 'it's not official, just friends parking together in a car-park for a chat, like.'

So it was arranged. I didn't really expect anything to come of it, but at least I'd have the feeling that I was doing *something*. And Alfie knew I had him by the short and curlies and he had to do almost anything I asked. Apart from that, it was a pleasant quiet evening, with the twins hardly bickering at all, and Muriel the cat not even biting my ankles once. She'd probably accepted me as a member of the family by now, like the others had.

Just to cap things off, when I got home there was a message telling me to call Derek back. 'We don't go to bed early,' he said, 'so don't worry about the time.'

I thought a bit about that. If they didn't go to bed early, and she was so gorgeous and he was such a nosh, what did that tell me about their sex life? Was it a bit lacking? Maybe she wasn't as perfect in that department as she was in every other way? Small consolation, but the best I could offer myself.

'Tell me about this button,' Derek asked, and I described it.

'It's pretty hopeless,' I said, 'there's just nothing useful about it.'

'Never mind,' he said, 'post it to me in a jiffy bag at this address,' and he dictated the address in Highgate.

'It should be in police possession anyway,' he said, 'Anapolis was wrong to give it to you. We've got his statement now, by the way, and who knows, maybe forensics will find something useful from this button.'

'What was in his statement?'

'Only what you'd expect,' he said. 'He came out of the pub where he usually has a pint with a work-mate when they leave the office, and somebody hit him and threw a sack over his head. He tried to fight back and there was a bit of a scuffle, but he thinks there were two or three of them and they overpowered him and got him in the back of a van. Then they tied his hands to his body with the bottom of the sack, tied his feet together and drove somewhere, not far, he says. They carried him in and up some stairs. Of course he gave them trouble, struggling and trying to kick and so forth, but they got him up somehow, dumped him on a bed and left him.'

'But he had no idea who they might have been? No sight, no distinctive smell, no voices? What about the van or the sack? No clue there?'

'No, and the worst of it was,' said Derek, sounding sympathetic towards Ari at last, 'the poor devil didn't even understand the danger he was in at first. He just thought something else was going to happen, and it took him literally days to realise that they'd just left him there to die. In the meantime, of course he'd tried to manoeuvre himself out of his predicament, but all he managed to do was untie his ankles and get himself off the bed and on to the floor.'

'Or maybe they didn't leave him to die,' I said. 'How about if they expected him to be found sooner, and they just wanted him out of the way for a while?'

'Maybe, but it's hard to think of a reason for anyone to go to that much trouble, getting into the Bennetts' house, to dump him there. Why bother? They could have left him somewhere more accessible,' he argued. 'Anyway, on a different subject, I've got something else to tell you, Greta. I don't know if you'll be glad to hear this or not. DCI Chester told me today that, if you hadn't blotted your copy-book, he'd been considering you as possible future sergeant material. Apparently he's got a very high opinion of you, whatever you might think of him.'

'I wonder,' I said slowly, 'I wonder if that's a bit of butter in the works.'

'Butter?' said Derek. 'What works?'

So I told him, and he said he thought it was an interesting hypothesis.

'Yes, I suppose possibly he thinks it's a good idea to get your loyalty that way. It's not very likely, but a possibility. But anyway, don't build too much on that theory,' he warned me. 'There's such a thing as getting too fanciful and far-fetched.'

I decided not to tell him about the stake-out Alfie and I were going to do at the car-park in Old Redding. I didn't want him thinking I was a complete loony.

Just as well, because that turned out to be a duff inspiration, too.

Alfie and I sat there in his car from ten o'clock right till three in the morning, and all we saw was cars driving in, bouncing up and down a bit, and driving out again. The only variation was when a car bounced sideways instead of up and down. We discussed that for a while, but only to help pass the time.

Nobody got out of a car, and no contact was made between cars. It was all strictly sex. As Alfie said, a wasted night.

Only for us, I pointed out.

Not for the other users of the car-park.

Chapter 17

I'd been reinstated with only a reprimand (what did I mean, only! – what would Grandpa have said!), and suddenly I'd been in the Department and Alfie's partner for a year, and everybody was talking about summer holidays. I wasn't about to let on to anyone, even Alfie, that I'd never had one.

'So I s'pose you'll have to go on your own,' Dusty sneered. '*I'm* going to Orlando with my sister.'

This gave me the chance to steer the conversation away from myself. I'd never been anywhere, but I'd read a lot of holiday brochures and travel stuff.

'What!' I scoffed. 'Not going to Florida in August, are you? You'll melt. That time of year no Americans would dream of going there. *They* know what the weather's like there in the summer. D'you mean you didn't know they all go to Florida in the *winter*, to get the best weather?'

I was glad to see she looked a bit worried. 'No, go on, you're kidding,' she muttered. Then she got another thought that brightened her up. 'My sister must know, she once worked in a travel agents.'

'Oh, yeah? How long for? A week, I bet—'

But just as I was getting into my stride, Alfie came along and scooped me up, telling me breathlessly we had an urgent call to make.

'What? Where?' I managed to ask as Alfie kangaroo'd the car out of the car-park. Then before he had a chance to answer, I said, 'Oh for goodness sake, Alfie, let me drive,' so we got out and changed over. Now he had to tell me where we were going.

'Eastcote?' I said. 'What business can we have in Eastcote? You'd better tell me the address and then explain as we go along.'

He gave me the address, I looked it up in the A to Z, and we set off again. He'd calmed down a bit by this time, but he was still pretty excited. This was all very unusual for Alfie, so it had to be something important. It certainly was. Practising my powers of cross-examination, I managed to get the whole story out of him before we pulled up in front of an impressive-looking house, not the sort of thing I would have expected in Eastcote. Although according to my A to Z, Eastcote didn't exist, being actually part of Pinner. Even so, fairly grand even for Pinner. Had its own in-and-out driveway with pillars and the lot.

Turned out it was the residence and consulting room of a doctor who was also a psycho-therapist and hypno-therapist, and he'd been treating Ari. I hadn't known about it because Ari and I had been out of touch since he'd come out of hospital.

Poor Ari had been in a rotten state, mentally as well as physically, and he'd gone back to live with his parents so that his mother could look after him. This meant I wasn't welcome to visit him, though I did phone a few times to ask after him and got the brush-off from his mother. And it seemed as if he hadn't fancied even phoning me himself, never mind coming to see me. Probably his mother never gave him any of my messages.

Anyway, this Dr Rose, who I saw from his brass plate had a string of letters after his name, had been trying to help Ari to get over what had happened to him. Well, he must have been OK at his job, because he'd managed to get Ari to remember things about the attack that he hadn't known he knew.

Now Alfie and I were going to be there while the doc put Ari in a trance or whatever it was he did, and Ari would tell all he knew. Of course it would all be tape-recorded, so what was the purpose of our being there as well?

'See, we can ask Ari things too,' Alfie explained. 'He doesn't only respond to the doctor's voice, he'll answer anyone. So if we think of any other questions, we can ask him on the spot.'

Sounded useless to me, but still, it would be good to see Ari again. That's what I thought, but I wasn't so sure when I saw him. Physically he looked the same old Ari, but there was something missing. The warmth had gone from his look, there was no light in his eyes, even his smile when he saw me wasn't the same beaming look of pleasure he always showed before. What had those buggers done to this poor mug, to take all his spirit away?

All he said to me was a small 'Hallo', as if we hardly knew each other. Pathetic.

Well, I'd had all the wrong idea about what was going to happen. I'd expected something like those stage hypnotists do, putting people to sleep. But this doctor just moved his hand a bit in front of Ari's eyes and started talking to him. And I could see Ari wasn't asleep or in a trance or anything like that. He looked as alert or as unalert as he had beforehand.

'Tell us what happened when you came out of the pub, Ari,' the doctor said. He didn't do any of that business about 'You're going into a deep sleep and you will answer my questions' or that sort of stuff. Just spoke in a chatty kind of voice, like you do in the regular way.

Ari said, not speaking like a zombie in a trance, but in his ordinary voice, 'When I came out I thought old Steve was behind me, so I went to turn round to say goodnight to him, and he threw a sack over my head. I thought that wasn't much of a joke, and I started to tell him off, then some woman came and punched me in the gut. So I started to struggle—'

'How did you know it was a woman, Ari?' the doctor asked.

I was amazed. I would have thought interrupting somebody like that would have thrown them right off the track, but nothing of the kind. Ari just answered him straight out.

'By the smell,' he said. 'She had on some cheap mucky make-up or hand-cream or scent. It was really tacky. Not like Greta smells.'

'Go on, then,' the doc said.

'Yes, I started to struggle,' Ari went on. 'And I think I landed one somewhere, I'm not sure, but then I got hold of this button off his jacket, and I just hung on to it. Even when they tied the bottom of the sack round my wrists I kept hold of it, and they never noticed. Then they tied my feet. Then they carried me into the van and we drove a little way. Then they carried me into the house and up the stairs and dumped me on a bed. I made it as hard for them as I could, but with the sack and my hands and feet being tied, I couldn't do much. After I heard them go, I tried to get out, but all I managed to do was undo my ankles and fall on the floor and roll about a bit. Never did find the door. Course, I shouted a lot at first. That didn't do no good, neither.'

He stopped.

'That's not all, though, is it?' the doctor asked.

'No, I remembered something else,' Ari said. 'I thought all along it was old Steve that threw the sack over me in the first place, but I couldn't be sure, so I didn't tell the police that. But now I've remembered something else. I always used to tease him because he only wore dark brown jackets with light brown trousers, and I used to kid him and say if he liked brown so much, why didn't he wear brown suits?'

'And the significance of that?' the doctor prompted him gently. I could tell they'd been through all this together before, but this time the doctor needed him to repeat everything for our benefit and for the tape.

Ari said simply, 'All the rest of us wore grey or navy to work.'

There was a bit of quiet while we all digested this. Then Alfie said, 'Tell us again about the woman. How could you tell it was a woman, just by the smell? Could have been a man. Some men wear cheap-smelling hair stuff or aftershave.'

'She swore once, when I stamped on her foot,' Ari answered, sounding a bit surprised. 'Do I have to say exactly what she said? She didn't speak like Greta.'

'Why do you keep talking about Greta?' the doctor asked. 'Who is Greta?'

Of course I'd been introduced to him as DC Pusey, so he couldn't know it was me Ari was talking about. I was glad he was still thinking about me, even if he hadn't had much to say to me when I came in.

'She's in the police. She'd been accused of letting them in to the house where they dumped me,' Ari said, 'and I knew if I told the police one of my attackers was a woman, they'd think for sure it was Greta. But I know it couldn't have been. It was some other woman.'

'This is good stuff,' Alfie said. 'When the tape has been transcribed, can you come up to the station in Watford to sign it? This is enough for us to get a warrant to search this chap Steve's house, and maybe find his jacket with the button missing.'

'How do you feel?' the doctor asked Ari. 'Can you remember everything that's been said?'

'Yes,' Ari said, 'I can remember everything now. And I feel much better. Thank you, doctor.'

As he was saying that, he was looking round the room like someone who's looking round at the films when the lights go up, and he suddenly saw me. It was as if he hadn't known I was there before. His eyes lit up and he practically leapt towards me with a big grin.

'Greta!' he said. We could see this confused the doctor, but I certainly didn't care, and I don't think Ari did either. 'Hallo, lovely girl, how are you?'

And he put his arms round me and gave me a big kiss. I felt better than I had for weeks.

We gave him a lift home, all the way back to Camden Town, and Alfie didn't speak a word of complaint at our going so much out of our way. Quite the opposite, the two of them gabbed away to each other like a couple of old pros. When we dropped Ari, he promised to phone me soon.

Then it was back to business. Didn't take long.

When Stephen Thompson was arrested, he right away put his hands up to the whole thing, but of course denied attempted murder. He claimed he thought their captive was going to be found and released by the owners of the house the very next day. Asked why he thought that, he fudged and stammered and muttered. But when asked why he'd done it, he said it was just meant to be a practical joke.

'That Aristotle,' he said, 'he was always larking about and laughing and joking, so we thought we'd play one on him. We never meant no harm. But when we heard what happened to him, we got scared to own up to what we'd done.'

Had anyone put him up to it, he was asked. No, all his own idea, he claimed.

Then came the big surprise. He'd kept talking about this 'we' who'd been playing this so-called joke. Who else was in it? And who was the woman who'd helped him?

Just the two of them. Him and a friend of his, he said, just a friend. And her name?

Dorothy Miller.

Her occupation?

'You ought to know,' he said. 'She's one of yours. Detective Constable Miller, Shady Lane CID.'

Dorothy? Dusty Miller's name was Dorothy? And she was the woman?

Ever since we'd been working together, Alfie had clung to the idea that Dusty Miller and I were buddies. He'd never noticed that she'd been bitchy to me from day one. Every time he'd come across us having one of our usual slanging matches, he'd obstinately seen it as just two girlfriends having a gossip and a giggle together. So now of course he thought I was upset that my pal was in trouble.

Whereas in fact what I was bothered about was that I wasn't going to be allowed to be there when she was questioned. Still, some of my unhappiness over this was eased by DI Derek Michaelson's promise to tell me every word that was said. And I knew I could trust him for that, with his memory like an elephant.

I wondered whether to show Derek the postcard from Joan Smith in Wales. It did seem to mean that she knew something about what happened to Ari. Or maybe I was just reading too much into it. But if *she* knew, Gerry Graves knew. What could be the significance of that? I decided not to muddy the already scummy waters with one too many clues. Life was complicated enough.

Ari had referred to his assailant, Stephen Thompson, as 'old Steve'. This had to be because Steve looked every one of his sixty-three years, looking forward to his retirement just over the horizon. And somehow I wasn't a bit surprised that this old geezer was the best that Dusty could do for herself by way of a boyfriend. It turned out that they'd been 'seeing each other', as she coyly put it, for about ten years. I didn't really know how old she was, but she looked like thirty going on sixty, so they made a good couple.

What wasn't clear was whose idea it was to set about Ari in the way they had. They didn't seem too sure of that themselves, although that could have been a deliberate fudge. Anyway, they were both up for a serious charge, although the CPS was in its usual dither whether it was going to be Grievous or Actual Bodily Harm. Not Breaking and Entering, though. They'd got in with keys, hadn't they. Anyway, whatever the charge was, it was all very satisfactory.

And another plus for me was that Dusty Miller wasn't going to be in CID to torment me any more. But that was small compensation for all that poor Ari had been through.

One evening soon after that I was delighted to find him on my doorstep again, just like the old days. And his real beaming smile was back in place, too. Just to add to the pleasure of our reunion, it was one of the times when Jim wasn't making one of his too-frequent visits. I didn't know what Jim was up to, but he seemed to arrive at my place more and more often.

'I've come to take you out to dinner, lovely girl,' Ari said, 'and we can tell each other all our news. Put on your glad rags, and we'll be off.'

Of course it didn't work out exactly like that. After all, we hadn't really seen each other for such a long time. When he came wandering into the bedroom just as I came out of the shower, I didn't chuck him out. So what with one thing and another, by the time we actually set off for dinner, it was pretty late and we were both very hungry, and we hadn't exchanged a word of news.

Well, first I told him all I knew about the arrest of 'Old Steve' Thompson and ex-DC Dusty Miller.

And I could see that he had something important to tell me, but he seemed unusually reserved about it.

'Come on, Ari, out with it,' I said. 'I can see there's something you've got to say. Don't be shy.'

The idea of Ari being shy, on top of all that wine, made me laugh for quite a long time, until I noticed he was serious.

'I've applied to re-join,' he said.

Then, seeing me looking blank, he explained, 'The Met. I was in before I went private, you remember? Anyway, I had to have a medical, and they said I'm not quite fit enough yet, but I should try again for the fitness test in about a month.'

I couldn't believe it. I must have been looking gob smacked, because he seemed to feel he had to explain himself.

'I never should have left, I can see that now,' he said. 'I wasn't no good as a private detective, and seeing you so happy in The Job, I said to myself, that's best for me, innit? And my lovely girl will respect me more if I've got a proper job. I didn't do anybody any good at the HSE, neither, innit?'

I was just beginning to get my breath back. I wondered why he thought I hadn't respected him before, and why it was so important to him, anyway.

'But Ari,' I argued, 'are you sure? I mean, there must be lots of other jobs you could do…'

'Yes,' he said firmly, 'that's the one for me. Back in the Met, where I know what I'm doing and what for. Then I can propose to you proper, right?'

I didn't get it. It must have been the wine.

'Propose? Propose what?' I asked.

'Propose you to marry me, lovely girl,' he said, taking my hand.

It was a long, difficult and tearful night. Not that I did any crying. I don't cry. At least not since Gran died. No, it was poor Ari. He probably wouldn't have got so mushy at any other time, but I could tell he was still suffering from the after-effects of his kidnapping. And that made him a bit soppy.

'It's that Jim, innit,' he sniffled, hanging on to my hand like a drowning man clutching a straw. 'You've got all settled down with him, and you don't want to break off now.'

'No, honestly, Ari,' I tried to reassure him, 'Jim really isn't all that serious for me. Really, I'm much keener on' (I couldn't bring myself to say 'more attached to') 'you than I am on him. He's really a sort of old habit, you know, useful but not important. Sometimes he's even a bit of a nuisance,' I added, laying it on a bit thick to try and make him feel better.

Ari blew his nose, but still looked a bit bleary.

'Well then, why him and not me?' he wanted to know.

'No, you don't understand. It's commitment I don't want. See, it's easy with Jim, he's already married and he goes back to his wife and kids somewhere up North, regular as clockwork, and no harm done. But it was when you mentioned marriage…'

I couldn't help it. I didn't mean to injure his feelings, but I just couldn't stop myself shuddering. That did it. His hurt changed to huff.

'Well,' he said, getting up to go, 'if it looks that bad to you to think of living with me for the rest of our lives…'

'No, Ari, please don't take it like that!'

Too late. He'd gone. Slammed out in a jumble of injured pride and anger. Maybe this meant I'd lost him altogether. How did I feel about that? I asked myself. I was surprised at the answer. The idea of never seeing Ari again made me quite miserable. This was puzzling.

I was madly in love with Derek Michaelson, having a sort of mechanical affair with Jim Robinson, and yet absolutely choked at the thought of losing Ari. There was only one thing for it. I went to bed. Disappointingly alone, this time.

But there were more important things to think about than my mess of a personal life. I'd had a note from Derek suggesting another meeting. This time, because I wasn't under suspicion any more, it need not be at the Archway café, which would be a relief to Alfie. He'd told me the food was all right there, but he didn't think it was special enough to justify the long journey. When I'd explained to him that it was a sort of security thing to meet there, he'd grumbled that he still didn't think it was worth the trouble. I gave up on that one.

Anyway, I got Alfie to ring Derek and suggest coming round to my place for a drink and a chat that evening after work. Of course Alfie still couldn't see we had anything to talk about, but the offer of a few cans of Guinness soon convinced him. So our meet was on.

One look at Derek was enough to make clear to me that he was the one I really loved, even if I never stood the slightest chance with him. Jim and Ari could hold hands and jump out of the window, for my part, if I could get Derek to take a second look at me. So I could stop feeling sad at losing Ari.

To business.

'I've spoken at length with Cheerful Charlie about the Aristotle Anapolis case,' Derek started, 'but I can't seem to convince him that it was connected in any way with the Jonathan Bennett case. And yet it seems to me there's a good chance that someone was afraid that Anapolis would discover something at the HSE that would not only clear Bennett, but show up a different guilty party—'

'What do you mean, guilty party?' Alfie interrupted. 'Guilty of what?'

'Well, it did seem fairly well established, from the evidence,' Derek explained, 'that there actually *was* some venality going on at the HSE, and if Bennett was innocent, somebody else must have been guilty.'

'Venality! That's a good word!' Alfie exclaimed in admiration. But that was his only contribution to Derek's theory. He was silent for quite a while after that, except for slurping his Guinness and munching up all my crisps.

'Do you think DCI Chester is just unconvinced,' I asked, 'or is helping some mates at the HSE to cover up? Do you think he's our inside man? The one in cahoots with the late Councillor Bennett as well?'

'I know you'd like it to be him, Greta,' Derek said, 'but I just can't go along with that. I could be wrong, of course, but after all, I am more experienced than you, and my gut feeling is that he's straight.'

'But—' I started, but he talked over me.

'I know, I know, you think you saw him up to something at that car-park in Harrow. And maybe you think he was a bit harsh with you over that set of picklocks you got from Gerry

Graves. But none of that adds up to anything really solid, Greta, you've got to admit.'

'What about Dusty Miller?' I put in, I thought rather shrewdly. 'Isn't it possible that someone higher up in our lot put her up to that business with Stephen Thompson? One thing we seem to agree about is that it wasn't the joke gone wrong that he and Dusty claimed it was.'

Derek sighed. 'That's true. But it need not be anything to do with Dusty being police. She was already more than friendly with Thompson, and if one of his bosses got him to have a go at your friend Ari, it would have been easy for Thompson to persuade her to help. Look, Greta, I can see your point of view about all this. But you've got to stop having a bee in your bonnet about DCI Chester. It's clouding your judgement. What do you think, Alfie?'

'I just can't understand Greta,' Alfie said. 'With her background, you'd think the last idea she'd have would be about police corruption. But she's been on about it for months now. What's the matter with you, girl?'

I didn't know what to say to convince them. It was true I had no hard facts, and I wasn't experienced enough to trust my intuition.

We sat quietly for a few minutes, then I said to Derek, 'How's the golf going?'

He looked embarrassed. 'Not too well, I'm afraid. I'm having to take lessons. Erica's paying for them, of course. But I'm certainly not good enough yet to go a round with Cheerful Charlie or Superintendent Wood or Roger Winters.'

'Roger who? Who's he?' Alfie asked.

Then something strange happened. As Derek was explaining to Alfie that Roger Winters was Chief Area Officer of the Health and Safety Executive and Jay Bennett's boss, Alfie's expression changed. As I looked at him, his whole manner looked different. His body language seemed to be saying something I couldn't decipher. He looked a bit like a dog outside a butcher's shop – alert.

'Have you met a lot of important people at this golf club, then?' he asked Derek, in a funny voice I'd never heard him use before.

'Well,' Derek replied, looking as puzzled as I felt, 'it depends what you mean by important. It does seem to be the favourite club in the area for upper management. You know, there's our own Super, this Roger Winters, a couple of local Councillors, the Chief Executive of the Office of Fair Trading, and of course quite a lot of executives in, er, food industries, land development companies, that sort of thing. Couple of City blokes, too, I think.'

It was only when he'd finished talking that Derek seemed to get the significance of Alfie's question and his own answer. When we sat in silence again, it was a different kind altogether. Before, we'd all been quietly avoiding each others' eyes. This time, we kept looking from one to the other in growing suspicion.

Finally, Alfie, never one to leave anything unsaid, spoke up.

'Maybe when our Greta here was talking about conspiracy, she was pitching it too low, eh, Derek? Can we be talking about something as big as what we're all thinking now?'

There was a pause while I was doing some hard thinking, and Derek looked doubtful, then Alfie answered himself.

'No, it's rubbish,' he said, but not in his usual positive way. It seemed to me there was a kind of undertone of doubt in his voice. 'It's you, Greta, putting barmy ideas in our heads. All this crazy talk, it's got us going. Why shouldn't all the most important people in the area go and play golf at the same club? We've gone conspiracy-mad, that's what it is.'

While Derek still stayed silent, I took a deep breath and blurted out, 'A sort of Rotary Club for suppressing investigation! If all the members run things to their own advantage, and whenever things look fishy, nobody follows up… Or if they can find the occasional fall-guy to seem like the villain…'

My voice tailed off as I saw that Derek was shaking his head.

'Using the word fall-guy is a dead giveaway, Greta. That's your trouble. You've been seeing too many American films where the one honest cop unmasks a crooked conspiracy involving his whole department. That's Hollywood. This is Watford. Your accusations would be laughed at if you tried to go public with them.'

He stood up and made for the door.

'I'll keep on at the golf club, and I'll keep my eyes and ears open. You may be right about something fishy going on, but when you start us imagining along with your wild fantasies… That's a film script too far, Greta.'

And he left. To say that I was crushed would give no idea of how I felt. You could have slid me under the door without opening it.

'Don't worry, girl,' Alfie said in his kindest most superior-male sort of voice. 'We won't think any less of you. All beginners get barmy ideas sometimes.'

And he left, too. I ran after him.

'Alfie!' I shouted. 'Come back! I want to ask you something.'

He trudged back up the path and looked at me with his eyebrows up. I was thinking that he really was a nice good-natured chap, even if he didn't always seem like it. And when he thought I was off my rocker, he still tried to tell me in a kind way.

'Do you still see the Widow Varney?' I asked him in an unreasonably hard voice. I saw from the way he flinched that I'd touched a tender spot.

'What if I do?' he asked defiantly.

'Don't worry, I wasn't going to interfere,' I assured him. 'I just wanted to ask you to see if there's any more you can get out of her that her late husband might have mentioned about his work at the HSE. I'm not going to forget it, Alfie, just because you and DI Michaelson think I'm living in a dream-world.'

'OK, I'll try,' he grumbled, and marched off again. I would have called him back again for a more thorough briefing, but my phone started to ring.

If I'd guessed it might be Jim, I wouldn't have bothered to run to answer it. He was showing unusual consideration in letting me know he'd be joining me late that night. Oh boy, something for me to look forward to. Big problem. Should I wait up or go to bed and straight to sleep and let him try to wake me when he arrived? I was feeling too restless to sleep anyway, so I compromised by going out for an airing on the roller-blades.

I had a lot on my mind, so I must have stayed out longer than I thought. By the time I got home, I saw from the lorry outside the door that Jim was already there. What I didn't expect was that he was using my phone. What a cheek, I thought, phoning little wifey up North from my place. But then I realised from the way he waved at me and the faces he was making and the way he was talking, that he was actually answering a call.

'So she left you and went off to Wales, did she?' he was saying in a sympathetic sort of voice. Could he be talking to Ari? 'What, not with another feller? On her own? Why don't you go after her then? She seemed keen on you, I bet she'd have you back like a shot.'

This was great. Jim the relationship counsellor, advising Ari how to get Joan Smith back! But more interesting than that was, why was Ari phoning me in the middle of the night? Not that this was unusual lately. This was when most people seemed to think was the best time to phone me. I signalled to Jim to give me the phone – that is, I snatched it out of his hand.

Ari was very excited. Not by Jim's advice to the lovelorn. Something much more important.

'You know I told you I got all these crazy letters after it was in the papers about how little Rosie Bennett found me in her bedroom? Well, I read some of them and they were from stupid women saying like they wouldn't mind finding me in theirs, you know I told you,' he started babbling, and then of course he had to stop for breath just when I was wondering if he'd ever get to the point. 'Well,' he went on, 'I thought I'd read a few more tonight, have a laugh, cheer myself up, innit. And one of them wasn't one of those, it was a serious one. Can I read it to you, Greta? Now? Is it OK with Jim there? I think it's important.'

I gave him the OK, and he read out to me:

'I read what happened to you, and I read all about the Jonathan Bennett HSE bribery case, and you can forget any idea you might have that the police will investigate any of it. I tried to get the police to look into something like that going on at the Town Hall, and offered them evidence and to be a witness, and nothing happened. I tried to interest the local press, and nothing happened. Then something happened all right. My car was stolen, my house was broken into, and I was mugged in the street. The police were 'unable' to find any culprits. What do you think? Keep your head down, otherwise you are in danger. I'll be in touch again. Don't show this to anyone and don't try to find out who I am.'

'Is it in writing or typed? Did you keep the envelope? Has it got a date or a postmark on it?' I was firing questions at Ari without giving him a chance to answer. 'Have you told anyone else about it?'

'Calm down,' Jim interrupted.

'Shut up,' I snarled at him. 'Ari, are you going to answer me?' I shouted into the phone.

But of course he wasn't going to tell me what I wanted to know. Not just then. If I hadn't been getting so overheated and had just stopped to think for a moment, I would have worked out what he was up to. Of course he wanted a real excuse to see me again. But if I'd thought that at the time, I might have even wondered if the letter he'd just seemed to read out to me really existed. It was only later that I started to think, could he have made the whole thing up, just to keep me interested?

'That's the lot, innit,' Ari sighed. 'I'll keep it safe till I see you again, lovely girl. Sleep well. Give my best to Jim,' he added just before he hung up, and if I didn't know Ari better, I'd have thought he was being sarcastic.

I looked at the time. Three o'clock. No good going to bed, whatever Jim felt like. My head was buzzing too much for sleep or anything else.

'I'll make us a cup of tea,' Jim offered, right out of character.

That was an amazing end to a really weird day.

Chapter 18

From the day I'd joined the Department, Dusty Miller had been the curse of my life. And yet now that she was suspended from duty, it was peculiar without her. You'd think I'd be pleased to be rid of her, but no. There was an odd gap where there'd been all those snide sneery remarks. Like when you take a pebble out of your shoe, it seems at first as if something's missing. I suppose that said something about me. Maybe I needed a bit of something scratchy in my life, like the grit that made the pearl in the oyster. Of course Alfie still clung to the belief that Dusty and I had been friends, so he thought it was natural that I should be pining for her. Pining!

I probably wouldn't have noticed her absence so much if we'd been busy. All this moody thinking came from not having enough to do. It was another one of those infuriating days, when everybody else seemed to be rushing about, too busy to say a word, barking into phones, slamming doors, driving off with squealing brakes, and Alfie and I were high and dry. At least I had him to talk to, even if it meant buying him endless cups of tea and buns in the canteen. But it did make the day drag, particularly when I was so anxious to get to the evening to see Ari.

Not for personal reasons, of course, even if Jim would have left by then and Ari and I would be alone together for the first time since I'd refused his proposal. No, it was about this letter that Ari had read to me on the phone the night before. Was it authentic? Who was it from? How had Ari got it? What could we do about it? What made it even worse was that, until I knew more, I'd made up my mind not to say a word about it to Alfie, so I was just busting with frustration.

And all that Alfie wanted to talk about was the Widow Varney, who he thought was a little doll and I thought was a pain in the neck. Just to make me even more irritable, he had to admit he hadn't got a word of information out of her about her late husband's job at the Health and Safety Executive. So every time he started drivelling on about her, I went back at him about Betty and his lovely home and the twins. I even managed to find a couple of good words to say about their horrible pets, Freda the dribbling dog and Muriel the ankle-biting cat.

The day finally dragged to a miserable close, with Alfie and me not on the best of terms. But I was free to phone Ari and arrange to see him. The surprise was, he didn't want to come to Watford, he wanted me to go to Camden Town to meet him at an address he gave me.

'My cousin's place,' he explained, and that was all I could get out of him. I thought it would take too long to cycle there, but by the time I got a train to Euston and then a Northern Line to Camden Town, I probably could have even roller-bladed there quicker. I don't know how people can bear to do all that travelling to work by public transport every day the way they do, poor buggers.

The explanation was simple enough once I got there. The letter Ari had read to me, forwarded in a batch from the newspaper where all his fan-mail had been sent, only had an email address for contact. Ari reckoned we needed his cousin George to help us, because he was on the internet and had a bang-up-to-the-minute computer. It turned out that Ari had already had some on-screen chat with the letter-writer, who was using the name 'Fly' – full address: *flyonthewall@btinternet.com.*

'Course,' George said, 'we don't even know if it's a man or a woman, old or young, let alone if what they say is the truth or all made up. That's the thing about the internet, you can be whoever you like.'

Some detective I was! It hadn't even occurred to me to wonder who the writer was, only if he/she was telling the truth. Anyway, off we went, with George doing all the keyboard work and me and Ari telling him what to say. Once we were in touch with Fly, it went just like a conversation. Most of the time we were trying to persuade him or her to meet us, but he/she was too cautious.

George had kindly printed out the first conversation Ari had with Fly, and I read that before we got started. But from then on we didn't print anything, just read it straight off the screen.

Ari had started off by asking Fly: 'Why did you contact me?'

Fly said: *'I wanted to warn you not to expect anything from the police. I told you in my first letter what they did to me just because I wanted them to look into what was going on at the Town Hall.'*

Ari: 'But how did you know all those things that happened to you were anything to do with the police? You could have just been having a run of bad luck. And there's nothing unusual about the police not being able to find culprits. Are you sure you're not just paranoid?'

Fly: *'When I first went to the police, I could tell from their reaction that they weren't going to follow anything up. When you add that to the other things that happened, you don't need to be brilliant to come up with the obvious answer. But of course you can choose not to believe me. I just wanted to warn you. I felt sorry for you when I saw your picture and read about what happened to you, and I thought you might expect some result, and I didn't want you to be disappointed.'*

Ari: 'Can you tell me the names of any of the police you spoke to? What police station did you go to?'

Fly: *'I went to Shady Lane in Watford and asked to see a detective. The first one I saw was a woman, a Detective Constable Miller. Then she brought in a Detective Inspector Graves. They both asked me a lot of questions and made a lot*

*of notes and said I'd hear further from them. But I never did.
After a few weeks, I wrote to the local paper, but they took no
notice.'*

It was at this stage that Ari decided not to go on until I
could be there to join in. Before George got online with Fly,
we had a little conference to decide what we wanted to ask,
apart from keeping on requesting a meeting. Then George
sent Fly an email asking for a reply. Fly must have been
sitting waiting, because we were in contact right away. Of
course the most important question was, what did Fly want
the police to investigate in Watford Town Hall. And I
shouldn't have been surprised at the answer, in view of how
much I already knew. It was just that the cover-up was
incredible.

Fly said: *'I was just a low-grade clerical worker, but I
couldn't miss what was going on. Councillor Rodney Bennett
and Anderson and Gustafson talked quite openly about the
pay-offs they were getting for helping with planning
permissions. Sometimes Anderson would do two lots of blueprints, one for the Planning Committee and one for the
architects. It was big stuff, with lots of money in it for
everyone, because the developers were making trillions out
of it. I was sure that if the police investigated, they'd uncover
a big ring of crookedness.'*

We asked: 'Trillions? Did you try to get a cut for silence?'

Fly: *'Well, I don't know how much was involved. But a
lot. And I didn't try to get a cut. Just as well, as it turned out.
They had nothing to fear from me or anyone else, because
they obviously had protection from high up.'*

We: 'Do you still work at the Town Hall?'

Fly: *'Of course I do. I have to eat, don't I. And anyway,
it's all over now, since Bennett and Gustafson died and
Anderson went to prison. Pity he didn't go for what he really
did, though. But the high-up protection is still in place, all
right.'*

We: 'How can you know that?'

Fly: *'I don't want to tell you any more. Why are you asking all these questions? Have you said anything to the police? Have you told them about me? They know who I am, you know. If you say you've had anonymous information, they'll know it's me. I could be in a fatal car accident if you say anything about this correspondence. I'm sorry now I tried to help you.'*

We: 'No, I'm just Aristotle Anapolis who was tied up and left to die in an empty house. Won't you meet me some time? I feel as if we're friends. I haven't told the police anything about you. Please trust me. I'll meet you anywhere you say. I live in Camden Town, but I'll meet you in Watford if you like.'

'Fly's gone,' George said. 'Closed down, switched off, gone. We can try again later if you like. I sent your last message, anyway. Maybe there'll be a reply later on, or tomorrow. Haven't you got a computer, Greta?'

I had to admit that I did have one, but had only just started classes and wasn't very good at it yet.

'Come on then,' he said, 'sit down and I'll give you some coaching. You too, Ari, do you good to learn something. Stop you moping.'

I gave Ari a good hard look. It was true, what George said. He looked mopey. Was it still the physical effects of what he'd gone through, or was it my fault because I'd hurt his pride? No time to wonder about that, George was putting us through an intensive internet course for the next three hours, until we could hardly hold our eyelids up.

Just when Ari and I were fit only to stagger off to our beds and get a bit of shut-eye, George said he thought we should make one more try to get in touch with Fly again.

'Can't we leave it till tomorrow,' Ari groaned, but George like all computer buffs didn't know when to stop, and insisted he thought it was worth another go. Wouldn't you know it, we got Fly right away – he must have been another nerd. So after a bit of chat and finally managing to convince

Fly that it wasn't a trap, Ari got a date fixed up for the following evening in a cyber-café in Tottenham Court Road. Fly chose the place and we didn't think we should argue, though it wasn't exactly a convenient area for us.

'I'll bring my girlfriend,' Ari wrote, 'you'll know us because we're both tall and handsome, and I'm dark and she's fair. How will we know you?'

Fly answered, *'You won't. I'll find you.'*

'There you are,' George gloated. 'All fixed up.'

I was giving Ari a bit of a cold glare.

'Girlfriend?' I gritted.

'Got to say that, innit,' Ari pleaded. 'Can't let him get suspicious, think you might be police, eh?'

Only just in time remembering to thank George for all his help, I grumped off. I was tired, I had a long journey back home, and I was still a bit worried about my state of affairs with Ari. If there was a state of affairs.

Still, I managed to sleepwalk my way through the next day well enough to get to the cyber-café well before our appointment time with Fly. No surprise to find that Ari had beaten me to it and was fighting his way through the mysteries of cyber-space to send an email to his cousin George to show him what a good lesson he'd given us the night before.

'Hallo, lovely girl,' he greeted me, and looked surprised and hurt when I said coldly, 'Stop that, Ari.'

'What?' he said. 'What I done now? Just because you won't marry me, does it mean I can't call you lovely girl any more? Aren't we friends any more, Greta? I can't help it if I love you, innit. I think you love me a bit, too.'

And he gave me that beaming smile that always made me feel warm and mellow. Then of course I had to give him a little kiss just to show that I wasn't really cross with him, only uncomfortable about him wanting to marry me. Maybe I should try again to explain to him why marriage wasn't part of my life-plan.

A female voice said, 'Excuse me. Are you still using this screen?' and we both turned to see a tiny dainty little creature, blonde and smart, with four-inch heels just bringing her up to Ari's shoulder. It can't be, I thought. But it was.

'Ari?' she said. 'I'm Fly.'

I nudged Ari. 'Ari, your mouth is open,' I reminded him. 'Hi,' I went on to Fly, 'I'm Greta.'

She was obviously still not happy about this meeting. I suppose small people are naturally more nervous than the rest of us, and particularly in her case, if all she'd told us was true. And Ari and I had hardly got our wits together after the shock of seeing that she was a female and such a little dolly one, too. So there was a certain amount of uneasiness all round. And I have to say that it did cross my mind that maybe she wasn't really Fly at all, but perhaps his sister or girl-friend, and he'd sent her to suss out if it was safe to talk to us. Because her appearance and her voice didn't match the image we'd got from our email contact.

So what with one thing and another; when she asked Ari if he had a car here and if we could go for a drink somewhere out of town, we were well pleased with the idea. She suggested a quiet pub right out at Rickmansworth, and on the way she said we could call her Marion. Then she asked Ari to tell her all about what led up to what she called his kidnapping. We'd decided he'd be absolutely straight about his connection with Ariadne and the HSE/Bennett case, only leaving out anything to do with any police connection. If she asked, we'd agreed to say I was a hairdresser, being the furthest we could think of from the truth.

'And was I right about the police?' Marion asked. 'Have they done anything about finding your attackers? I bet they haven't.'

'Well, no, Marion, you were wrong,' Ari said uncomfortably, and I could see he hated seeming to make her look silly. But he went on bravely, 'They really have already arrested and charged the two people who did it, and one of them is actually a police detective. I think she might even be the one you first saw at Shady Lane. I'm sorry if that doesn't fit in with your theory of high-up police corruption, but that's what's happening. DC Miller wasn't tied up with any conspiracy, it was just a stupid practical joke that went wrong.'

She was silent for a while, then she burst out, 'So what's this meeting for, then? Why didn't you tell me by email that my warning about the police wasn't necessary? Stop the car. No, don't stop it. Turn it round and drive me back. No, not back to where we met. Drive me home. No, that's no good, I don't want you to know where I live. I should have known I was right not to trust you in the first place! Now what shall I do?'

Then I was horror-struck when she burst into noisy tears. She sobbed and snuffled and muttered incoherent words, and snatched the handkerchief Ari offered her, and held her head. This went on for quite a while as we all sat in the stationary car, Ari getting more and more embarrassed and me wishing I was somewhere else. Finally she blew her nose quite loudly for such a little one, and suddenly thumped poor Ari on the chest with both tiny fists. I leaned forward from the back seat and pinned her back.

'Stop it,' I ordered. 'Stop all this hysterical stuff and listen to me. You've got to help us. You're our only hope. I'm going to trust you and tell you everything.'

And I did, the whole long story from beginning to end, in all its muddle and baffling haziness. Of course I left out the personal bits. But when I'd finished explaining, I could tell that Marion, if that was really her name, felt quite different about everything. What made this clear was the first thing she said after listening without a word for all the time it took me to explain.

She said, 'I don't think Gustafson's death was an accident and I don't think Councillor Bennett died from natural causes.'

Chapter 19

Alfie and I got packed off to Hatfield again to lend our priceless support to the Fraud Squad there. How had they ever managed without us, I wondered, as we were briefed about inconspicuously following people as they left the Job Centre.

'This is so boring,' I groaned to Alfie, and got a sharp lecture in return, all about if I wanted glamour I should have joined the Homicide Division of the Los Angeles Police Department.

The fact was that normally I didn't care what I was given to do, I was always keen, but at this particular time I was simply busting to have a conference with Derek, Alfie and Ari. Anyway, Alfie and I slogged our way through the endless day until we were allowed to return to Watford – although with the reminder that we were going to be seconded to Hatfield for at least another week. On the way back I explained to Alfie that we had to get hold of Derek and have a meeting with him and Ari.

'No, that won't do,' Alfie said firmly. 'You can arrange as much as you like with me and Derek, but we can't include a civilian in police business, even if he is a good friend of yours.'

'But he used to be in the Met, and he's applied to re-join...' I started, but Alfie kept shaking his shaggy head and repeating that he wouldn't have it, and he didn't think DI Michaelson would, either.

He was right, too. I kept explaining to Derek on the phone that evening how Ari was involved, but he was on Alfie's side.

'I'll give you as much of my free time as I can, to listen to your theories,' Derek said, 'but this is police business. Now, do you want to arrange a meeting of the three of us, or not?'

What made me even more furious was that when I started explaining to Ari, all apologetically, he actually agreed with Derek and Alfie.

'I'm still a civilian, and it's not proper,' he said, and that was that.

That left it up to me to explain to Derek and Alfie all about the letter Ari got, and our exchange of emails with Fly, and how she turned out to be Marion, and all that she'd told us. It took ages, because Derek kept asking questions and Alfie kept saying he didn't understand. But when we finally ground to a halt, we were left with Marion's last statement that she didn't think Gustafson's death was an accident and she didn't think Councillor Bennett had died of natural causes.

'You mean she wouldn't explain any more than that?' Derek asked, and when I shook my head, he went on, 'Well, in that case, I can't see any possible reason to attach any credence to her opinion.'

Then he thought a bit, and added, 'On the other hand, if I look through the station records and find no report from Graves or Miller about her visit, she's entitled to claim there's something fishy going on.'

'That's if she didn't dream up the whole thing,' Alfie put in, 'including going to Shady Lane and making her statement to Miller and then Graves. Why should we believe her? Why not give Graves and Miller the benefit of the doubt? We should all be sticking together—'

'Well,' Derek interrupted, 'there is something else. I hadn't intended to tell either of you about this, but after what Greta has told us this evening, perhaps I'd better. DCI Chester told me, in confidence mind you, that the Sergeant who retired, what was his name, oh yes, Forbes, came to him a month before he left and made allegations about DI Graves.'

Listening to this, Alfie had started to go a funny colour.

'I don't believe it—' he started, but Derek cut him short again.

'DCI Chester wouldn't tell me the exact nature of the statement DS Forbes made to him, but it did partly concern sexual relationships with one of his informants, known as Joan Smith, and also with DC Miller. There were other matters which he thought best not to disclose to me.'

He paused.

I asked, 'But didn't he say anything about pursuing the matter? And if he didn't, isn't that alone a bit fishy?'

'No, I don't think so, Greta, in spite of your hobby-horse about DCI Chester being at the bottom of all wrong-doing,' he said, with a sad sort of smile. 'He knew Forbes was retiring and Graves was being transferred, and he thought best to leave it all alone, and once Graves was out of temptation's way, he'd straighten out.'

'I see,' I said sarcastically, 'what a good idea. Not to let them know in Wales what they were getting, eh? And now look what's happened to Dusty Miller. And by the way, perhaps you didn't know that Joan Smith is in Wales now?'

The air between us was thick with hostility. How could I ever have imagined myself in love with this stupid, pompous, loose-moralled little prick?

Alfie gave a loud groan.

'I'm going to see Freddy Forbes, and ask him,' he said. 'I don't believe a word of any of it.'

'Can I come with you?' I asked eagerly. 'Three heads are better than two.'

'Course not,' Alfie said. 'All right if I drop round on an old pal, but a bit fishy if I turn up with my new young partner, specially one looking like you, girl.'

I decided that this was meant as a sort of compliment, probably the nearest Alfie could get to saying that I was suspiciously attractive. Difficult to argue, anyway, even if Freddy Forbes remembered me.

Derek had been making careful notes in – of course – a leather-bound dinky little notebook, probably yet another expensive gift from his darling Erica.

'I'll check up on our records to see if I can find anything about Marion's call at the station to report her suspicions, and also about her car being stolen, her house broken into, and her mugging. You say she reported all of these events? And you can give me approximate dates? Well done, Greta, good reporting.'

Condescending little twat, I thought.

'And anyway, Alfie,' I said, 'if she made the whole thing up, how did she get DC Miller's and DI Graves's names?'

'That's a point,' Derek said. 'One other thing,' he went on, 'you haven't told us Marion's surname.'

Oh bugger, I thought. I've forgotten it, and I didn't write it down. Now what the hell was it? Something Italian-sounding. Pastrami? Albino? Cortina? There was a painful silence while I racked my brains. Alfie was looking surprised, probably because he knew I was brighter than to overlook something so important, and Derek was beginning to smirk in a supercilious sort of way. I'd gone right off him by then.

'Got it!' I shouted, jumping to my feet and punching the air in my relief. 'Sestina!'

Derek burst out laughing. I was mortified. I thought he was laughing at my football hooligan-type behaviour, but it wasn't that bad.

'She's having you on,' he said. 'That can't be her name. She's given you a false one. She doesn't want you to check up on her. Tell you what, Greta, you phone the Planning Department at the Town Hall in the morning and ask if they've got a member of staff there called Marion Sestina, and I'll take a bet the answer will be no.'

'What makes you so sure, Detective Inspector Michaelson?' I asked politely but with ice dripping from every syllable. 'How can you possibly know that?'

'I'm sorry, Greta, I didn't mean to hurt your feelings,' he said, much quieter. 'But a sestina is a little-known form of poetry. It's like if you arrested someone and asked his name and he said Iambic Pentameter or William Shakespeare.'

'I'm off,' said Alfie, lumbering to his feet. 'This is all too deep for me.'

But I got it. I didn't go to university, like Mister Clever-Clogs Michaelson or his precious Erica, but at least I understood that much. And I was willing to bet that Marion hadn't lied, and her name really was Sestina. Why shouldn't it be? I believed all the rest of what she'd told us, so why not the name too?

Derek said, 'Well, it's time I left too,' but I was already on my hands and knees lugging out the local telephone directory.

'She still lives in the same house where she grew up,' I said, leafing through the pages. 'She told me she kept everything on her father's name after he died, so it should be – ah, here it is! See, look, Sestina, George H. You lost your bet.'

'OK, quite right, Greta,' Derek said quite calmly, without the slightest embarrassment at having made a complete idiot of himself, showing off his superior education and trying to make me feel a fool. 'Well, we've all got plenty to think about now, haven't we. Goodnight.'

And they'd both gone, leaving me feeling let down, fed up and confused.

I phoned Ari to bring him up to date, but his mother was pleased to tell me that he was out and she didn't know when he'd be home. If she'd said in so many words, 'That's one in the eye for you, Greta Pusey,' she couldn't have made it clearer that anything Ari did that didn't include me was all right with her. I didn't even bother to leave a message. She probably wouldn't have told him, anyway.

What to do? Too early for bed. Didn't feel like a cycle ride or a turn round the houses on the roller-blades. Didn't feel like karate or computer practice or watching rubbish on the TV or reading a book. I couldn't remember ever feeling like this in my whole life before. Boredom was for boring people, my Gran used to say, and generally I agreed with her. But on this particular evening I simply didn't know what to do with myself.

Then I had a bright idea. I looked up that number again and phoned Marion Sestina. Since talking to Derek about her name, I'd managed to stop thinking of her as Fly.

'Greta! What a nice surprise!' she said. 'Did Ari tell you to call here? Just a minute, I'll fetch him.'

Well, it might have been a nice surprise for her, but it wasn't quite that for me. What was Ari doing at her house? And why was she so friendly? And why should he have told me to phone him there? I didn't like any of this. It got better when I heard her in the background telling him to ask me to join them, but it still smelled a bit. I felt that Ari was up to something, but I couldn't think what. Or why.

By the time I'd cycled round to her house I'd calmed down and realised that I was only getting suspicious about everyone, even including poor Ari, because I was so fed up and frustrated about everything. It turned out that Ari had been feeling at a loose end, too, and had phoned Marion to see if he could get any more information from her. She'd invited him round for a drink, but they'd only just started chatting by the time I phoned.

She was not a bit like the first impression I'd had of her. She was really friendly and welcoming, and told us a lot about herself and her late parents and her job at the Town Hall. Nothing useful for our investigations, but interesting just the same. It turned out we were pretty much the same age, and having both been born and brought up in Watford, it was a bit surprising that our paths had never crossed before. But we'd gone to different schools and followed quite opposite career paths. Both her parents had been Civil Servants, and her older brother was a headmaster of a private school in Bushey. Quite a contrast to my own life. But I didn't tell her anything about that, though she did ask me a few questions.

'Wasting your time talking to Greta about her private life,' Ari advised her. 'We're close friends, but I don't know a thing about her.'

Anyway, it ended up quite a cosy and chummy evening for the three of us, after we'd agreed to avoid talking about the heavy stuff that had brought us together in the first place.

Of course, from the start Ari and I tried to ask Marion some more questions, particularly about her theories on the deaths of Gustafson and Councillor Bennett. But she was firm that this was going to be a social evening, and she didn't want to talk about anything serious.

'Let's just get to know each other,' she said. 'I've got a feeling we're going to be good friends, after all.'

I suppose she meant that we hadn't really got off on the right foot, and she wanted to make up for it. I'd never had a close girlfriend before, and it felt so comfortable, it made me wonder why I'd spent all my life holding people at arm's length. When I left, Marion and I arranged to go shopping together next time we had a non-working day coinciding. Ari didn't offer to come home with me, but I was in a much better frame of mind by the time I went to bed that night.

Next morning there was a note in my letter box. Unsigned, but I knew it was from Derek. He must have come by at some weird hour to have beaten my alarm. It said: 'New developments. New action. See you soon.'

I asked Alfie if he knew what it might mean, but he had no idea. He did tell me, though, about his evening with his old mucker, ex-DS Freddy Forbes.

'Seems as if that Gerry Graves was not what you might call discreet,' Alfie guffawed. 'After what old Freddy told me, I can well believe he picked your lock to get into your place to tell you to mind your own business. Lucky he never tried to get in bed with you, an' all. Freddy caught him at it twice, can you believe it! Once he was going at it with that Dusty Miller on the floor in the food store at the back of the canteen kitchen.'

'Huh,' I said, 'that's no surprise. I expect she'd be only too pleased to get that much attention from anyone, wherever she could.'

Alfie's eyebrows shot up, and I could see him at last re-thinking that daft idea he'd had that Dusty and I were friends.

'What was the second time, not with Dusty again, surely?' I asked, and Alfie was only too eager to tell more.

'No,' he said, 'the other time was when Freddy found him humping that little scruff, his nark, you know, the one who calls herself Joan Smith sometimes, up against the wall in the car-park!'

'What, our own car-park?'

'Yes, right outside the back door of the station house,' Alfie chortled, wiping his eyes. 'It's a wonder he got away with it. I mean, anyone could have fallen over them, could have been the Super, anyone, couldn't it? But old Freddy said to me, he reckoned a person's sex life was their own business, and he wasn't going preaching to anyone.'

'So then why did he say anything to DCI Chester at all?'

'Well, see,' said Alfie, sobering down a bit, 'then he got wind of something more serious, like suppressing a complaint from a member of the public. And as it was near the time he'd be retiring himself, he thought he could safely pass it on up higher and let them deal with it.'

'What do you mean, safely?' I asked.

'Well, you know, like not having any repercussions on himself,' Alfie explained vaguely.

Repercussions, I thought. Did that mean being sent to Coventry for lack of loyalty, or actual physical punishment for blowing the gaff that there were real criminals amongst us, not just sex-mad officers who'd have it away with any available female?

'Did he tell you any details of the part about suppressing a complaint?' I pressed Alfie, but he just sighed and shook his head.

'Come on, girl,' he said. 'Time we was at Hatfield.'

And he wouldn't say another word about Freddy Forbes and what he did or didn't tell him about the serious stuff he'd discovered about DI Graves.

*

The following evening when I got home, Derek was sitting outside in his car. This was something new. He'd never just turned up before. Could it be a personal matter? As I walked towards his car, my heart started racing.

If he wanted to talk to me about police matters, he would have called a meeting with Alfie as well as me. So if he'd just arrived without warning, it must be that he wanted to see me alone. My mind was churning out possibilities at an even faster rate than my heart was thumping. Maybe he'd broken up with the fragrant Erica and had finally come to appreciate my more well-built charms? Was this the change in my emotional life I'd been longing for ever since I first set eyes on him? I'd absolutely forgotten by then that I thought I'd gone off him at our last meeting.

By the time I'd got level with the driver's seat and he'd caught sight of me, I was so wound up I could hardly breathe.

'Oh there you are, Greta,' he said irritably. 'Why does it take you so long to get home? I've been waiting ages for you.'

Even while I was explaining that Alfie had dropped me at Shady Lane and I'd walked home from there, my fantasy of why he was there was draining out of the tips of my toes. I'd been building a dream on nothing again. I made a mental note to stay in character in future, and go back to being the down-to-earth Greta I'd always been before this hateful man came and turned my life upside-down.

It was strange the way I sometimes dreamed of having his arms around me and the rest of the time I hated and despised him. Maybe that was what love was really like. Was that how Ari felt about me?

'Anyway,' Derek said, still without a clue of the havoc he'd been causing in my innards, 'just get in the car for a minute while I tell you the latest. No, I won't come in to your place, I haven't got time. I've got an appointment with one of the Assistant Chief Constables in forty minutes, so we'll have to be quick.'

My heart started its thumping again, but this time to a different tune. Assistant Chief Constable? Something was buzzing now. I was so hyped up by this time, I didn't even realise that Derek was talking faster than I'd ever heard him before. It was only when he'd driven off and I slumped down on my couch to mull things over that I realised I'd only been in his car for less than five minutes.

'You might not think I've been taking notice of everything you've been telling me, Greta, but it's all in there,' he'd said, tapping his head, 'as well as in my notebook. Two things have been added, and that's enough for me to request a confidential interview with an ACC. The first thing was that DCI Chester asked me if I was on the square, and when I said I had no interest in being a Mason, he said that was good, he wasn't either. But I wasn't sure if I believed him. Then at the golf club, Superintendent Wood asked Roger Winters, pointing at me, "Is he a member?" Mr Winters, who you may remember is the Chief Area Officer of the HSE, answered quickly, too quickly, I thought. Like someone trying to cover a mistake. He said, "Yes, Willy, of course he's a member here, you remember when he joined soon after he came to work at Shady Lane". And that was—'

'But just a minute,' I'd interrupted, 'I don't get it. The Super wanted to know if you were a member of the golf club. So what?'

'No, come on Greta, I haven't got time for you to start acting dumb,' he'd said, switching on his motor. 'It was the emphasis that was important. The Super wasn't asking if I was a member of the golf club, but Roger Winters was telling him *that was all I was a member of*, you see. Maybe I didn't make clear just how he said it. But I can tell you that on top of everything you've told me, it's the clincher for me. That, plus the fact that I couldn't find any record of complaints from Marion Sestina.'

'What! Not even her car theft?'

'No, not a word. Her name simply doesn't appear in any of our records. So now I'm going to ask the ACC for an investigating officer to come to Shady Lane, a.s.a.p. Buck up, Greta, get out of the car, I must get a move on.'

And I was out and he was off. And I was puzzled. He'd accused me of over-interpreting everything I'd told him, and now he was going to the top with the same information!

I was no wiser when he phoned me later that evening.

'Apparently the ACC had already asked Superintendent Wood why we weren't investigating the HSE more closely, and he'd said we were under-manned,' he said. 'And when I told him you and Alfie kept getting seconded to the Fraud Squad in Hatfield, he admitted that didn't add up. So we'll be getting a new DI soon, but he won't be what he seems. And that's all I can tell you just now, Greta, so you'll have to make up your own mind whether you want to pass it on to Alfie or not. By the way, did he see his old friend Forbes?'

I told him what Alfie had told me he'd got from Freddy Forbes, and he laughed quite a lot. I wasn't sure if it was all the humping or my comments on it that he found so amusing, but it was good to hear. Come to think of it, I'd never heard him laugh before, and it was a big laugh for such a little geezer. Warm and hearty, like I imagined he'd be in a clinch. If I ever got the chance to find out.

I got another phone call that evening, from the last person in the world I'd expect to hear from. Dusty Miller. Not the sneery pain in the arse I'd known, but a much quieter, friendlier Dusty. More of a creep, really. She said she'd like to see me while she was still on bail.

'Come on, Dusty, you know I can't do that,' I said at first, but she said it was nothing to do with her case, it was personal. So I got her address and said I'd call round right away. Why not, I thought. I had nothing better to do that evening, and I certainly couldn't expect another exciting call from Derek.

Turned out she lived in one of those nasty blocks of Council flats down towards Croxley. Too far to roller-blade, so I cycled. Only took ten minutes. She was surprised to see me arrive so quickly. When she asked how I'd got there, she seemed strangely pleased when I told her. No more snide remarks about my not having a car, I noticed. I soon found out why.

She lived with her old dad, who must have been about ninety and had a terrible wheezy chest. This didn't stop him taking charge of the conversation, though. It was from him that I finally found out what it was all about. Simple really. Dusty had worked out that she was probably going inside for a while once her case came up. She'd have no use for her car, and her dad wasn't fit to drive. She wanted to sell it to me, that was all. It wasn't a bad offer, and I knew the car was in good nick, having driven it once for her when she wanted to show off that she had a driver.

'See, what we thought was,' her old chap puffed out at me, 'if you don't want to pay cash, you can let me have the money in instalments. We can come to an arrangement, see, benefit us all.'

It was a reasonable suggestion. The trouble was, did I really want a car? I'd got on so happily with my bike and my blades, did I want the expense of running a motor? On the other hand, it certainly would be more dignified to graduate to four wheels, even if it was only a little Ford Fiesta. It was the old boy who clinched the sale.

'My Dorothy's worried about me,' he wheezed, 'not having enough income to manage on week by week while she's away. And I don't want to start applying for the supplementary, my time of life, do I.'

It was pathetic. And such a come-down for the rude, jeering, scoffing Dusty Miller who'd been so set on giving me a hard time when I first joined the Department. How could I refuse. Easy. She asked for an amount which was far from reasonable, specially when I saw it had a 'D'-reg. number-plate, which I'd never noticed before.

'No, that's not the year,' Dusty explained, 'it's only two years old, and you can see it's in good nick. You drove it yourself once, so you know it's OK.' She went a bit coy-looking, a hard job for someone with a face like hers. 'The number-plate was a special present,' she added, 'like, you know, personalised.'

I went downstairs and looked at it again, and sure enough, the number was D11STY. The nearest somebody could get to spelling DUSTY. But even though it wasn't exactly her name, someone had gone to some expense to buy it for her. Pity I couldn't coax her to tell me who'd paid for it, or why.

'Listen, Pusey,' she said, reverting to the original Dusty I'd known and not loved, 'either you'll buy it or you won't. You don't need the history of the number-plate, right?'

So after a bit more haggling, we came to terms and wrote out an agreement on the spot, and I ended up not just shaking hands with old Mr Miller, but wishing Dusty well before I left. That was easy, because she seemed so sure she was going to be put away, which didn't upset me at all. Although privately I thought she had a good chance of getting off scot-free. So it didn't hurt to offer her good wishes. Am I a softy or what? I'd got myself a set of good second-hand wheels at a bargain price. Of course I'm not a softy.

First thing next morning, before I'd even made up my mind whether or not to tell Alfie what I'd done, we all had to go to yet another meeting to listen to a talking-to by Superintendent Wood.

As usual, he waffled on and on and I noticed several pairs of eyes getting very slitty and a few heads nodding while he stood there, waving his arms with his knobbly wrists sticking half a yard out of his cuffs. Every time I saw him he looked more like a leafless tree with partly animated branches. How could Derek have found anything suspicious in anything this man said? Everything that came creaking out of his skinny jaws was only boring fragments of sentences. Goodness knows how he'd got to be a Superintendent. Still, he finally got to the point.

'Not only do we have an increasing load of work, as you all must know,' he droned on, 'with a tight budgetary grip on overtime, but also our numbers have recently become seriously depleted.'

'What?' hissed Alfie. 'Is he saying what I think?'

'Tell you later,' I whispered. I saw DCI Chester frowning at me, and quickly put my head down, making out to be taking notes. Notes on what? What was the message? Had we been listening to this all morning? I glanced at my watch. Amazing. Only ten minutes had gone by since we settled down to listen to Sir.

'I am therefore delighted to tell you,' the Super was going on, 'that two sterling officers from the uniformed branch will be joining CID, whom I'm sure some of you already know. They will be PCs Kevin Burton and Frederick Archer, and will form a team with DI Michaelson.'

A sort of groaning murmur came from the ranks. Probably the nearest we could get to applauding. I knew Kev and Fred, and thought we should be pleased to get them. I hadn't known they wanted to go plain-clothes, but why not.

'But most important of all,' Superintendent Wood raised his creaky voice a little, 'our numbers will shortly be augmented by a new Detective Inspector, a Mister Moon, joining us from Birmingham. His team will consist of DS Partridge and DC Pusey. That team and DI Michaelson's team will, of course, report to DCI Chester. I am sure our efficiency and arrest and conviction rate will be greatly improved by these additions. Thank you.'

There was a splatter of half-hearted applause, as if we couldn't make up our minds if that was the right thing to do or not, and then we started to disperse.

'Right,' said Derek to me and Alfie, 'our first port of call is the fairground.'

'What? What you mean, *our* first—' Alfie started to protest, but Derek cut in with, 'Yes, Sergeant, I am well aware that Superintendent Wood just said that my team will consist of Burton and Archer, and you will be working with our new DI, Moon. But in the meanwhile, until they are actually here in the flesh, you and DC Pusey will be with me. So we will now go to the fairground and talk to people there about the accidental death there of a certain Mr Danny Robbins. You drive, Pusey.'

'This Danny Robbins, Guv,' I noticed Alfie was now using a different tone to Derek, and he obviously felt more comfortable calling him Guv than Derek, 'is he the one who first said he'd taken a bribe from that Jonathan Bennett?'

'Yes, and wasn't it convenient for someone that he had a fatal accident before he was called to testify to that on oath. But who was it who benefited from his death?' Derek said. 'I think it's worth asking a few questions about it, even if it was so many months ago.'

'Talking of deaths, Guv,' I put in my own contribution, 'can you tell us how much investigation there was into the car crash when Gustafson was killed? Was it regarded as suspicious at all by your lot in Durham?'

'The usual scrutiny was employed, Pusey,' he said coldly in his usual lofty way. 'Do you have a reason for asking at this point?'

'Only that Marion Sestina seems convinced that it was no accident that killed Gustafson. It seemed as if she's sure that Anderson was deliberately responsible for Gustafson's death in some way, and that he knows more than anyone suspects about Rodney Bennett's death, too.'

'Councillor Rodney Bennett died of natural causes,' Alfie put in reprovingly. 'There was a proper inquest and we all heard the coroner's conclusion.'

'I'm not so sure about that, Sergeant,' Derek said. 'I think the time has come to take another careful look at everything that's happened in Watford in at least the past year.'

No need to point out that the Anderson/Gustafson car crash wasn't in Watford. We all knew what he meant, and I for one was dead chuffed to hear it. At last, we were going to get somewhere!

I noticed that Alfie was looking unusually thoughtful.

'Now that you mention it, Guv,' he said, 'I've just remembered something. I don't know if it's useful, but—'

'Well, get on with it, man!' my little sweetheart snapped.

Alfie wasn't put out by his tone, but went on slowly, 'When we first got notice of that so-called accident at the fairground, you remember, Greta, it was round about your first day in the Department, guess who went to interview the fairground owner? It was Gerry Graves, Freddie Forbes and Dusty Miller! That's an interesting trio, if you like. What do you think of that, Guv?'

'I think that's pretty significant in the light of what we know now, Sergeant,' Derek said with a noticeable change of tone. 'Seems to me you'd better go and have yet another friendly chat with your pal Freddie Forbes.'

The widow of Danny Robbins, the fairground owner, was as different from Alfie's favourite widow, the apricot-favouring Vera Varney, as it was possible to be. She was dark-skinned, black-eyed, with obviously dyed black hair which made her wrinkly old face look even more ancient.

'About time,' was her greeting when Derek introduced himself. 'Took you lot long enough to come and ask questions, didn't it. Very handy it was for everyone, wasn't it, that my Danny met with a accident. First them HSE buggers come and got him to say one of their own was a crook—'

'You mean Jonathan Bennett who was on the Devil's Ride with his whole family?' Alfie interrupted, but she swept on with, 'Yer, him. Then the cops just leave it. Not another dicky-bird after that.'

'But if you thought your husband's death was suspicious, madam,' Derek started politely, to be screeched down with, 'Don't you start madaming me, you lousy pig! You know bloody well none of your bunch wouldn't take no notice of me, you never do, us Romanies!'

Oh Gawd, I thought, here we go with another persecuted minority. They never seem to work out that the more they say we're prejudiced against them, the less notice we take of anything they say. Just the same, picking the bones out of the chip on her shoulder, it was quite interesting. I had to admire Derek, the way he patiently worked his way through all her carryings-on to try to get to what might have been the truth. It took ages, and I couldn't tell how he felt at the end of it, but I could see Alfie was as worn out as I was.

'Have you noted all that, Pusey?' Derek suddenly snapped at me, giving me a nasty turn until I saw from a glint in his eye that he didn't expect me to have taken verbatim notes.

'Yes sir, certainly have,' I came back at him smartly without a crimp in my straight face. But of course none of it was useful stuff, just all wild accusations and suspicions and resentment. What it boiled down to was that the Widow

Robbins thought that her husband's so-called accident had been arranged somehow because it was feared that his evidence wouldn't stand up in court.

'Been in this business all his life, his father and his grandfather before him,' she explained, 'and he bloody-well knew enough to keep out of the way of a wagon what could smash him flat. No, obvious, he got pushed, didn't he. And who would have done that, ask yourself. Somebody who was afraid he wouldn't be able to keep up his story with all that cross-examining they do. Truthful man, he was, and lying never come natural to him. They must have known that and got him out of the way after he signed his statement.'

'But may I ask,' Derek put it as delicately as he could, 'how you came to the conclusion, if it *was* foul play, that it was instigated by the people from the Health and Safety Executive? I mean, if I might suggest, even if it wasn't an accident, perhaps somebody closer to home might have profited more than those conspirators?'

Well, her opinion of that theory would have shrivelled the pages if I'd tried to put it down in my notebook. Derek must have regretted even implying such a thing. Who inherited the fairground and all the machinery and the rides and the wagons? Well, her sons, of course, and God help anyone who hinted they might have pushed their father under the caravan wheels!

'Well,' said Alfie gloomily as we finally left the field, 'we didn't get much out of that long do, did we?'

'I rather thought we did, Sergeant,' said Derek, and clamped his jaws shut as if he was using all his will power not to say any more. I could see his point of view. Alfie could be a bit downbeat sometimes.

I was glad to be spending that evening alone, for a change. There was a lot to think about, and not just about the widow of the late Danny Robbins and the other Romanies at the fairground, either. For example, how could any of this stuff ever be proved? All those deaths, Gustafson, Danny Robbins, Councillor Bennett, and not a speck of evidence that any of them were down to foul play.

I wasn't best pleased when the phone rang, but I perked up when I heard Marion's voice.

'When can we have our shopping outing together, Greta?' she asked, and I had to explain that work was getting too heavy just now to make any arrangements that included days off. I wasn't going to tell her that I wanted to be available day and night for Derek, as long as I had the chance to be on his team until the new set-up started. I'd never tell anyone how I felt about him. So I just suggested she might like to come round to my place that evening for a drink and a chat. She jumped at the invitation. It was nice, the way we'd taken to each other.

Well, we were jawing away about clothes and make-up and computers and all kinds of stuff, when she suddenly slipped a question in that took me aback. She must have thought she'd sounded very casual, but she was no actress.

All airy and offhanded, she asked me, 'Is it serious with you and Ari? Only he said at the beginning that you were his girlfriend, but I couldn't really tell how you felt about each other. I mean, I wouldn't blame you, he's a lovely feller.'

So she fancies him, I thought. Well, even if I am madly in love with Darling DI Derek Michaelson, I'm not going to share Ari with anyone.

If she's hard up for a feller, I'd rather hand Jim over to her.

I could always spare a long-distance lorry driver – or two, come to that.

Chapter 20

Our new DI, Monty Moon, was a joke. Everything about him was unbelievable, even as a civilian, let alone the police. Of course the height restrictions were relaxed long ago, but what about the fitness test? A little round plum pudding like that couldn't possibly have passed. He couldn't have been many inches taller than five foot, and his girth was about the same. How could those little legs support all that weight?

And Alfie and I were his team. Alfie is about six four, and I'm five nine even in flatties and with my knees bent. What a trio we were going to look. Somebody was having us on, I was sure. If I needed anything to add to my gloom at not being on Derek's team any more, it was this. There's nothing to beat looking like part of a joke to lift a person's morale.

All this was my first impression when he sent for me on his first morning at Shady Lane. Me alone, mind you, not me and Alfie.

'Ah, Pusey,' he greeted me, 'I see you don't remember me. You've changed yourself since I saw you in training at Hendon. You've filled out a bit, and you look a lot happier. Just as pretty, though, I'm glad to see.'

These few remarks got my mind going in six different directions at once. For one thing, he didn't care about being accused of sexism by talking about my looks. He remembered me from Hendon, but I didn't... yes, I did! He'd come one evening to give us a talk about ethics. No wonder I didn't remember. It was so boring and seemed absolutely unnecessary. All about choosing between loyalty and integrity. What if a fellow officer did something wrong, he'd asked. Or worse still, if a senior officer commanded us to do something we knew to be dishonest? And a whole lot more like that. Now that I called the whole mind-numbing thing to mind, I thought again about the lecturer. Surely he'd been taller and slimmer than this man?

All this while he'd kept on talking and I'd been sort of half-listening and the rest of my mind had been sorting out all these recollections. He was right about one thing, of course. At Hendon I'd still been coming to terms with the loss of my Gran, and doing my best to feel that the police was my family now. I'd been throwing myself into all the physical stuff but maybe not paying enough attention to food.

So that ethical lecturer had been DI Moon? No, that wasn't what I remembered at all. There was something wrong here, but I couldn't quite work out what it was.

Meanwhile, his voice was going on.

'I get the impression, Pusey, that you've been looking for a culprit here at Shady Lane, without success. You seem to have suspected, in turn, a Sergeant Forbes, now retired, a DC Miller, now awaiting trial, a DI Graves, now transferred to Wales. Apparently you are running out of crooked police without ever clarifying to yourself what it is you think they have done or left undone.'

Ouch.

'But sir—' I began, but he talked me down.

'During this time, Pusey,' he went on, 'your own activities have been somewhat unconventional, I gather. And that's putting it delicately, as far as I can tell. You seem to have got in with a rather dubious crowd in Camden Town, you became far too friendly with the family of a man awaiting trial, you befriended the widow of a murdered man, and you encouraged a very inexperienced private detective to obtain employment at the Health and Safety Executive in order to look for incriminating documentation of corruption taking place there.'

He paused for breath. I'd been mistaken. He was at least five foot five, and growing as I watched. He was beginning to look quite imposing. And fierce. I was getting a bit anxious. Wrong. I was scared shitless. Alfie, Derek, Ari, help, I thought.

'We won't go into any of these matters any further at the moment,' DI Moon said, and passed me a small piece of paper. 'That will be all for now. Send DS Partridge in on your way out, please.'

The paper had a short message on one side and an address on the other.

The message was 'THIS IS ALL WINDOW DRESSING. COME TO TEA ON SUNDAY.' I guessed the address was his home. I was totally lost and bewildered.

Still, I did now have a car to go in, so I could posh myself up a bit for this worrying tea-party at his home, and not turn up wearing the sort of things that go with cycling or rollerblading. Looking my best might be a bit confidence-building.

I sat in the canteen to wait for Alfie. I didn't feel like talking to anyone, so I hid behind a newspaper. That didn't stop me hearing, though. Police never whisper, particularly in the canteen, so I heard quite clearly that nearly everyone was discussing the same topic. It was Gerry Graves again. The talk was that his wife had left him. Some thought she'd gone off with some builder bloke who'd been her chap years ago before she met Gerry, and others thought she'd just gone back to live with her folks because she'd got fed up with Gerry's shenanigans.

'But did you ever see that little scrubber, his nark? He was so keen on her, he sent for her to follow them out to Wales,' Fred Archer said.

His mate, Kevin, a man of few words, just added the descriptive comment, 'Nasty 'orrible piece, she was.'

I silently agreed. The tatty little bird I'd known as Joan Smith was pretty gruesome, and it was strange that anyone could fancy her as much as Gerry Graves seemed to. Still, we police should know better than most that there was no accounting for human behaviour.

The best item, though, was what came up just as Alfie joined me, so I wasn't sure I'd caught it properly. But it did sound as if someone was saying they'd heard that Gerry Graves and Joan Smith had gone off to Spain together, and not just for a holiday. That really was interesting, if true.

'Well, Alfie, what did our new man have to say to you? He gave me a right going over,' I said.

'No, girl, nothing much,' Alfie mumbled through a mouthful of hot buttered bun. 'He just wanted a recap of everything to do with the case of Jonathan Bennett and the HSE, and what I thought about that Anderson bloke and his car accident.'

'You must have talked fast to get through all that in half an hour,' I observed. 'So what does he want us to do now?'

'Go and politely ask Anderson if he'll accompany us back here for a chat with DI Moon. Make it clear he's not being accused of anything, just helping to clarify a few outstanding points. Why, what did he say to you?'

'Just told me to stop seeing corruption and conspiracies where there weren't any, like you always do, Alfie,' I told him, and he nodded approvingly.

Anderson came back to Shady Lane with us willingly enough, though he made clear on the way that there was nothing useful he could tell our new DI. Alfie explained that being new, Mr Moon just needed to get a few details clear in his own head. That may well have been the case, but I wasn't in on it. DI Moon asked Alfie to be at the interview, but my presence wasn't required.

I was politely told about some paperwork that needed doing, particularly as it was a Friday, and we needed clear desks to start the next week. I was getting some rum treatment here, and it was making me very fidgety. But there was nothing I could do about it but follow orders.

Plonking away on form-filling and reports in triplicate, I had a chance to rake back in my memory. I was able to recall the exact words that Derek had spoken after his interview with the Assistant Chief Constable. He'd said, 'We'll be getting a new DI soon, but he won't be what he seems. And that's all I can tell you just now.' So that could mean that Mr Moon was the undercover man who'd come to find out whether there really was corruption at Shady Lane. Or just that he wasn't really a DI.

*

Saturday I should have got stuck in with all those boring domestic things, like washing and hoovering and re-stocking the fridge. Instead I spent hours getting acquainted with the internet. Finally I felt confident enough to send an email to Ari's cousin George, telling him my email address and giving him a friendly message to Ari. Then I plucked up courage and phoned Derek at Erica's home in Highgate, where he'd moved in with her. He was out and I got an earful from her.

'I would appreciate it, Constable,' she said in her posh voice, 'if you would kindly refrain from telephoning Detective Inspector Michaelson at this number. Unless, of course, it happens to be an emergency. This is a private telephone, and we don't wish it to be used for police matters. He is at his golf club at the moment, but I will tell him of your call. I suppose you'd better give me your number, should he wish to contact you before Monday?'

And even while I was mumbling 'Yes' and 'Sorry' she hung up without even saying goodbye. I hated her.

I went back to the computer. Excitement! I was receiving my first email. It was from Ari, sent courtesy of George. It said, 'Dear Lovely Girl, I can't bear to see you any more now that I know you don't love me and won't ever think of marrying me. I will always love you. Ari.'

This was turning out to be a black Saturday for me. I phoned Marion and wasn't a bit surprised to hear that she'd invited Ari to dinner that night.

'You don't mind, do you, Greta?' she asked anxiously. 'But he did say that you'd chucked him, so I thought it would be OK.'

By this time I was really fed up. All that I'd need at this moment was for Jim to turn up and expect a roll in the hay, and I'd probably poison his ice-cream. So I went for a ride around in my new car. I have to admit that I was quite pleased to have got hold of it, even if it did have Dusty Miller's personalised number plate on it. I went up to Luton and looked at the HSE Area Headquarters there. That didn't tell me anything, but it was something to do. Then I went and had a nosh in a nice-looking fish and chip place, and that made me feel a bit better.

On my way home, I thought I might as well detour to have another look at that car-park in Old Redding, where Ari and I thought we'd seen some kind of 'pass the parcel' going on. It was quite nice there. I could see why snogging couples liked it. It was in a quiet and countrified part of Harrow, but it had a good distant view of all the lights of London. I slumped down in my seat and tried to sort out some of my thoughts, particularly in view of what might happen next day at Mr Moon's home.

A car came up behind me with its lights on full beam. Just as I was about to point out to the driver that this was unsociable behaviour, he dashed round, pulled my door open and started to shove something at me. Before I had a chance to register what it was, he'd looked at me, made a sort of gulping noise, took back his parcel and started to rush off again back to his own car.

But he hadn't reckoned on my long legs and quick reactions. He'd only gone two steps when I brought him down with a lovely flying tackle, though I say it myself. I knew who it was. I hadn't had a chance to see what his parcel could have been, but I'd recognised him right away. It was Anderson, and he was now underneath me in a sea of mud. So the day had turned out not to be black Saturday, after all.

What I wasn't ready for, after I'd cuffed him and got him in my passenger seat and turned off his motor and locked it up and pocketed the keys, was the first thing he said.

The little toe-rag said, 'I thought you were Dusty.'

What a cheek.

I drove back to Shady Lane and got the Duty Sergeant to open the parcel. If it wasn't icing sugar it was something that looked very like it. The Sarge wet his finger and dipped it in and cautiously licked it.

'Good stuff, Greta,' he said. 'You've got him bang to rights. Do you know him?'

*

I went home all puffed up with pride, even if I had to admit to myself that it was only luck that Anderson had thought I was Dusty, just because he'd recognised her number plate. Still, that gave me something positive to tell DI Moon next day over tea.

It did also put a little niggling thought in my head, that maybe I'd been wrong about it being DCI Chester that time when I thought I saw him playing pass the parcel in the Old Redding car-park. It was hard to admit it to myself, though, because I'd always fancied him as the bad guy.

Then it turned out to be black Saturday after all, because there was a message on my machine from the hateful Erica. She thought I would want to know that Detective Inspector Michaelson had been attacked on the golf course that afternoon, and was in the Clementine Churchill Hospital in Harrow. She was there now. No visitors. She couldn't tell me any more than that.

She *would* put him in a private hospital, I thought bitterly. I hated her.

Chapter 21

The address DI Moon had given me was in Moor Park. I'd
never been there before, even though it wasn't far from
Watford, but naturally I'd heard how expensive it was. It
certainly looked it, with huge houses each surrounded by
acres of private land, all manicured lawns, TV gardening
programme-looking landscaping and lots of topiary. That had
to mean gardeners working there. How could a DI afford all
this? And if he'd been sent from Birmingham, as the Super
had said, how had he acquired it so quickly? Who was this
mystery man, anyway?

So I parked carefully in the driveway and marched up to
the front door with question marks sticking up all over my
head like a punk hairdo.

And all the time I was worrying about Derek. Since that
message from Erica, I hadn't been able to get another word
of information about what had happened to him or how he
was. Perhaps the mysterious Mr Moon would know
something.

A lovely lady opened the door to me. She was about my
height but more kind of willowy, and really beautiful, not just
pretty or good-looking. And when she saw me, she gave me a
hundred-watt smile of greeting that looked as if she was
genuinely pleased to see me.

'Hallo, it's Greta, isn't it?' she said, and her voice
matched her face. She could have been a film star. 'Come in
quickly, it's cold out there. I'm Beth Moon.'

Daft as it might seem, the first thought I had was that she
and Alfie's wife, Betty Partridge, must have both been
christened Elizabeth, and two people less like each other you
could never find. Nothing against Betty, mind, who was a

really smashing person, but this Beth Moon was a stunner. And when it got through to my brain that she must be our DI Moon's wife, I was knocked out. How on earth – I wondered, but then I saw how she looked at him, and that answered the question.

They were a wonderful couple of hosts, offering me little finger sandwiches of smoked salmon, and scones with jam and cream, and all kinds of cake. It was like everything I'd read about tea at the Ritz, and I thought I'd died and gone to heaven. And no shop talk, either. Just chit-chat, like you'd imagine would go with tea at the Ritz, like had we read this book, seen that film, heard about the other play. We got on so well, I almost forgot who we all were and why I was there. But when we'd finished tea and I'd helped Beth clear the things away, Mr Moon invited me to come to his study for a talk, and I knew the honeymoon was over.

His study! What kind of establishment was this, anyway?

He soon clarified that for me. He was no fool.

'Now, Greta, you'll be wondering if I'm on the take, too,' he said, settling down comfortably in a leather armchair. 'The answer is that this house has been rented for us for a month through the good offices of the Chief Constable of Hertfordshire, and Beth and I actually live in far less grand style than this in a suburb of Birmingham. That's all you need to know to set your mind at rest. This isn't our usual life. We put on this swish tea for you just because we both wanted you to feel relaxed and comfortable with us.'

'Thank you, sir, and it worked,' I muttered. 'But why? What makes me so important that you have to go to all this trouble?'

'You have all kinds of good points,' he smiled, 'but what makes you so valuable just at the moment is that you are incorrigibly nosy. And that's a good quality in a police – er – person, at any time, but none more so than here and now. I've had a full report on how you pulled Anderson in last night, and you might say it was just good luck, but I think it's more that you can't let go of things until you've unravelled at least part of the puzzle.'

I couldn't bear it another minute.

I burst out, 'Oh sir, if you've heard about that, then you must know about DI Michaelson. Can you tell me—'

He grinned. I might say he smirked. I could have hit him, senior officer, generous hospitality and all. I thought I would explode with anxiety before he answered.

'Yes, yes, he's OK,' he said. 'He's had a CAT scan and there's no serious damage. But he's got a slight concussion so he'll stay in hospital for a day or two, just for a rest. Can't say I blame him, that place is like a luxury hotel. Good thing he's got a rich girlfriend, eh?'

I didn't agree but didn't let on.

'But what happened?'

'It's not quite clear. We know he was having a round of golf with Superintendent Wood…'

'…but he told me none of those experienced players would go round with him because his game was so inferior to theirs…'

'…well, I don't know anything about that, we'll have to wait for a fuller explanation. But anyway, the Superintendent has told me himself that Michaelson went behind some trees to retrieve his ball, and he'd been gone such a long time that he, the Super, went to see what the trouble was and found him lying unconscious. And apart from this good report on his condition, that's all we know at present. But now let's get down to what we do know, Greta.'

'You're not a DI, are you?' I said slowly. 'You're a Superintendent yourself, I remember now from when you came to Hendon to give us a talk on integrity versus loyalty. You've been sent to Shady Lane to investigate rumours of corruption, haven't you?'

'Let's hope nobody else is astute enough to have worked that out. Now,' he went on swiftly, 'tell me everything you know, you think, you suspect, you believe. Don't leave anything out just because you think it's unimportant or even personal. For example, start with your relationship with that Cypriot chap who used to be a private detective in Camden Town.'

He was so easy to talk to, so comfortable and understanding, that I found I was telling him a lot more than I thought I really needed to. I thought, this must be what it's like to have a father. I even told him about how things had been between me and Ari, and why it was all over, though of course I'd rather have died than tell anyone – even him – how I felt about Derek. Betty and Alfie Partridge had always been kind, and Betty was a good listener too, but now I found I was telling this funny little man a lot more than I'd ever confided to them. Later I thought maybe it was that sumptuous tea that had softened me up, but it wasn't really. He was a clever chap, this Moon. He really knew his job.

When I'd finished telling him everything that had happened from the day I'd joined the Department, and answered all his questions, he started telling me things.

'I had a long talk yesterday with that young chap, Anderson,' he said. 'He told me that he was pretty sure that Gustafson had caused the death of Councillor Rodney Bennett. He said that on their way up north, Gustafson had said that Bennett was becoming a liability because he was losing his nerve, and it was lucky that he'd managed to scare him into his fatal heart attack.'

'But that means that Anderson was an accessory after the fact—'

'Now, Greta,' he smiled, 'don't start teaching your grandmother to suck eggs. He knew that whatever he said on those lines, there was nothing we could get him for. As your friend DS Partridge told me several times, the coroner had found that Bennett died of natural causes, and after a cremation, there's no way for us to re-open the case. Unless Anderson actually admits to murder, he's in the clear, and even then, with no supporting evidence…' he shrugged.

There was a silence, gloomy on my part, inscrutable on his.

Then he said, with a broad grin, 'However, what happened in that car-park last night has put a different complexion on things. We now have DC Miller back in custody, and of course we're still holding Anderson. Obviously, when he saw you in that car he thought you were Miller and took what was probably his last chance to unload on her. What a happy coincidence that you had bought her car complete with personalised number plate and for your own reasons decided to pull in to that particular car-park.'

I was trying not to get elated, but I could feel this bubble of excitement growing inside me – unless of course it was just indigestion from too much tea.

'Do you mean that we've cracked some of the case?' I didn't mean to bark the question at him, but it came out like that. He didn't seem to mind, though.

'Well, yes, some of it. It looks now as if DI Graves and DC Miller and Anderson were part of a drug ring, and Bennett and Gustafson were taking bribes from property developers to pay Anderson for their habit. I think we'll have to try to get Graves back from Spain, but there seems a good chance that Miller and Anderson will lead us to whoever was higher up in their organisation.'

'And what about the attack on Aristotle Anapolis? Will we be able to get Dusty Miller for that, too, with her chum from the HSE?'

'Oh yes, I think we might even be able to get Miller to confess,' he said, but I could see he wasn't quite happy. He thought for a while, then must have made up his mind, because he went on smartly, 'But you see, Greta, none of that is what I'm here for. Finding out what Graves and Miller have been up to isn't good enough. For example, who attacked DI Michaelson, and why?'

I felt guilty. I'd got so excited about all this stuff, that I'd actually forgotten for the moment about poor darling Derek, lying with a bandaged head in some luxury hospital, probably being fed peeled grapes by the lovely Erica.

'DCI Chester?' I asked timidly. Derek and Alfie had both been so scornful of my suspicions of him that I didn't want to make a fool of myself by suggesting to Mr Moon that he might be the villainous mastermind of Shady Lane.

'It's possible,' he said, to my relief. 'I think what we have to do now is bring all that we have to Superintendent Wood, and ask him to take the initiative on our next action. Come to my office first thing, and we'll go to see him. Bring DS Partridge with you, and I'll arrange an appointment for us all to go to his office, with DCI Chester and DI Michaelson if he's well enough and back with us.'

*

It turned out that DI Michaelson had intended to stay in hospital for another day or two. But when he was told of the plans for the meeting, he discharged himself and joined us all the next morning in the Superintendent's office.

Mr Wood sat at his desk, unemotional as an old dead tree, while Mr Moon brought him bang up to date with everything, and we all sat round like a lot of naughty school-kids in the headmaster's study waiting for punishment.

When Mr Moon had finally finished talking, Superintendent Wood said, 'And what is your conclusion about all this? You seem to think that there is something further.'

'When we brought in Roger Winters, whom I believe you know is the Chief Area Officer of the Health and Safety Executive—' Mr Moon started, but the Super interrupted with, 'Brought in Roger Winters? How dare you? On what charge? This is monstrous!'

This was the first time I'd ever seen him show any feeling. His face went all mottled, and some spit gathered at the corners of his mouth.

'Yes,' said Mr Moon quietly, 'that's more or less what *he* said. He seemed to think that he was safe from all charges because he had some kind of protection. What do you think about that, sir?'

There was a silence, broken from an unexpected quarter.

Derek Michaelson suddenly burst out with, 'It was you! It was the Super who hit me over the head with his number three wood! Just finished telling me why it was called the "get out of trouble club", and then whacked me with it! Why? Why did you do that?'

Then things took a bizarre turn. If anyone had told me this might happen, I would have scoffed at them even more than Alfie would at such a notion.

Superintendent Wood stood up, opened a drawer of his desk and took out a gun. A gun! In Watford! It was just ridiculous.

'You think you've got me, Monty Moon,' he said in that creaky voice of his, and if it hadn't been so scary it would have been funny.

It was so Hollywood. The words and the voice and the tone, and the idea of a Superintendent of Police in Hertfordshire, England, holding a gun on his own officers, were all so ludicrous.

I couldn't believe what was happening.

'Put it down, William,' Mr Moon said quietly, but of course the Super did no such thing. He started to edge towards the door, still pointing the gun at each of us in turn, as we sat there like dummies. Then I saw out of the corner of my eye that DCI Chester – my favourite suspect until now! – was kind of gathering himself to leap towards the Super. And I could see that he wouldn't make it. He wouldn't cover the distance fast enough.

I've got long legs and a Black Belt in karate. As Chester jumped, so did I. I managed to get between him and the Super, give the Super a good karate kick, and fall. After I'd fallen, I heard a bang, then I felt a sort of a hot pain in my chest.

Then I didn't know anything.

*

It was all very surprising. Mr Moon confessed to us much later that if Superintendent Wood hadn't suddenly panicked, thinking it was all up for him, he wouldn't have known what to do. We had no provable case against the Super, and there was nothing we could do to trap him. It was just mind-blowing that a man with all his experience should have flipped like that and given us the whole thing on a plate.

So finally it wasn't good old detective work that closed off the case, but just crazy good luck for Mr Moon and the rest of us. Bad luck for ex-Superintendent William Wood, though. Once the shooting incident had been sorted out, he just caved in and confessed everything.

And I was some sort of reckless hero.

Almost as amazing was the way I woke up.

Jim was holding my hand. At first I thought I must be unconscious and dreaming. Jim just didn't do that kind of thing. Hand-holding and all that romantic stuff was no more normal for him than it would have been for me. Bringing duty-frees on his regular visits, yes. But actually doing something soppy and caring, never. Life was getting very puzzling.

Mr Moon was on the other side of the bed, though, and he clarified a few things before the nurse came and shooed them all out. One of the points that he didn't need to explain was that I'd been wrong about Cheerful Charlie Chester all along. I'd worked that out for myself by that time. He said he'd tell me all the rest when I was back at work.

My chest hurt.

'Not surprising,' the nurse said. 'You've got a nasty hole where they took the bullet out, and it's not long since you came back from theatre. You must still be a bit woozy. Lucky though, it missed your lung and an artery by a hair's breadth.'

Oh yes, I thought, that's lucky. A hole in the chest. The kind of luck I could do without.

Later on, I thought Mr Moon told me that Superintendent Wood had been giving protection to quite a few villains, all members of the club within the golf club. His guardianship had consisted mainly of not allowing enquiries to be pursued into, for example, corruption in the Planning Department of Watford and bribery in the Health and Safety Executive Area Office.

Possibly the HSE group trying to get rid of Jonathan Bennett by framing him with the fairground incident, was what started the whole thing unravelling. Wood was also currently admitting involvement in the drug business which had so gainfully employed Anderson, Joan Smith, Gerry Graves and Dusty Miller. But not DCI Chester. I'd been slightly wrong there. Just a bit off.

Maybe if Superintendent Wood hadn't lost his nerve the way he did, he might still have bluffed and somehow got his way out of trouble. But he'd lost his luck and we'd found ours.

Then afterwards I wasn't sure how much of all that I'd dreamed. So I had to wait till I was back at Shady Lane before I could hear Mr Moon spell it all out to us in detail.

'Quite a coup,' I think Mr Moon had said before he left my bedside. He seemed pretty pleased. I should have been, too, if I hadn't felt so feeble.

Still, when Derek popped in I started to feel a lot better, specially when he told me that the new team arrangements meant that Alfie and I would be working with him again. I wasn't sure about that afterwards, though. I kept dozing off. Maybe that was just another dream.

But there was one thing I *was* sure about, and that was what he said just before he left.

'You're a heroine, Greta,' were his parting words, and I felt we were getting closer, and who knew where it might lead.

After that, it was a bit of a let-down when Jim came back that evening. I was a bit more awake by that time, and I didn't feel I needed any more of Jim's company.

'I've brought you a present,' he said.

He seemed almost shy. Not his sort of thing, any more than hand-holding.

'It's no good you being all on your own all the time,' he went on, 'you've got to have some company when I'm not with you. I know you can't look after a cat or a dog, so I've brought you this little friend.'

Oh God, I thought, not a gerbil, please, not a hamster.

No, it wasn't.

It was OK.

It was a ferret.